# *Fatal* FLASHBACK

FRANK "SKIP" CRIST

For information, address:

The Preserve Publishing Company
316 Mid Valley, Box 184, Carmel, CA 93923

ISBN 0-9710819-0-5

Book design Siri Weber Feeney / Remen-Willis Design Group

Cover art DJ Simison

Printed by BookMasters Inc., Mansfield, Ohio, USA

10  9  8  7  6  5  4  3  2  1

▲

To
my loving wife,
Carolyn
and family

▼

# ACKNOWLEDGMENTS

There are so many people to thank for their time and effort in helping to write this novel. I started off with my guinea pig, Lou Fenton, an outstanding lawyer in the Monterey area. With his direction I began this tale. After I finished the transcript, Karen Gilleland, a very successful Book Doctor, took a lawyer's work product and taught me how to write a story for the reader instead of a judge.

' My wife, Carolyn, had a major impact on the story as she gave me insight into the sensitive side of the characters. From then on, ideas came from my friends and family as they read the manuscript. The list includes Tom and Sue Masters, Jim and Jana Gill, Nancy Tuck, Tress Barnett, and all of our eight kids and their spouses. All took time out from their busy schedules and gave great input.

Special thanks to my technical experts, Viola Mecke, an outstanding psychologist; Judge Steven Sillman of the Monterey Superior Court and my golfing buddy; my longtime friend, Charlie Page, who is enjoying his retirement from law by writing; John Hult, legal researcher; John Pearne, a fine San Jose private investigator; Beverly Cory, a detail-minded copy editor; and my sister-in-law, Kathy Peregrin, who proofed the manuscript.

Lastly, a special thanks to Ann Remen Willis, who not only gave me great insights into the manuscript, but also led me down the path to publishing this book.

# PREFACE

After thirty-one years of practicing law, I was cleaning out my desk for the final time. It was Saturday, July 2, 1992. I was remembering a remark made several years earlier by Ernie Arbuckle, former dean of the Stanford Business School, at a Stanford Law School reunion. His advice: "Ladies and gentlemen, in order to maintain your youth and enthusiasm throughout your life, you need to repot yourself about every twenty years." I was fourteen years late, but at least I was in the process of repotting myself.

When I was fresh out of Stanford Law School in 1958, I really enjoyed the challenge of practicing law. As the years rolled by, I became fascinated with trial practice and devoted most of my efforts to performing in an arena where a decent mind and a glib tongue paid big dividends.

As I tried cases through the years, I noticed the practice of law changing dramatically. People have become more litigious, lawyers more aggressive, and judges more insensitive. No longer is the courtroom an enjoyable arena in which two lawyers present their case before a judge or jury, seeking a just and fair result. Rather, the courtroom has become a battleground, the battle waged by aggressive lawyers before an impatient judge.

Pretrial discovery has turned into a nightmare with endless motions, countless interrogatories, and lengthy depositions. The defense lawyers, paid by the hour, have no urgency to finish any pretrial task. For example, big-city firms may have two lawyers and often a paralegal attend the endless depositions to make sure a proper deposition is taken. In addition, a judge sanctioning a lawyer with a hefty fine is commonplace during the course of pretrial discovery.

In the 1960s and 1970s you could try a significant case for less than $5,000. Today $50,000 is the minimum. When I began trial work, I always remembered that my colleagues were my best friends. We would try knock-down-drag-out cases against one another, then meet together for a drink after the case was over. Now lawyers are at each other's throats, behave discourteously to each other, and by the end of the trial hate each other.

My decision to repot myself took several years. After a lifetime of combat in the courts working twelve- and fourteen-hour days, I became aware that I was enjoying trial work less and less. When several of my legal cohorts began to have strokes and heart attacks, I developed serious doubts about the severity of the stress of trial practice.

The straw that broke my back occurred one day in a deposition in Salinas which was being taken by a young lawyer thirty years my junior. I quietly listened to him ask my elderly client, the plaintiff, the most inane questions, having nothing to do with the issues in dispute. I could see that this deposition was going to take several days longer than necessary. Looking out the window, I saw the gorgeous weather. I thought to myself, *What the hell am I doing in here, listening to this kid waste everybody's time. I could be out in the fresh air, playing golf and smelling the roses.*

That was the last deposition I ever attended. The next Monday, I announced to my partners, "I've lost my thirst for the practice of law. I'm retiring. I'll be damned if I'm going to practice law until I'm ninety-one like my father and die in the saddle, still practicing law when I pass away."

As I carried my last box out to the car, I was thinking about a case that significantly changed my life. It involved my wife, her housekeeper, the housekeeper's eleven-year-old son, and his teacher. It is a fascinating story and I decided to put it to paper. While parts of the story are true, I must admit I substantially embellished the facts. Enjoy.

# CHAPTER 1

It was a rainy and cold evening in March 1991 when Skip Massey and Susan Winters drove into the school board parking lot around 6:50 p.m. The old one-room stone building had been the first schoolhouse in the town of Los Gatos, California. In early 1970s it had been converted into the school board meeting hall. Massey spotted Sam and Leola Langley in an old Toyota Corolla parked near the entrance. He got out of the car, opened the umbrella, and splashed through a path of puddles to see if the building's doors had been opened. After several minutes, he returned and opened Susan's door. "I rapped my knuckles on the front door and finally got the janitor to open up. I'll get Sam and Leola. Take this umbrella and watch out for the puddles."

Once inside the large vacant hall, Massey found the janitor sitting in one of the chairs near the door. "Is there a school board meeting scheduled for seven tonight?" he asked.

The janitor, munching a sandwich, looked up and muttered through a mouthful of food, "Yeah, but they normally don't get started on time. They'll be here soon enough."

The hall was lined with wooden fold-up chairs. By seven, people started straggling in and taking their seats. Sam and Leola sat in the back row, where Massey knew they could remain anonymous. At the far end of the hall, three oak tables were elevated on a low platform. On top of the tables were name placards for the members of the board, the superintendent and the secretary, none of whom was yet present.

Massey checked his wristwatch. Fifteen minutes after seven. The hall was half-filled with spectators. After having been fined by several judges for being late to court trials, he was now a time nut. He and Susan had already taken seats in the first row. He turned to Susan. "Can you believe this? They schedule a meeting for seven and not a single board member is here yet."

Susan smiled at him. "Be patient."

The sight of her made him relax. She looked stunning in a black dress, her blond hair gleaming and the gold hoop earrings swinging slightly as she turned her head. "Well, at least the scenery's great," he said, reaching out for her hand.

▼

At 7:20 p.m., four board members, the superintendent and the secretary came out of a side room, stepped up onto the platform and sat down. Soon a fortyish-looking man, with glasses and a balding pate surrounded by black hair, pounded a gavel. "My name is Paul Jones," he said. "I'm the president of the school board. We are going to wait for the fifth board member before starting. He'll be here shortly."

Massey leaned over to Susan. "I can't believe this. They're going to wait for some tardy idiot. I know Jones. He practices in San Jose. He's a pompous ass."

"Shh, everybody can hear you!" she whispered.

"Look, they think they're having a damn tea party and are going to entertain us when they get good and ready." Susan winced.

Massey put his hand to the side of his mouth and made an effort to lower his voice. "See that gal next to Jones with the big rock on her finger? She's the wife of Art Sheppard, chief executive officer of Centurion Electronics. Fourth wife. Look at that outfit. Probably cost ten grand. I hear he's worth $500 million. It looks as though she loves spending his money."

"Massey, you think you're whispering, but you're not. Pipe down, or I am going to move to the back with Sam and Leola." Susan turned her head away.

10

"I'm sorry. I'm edgy and angry over the way Sam and Leola have been treated. I'll behave."

At 7:30 p.m. a man dressed in a red and white sweatsuit sauntered in. He took the remaining vacant seat behind the placard with the name Gary Fillmore on it and turned to the president. "Sorry, I got stuck in traffic coming down from Lake Tahoe." His tone was not humble, but arrogant.

*Not even an apology to us peons in the audience for being late,* Massey thought. Fillmore, mid-forties most likely, had blown-dry brown hair, a swarthy complexion and a powerful physique.

President Jones banged the gavel and called the meeting to order. "We have a short agenda this evening," he announced, "but before we begin, we'll take oral communications from the floor."

Massey immediately stood up, straightened his tie and walked to the podium on the right side of the platform. "Ladies and gentlemen of the school board," he said as though addressing a jury, "My name is Skip Massey. I'm an attorney representing Sam and Leola Langley, parents of a fifth-grade boy at Los Encinos Elementary School. Several days ago, the Langleys learned that their son was being sexually abused by his teacher, Mr. Stanley Arnold."

There was a loud gasp. Massey turned and saw a tall, slender brunette in a gray pantsuit put her hand over her mouth. Other parents were whispering to one another.

President Jones looked directly at him, eyes squinting. He banged the gavel and shouted, "Let's have order." Rising from his chair, he pointed a finger at Massey. "Sir, do you know what you have just done? Your slanderous outburst could ruin the reputation of one of our school's finest teachers. Don't you have the decency to communicate your suspicions in a private manner before making these charges public?"

Massey held the man's gaze a moment, then said, "For your information, Mr. Jones, my clients contacted both the school's principal and the superintendent, Mr. Garrity here." He pointed to the man with brownish hair and horn-rimmed glasses. "They were told that the boy was fabricating the story. Ever since the incident came to light, the parents have kept their son out of the classroom. Coming here tonight is their last resort before instigating legal action. My clients want this teacher suspended pending an investigation so that their son can return to class."

Superintendent Roland Garrity jumped to his feet. His hands trembled; the veins on his forehead seemed ready to burst. "This vicious attack is totally unfair," he managed. "These gross allegations against this outstanding teacher are total lies."

"Well, I can assure you they are true. Another boy in the class will verify that the teacher made an inappropriate contract with him."

The room grew quiet and the board members looked at each other.

Superintendent Garrity's face was now turning red with anger. "Members of the school board, I have personally investigated this matter, interviewed the persons involved, and I can tell you that both boys made up the story. They have a grudge against the teacher because they were disciplined for creating a disturbance in class. Mr. Massey, the attorney, is making a gross exaggeration of the situation. Mr. Arnold engaged in absolutely no illicit activity. His reputation is impeccable."

Suddenly, a short, blond-haired woman in a Stanford sweatshirt rose from her seat and walked to the podium. She gave Massey a look of disdain and grabbed the microphone out of his hand. "Members of the board," she said, "I'm Gloria Vincent, mother of two children in Los Encinos School. One of my youngsters had Mr. Arnold last year, and I have a daughter currently in his class. I know firsthand of Mr. Arnold's outstanding reputation. It is disgusting that this lawyer came here to a public meeting to vilify the character of a fine man." She threw the microphone back at Massey and returned to her seat. Several people began clapping.

President Jones then stated, "Thank you, Mrs. Vincent, for your comments." He turned his glance back to Massey. "Let me tell you, Mr. Massey, and the audience, of this teacher's credentials. For your information, Superintendent Garrity did telephone me about the incident with the Langleys. I immediately asked him to investigate the matter and had Mr. Arnold's file sent to me, and I can tell you honestly I was greatly impressed with what I read."

He pulled a thick blue folder from his briefcase, opened it and scanned the papers inside. Then he said to the audience, "In 1985, Mr. Arnold won the county's Teacher of the Year award. In 1989, he was named the State Teachers Association Math Teacher of the Year. In 1990, he was the runner-up for the same award from the American Federation of Math Teachers." He paused dramatically before continuing, "Mr. Arnold is a nationally recognized math teacher. This folder is filled with letters of recommendation from parents whose children attended his classes." He looked around at the board members. "Do I have any comments from other members?"

"Yes," said Gary Fillmore with a sneer. "So, Mr. Massey, you want an immediate suspension of this outstanding teacher? Who the hell do you think you are? You and your clients are way out of line. It is my opinion that you're out to do a hatchet job on an innocent man. I move that the teacher remain on the job pending any investigation."

"I second the motion," chimed in Snooky Sheldon, the board member next to Fillmore.

The president then asked if there was any further discussion. The motion passed unanimously.

"I would like to address the board again, Mr. President," Massey demanded, approaching the podium.

"The public hearing is closed. You have no right to speak," shouted the president.

"Well, I'm going to speak anyway," Massey barked back. "If you refuse to suspend Mr. Arnold right now, I am going to have the board served with a copy of a complaint seeking an immediate injunction preventing Mr. Arnold from teaching this class pending an investigation. In addition, the complaint requests monetary damages sustained by the Langleys and their boy."

Gary Fillmore's face contorted with anger. "You threaten us with a lawsuit? How dare you question this board's decision and authority! You of all people, an attorney, know that Mr. Arnold is presumed innocent until proven guilty. You can't come in here and try to ruin a man's reputation on the word of a young child."

A man stood up in the back row and shouted, "Get the lawyer out of here and let's get on with business." The audience clapped loudly.

Massey turned and walked back to his chair. He snapped open his briefcase and withdrew a stack of papers about five inches thick. "I had my staff prepare these today," he whispered to Susan. "Would you please give a copy to each of the board members. As the Langleys' lawyer, I'm not allowed to serve them."

Massey returned to the podium. "Members of the board, you leave me no choice. My associate is going to hand each of you a complaint and summons documents which set a hearing for next Friday requesting an injunction and then a trial for monetary damages."

The audience was now buzzing loudly. When Susan stood up and walked to the table where the board members sat, the room quieted, and the only noise was the sound of her heels clicking on the old oak floor. Without a word, she set the documents in front of each person. When she placed the papers in front of Fillmore, he picked them up and flung them back at her. Then he stood up and shouted at Massey. "You dirty son of a bitch, you ambulance chaser!"

Massey jumped up and shouted back. "You sarcastic, demeaning bastard!"

President Jones pounded the gavel, yelling for order as Fillmore and Massey continued shouting. The board secretary, who had been taking minutes of the meeting on a pad in front of her, threw her hands up in the air. After the president banged the gavel again, Massey grabbed Susan's arm and steered her toward the door. The Langleys, he noticed, had already left.

On the way home, he turned to Susan, "We certainly infuriated them, but at least they will have to hire a lawyer and go in front of a judge. This fact alone may make them realize their responsibility is to Billy."

▼

The following Monday morning, Massey stood at the opened window in his office in Palo Alto, California, taking in the sweet fragrance of the freshly cut grass. It was one of those awesome spring days that occur in the South Peninsula. Outside, a crab apple tree was in full bloom with white and pink blossoms glowing in the sun. The sky was cloudless, the bluest of blue. The air was crisp, the early morning temperature rising. It would be seventy-five degrees by noon, one of those days when it's hard to stay inside and work.

Reluctantly, Massey sat down at his desk and began the morning dictation for his secretary, Helen McGuiness. He was on the third letter when the phone rang. It was the school board president, Jones, his voice dripping with contempt. "Mr. Massey, Sergeant Cardoza of the Santa Clara County Sheriff's Department has informed me that their investigation of Mr. Arnold has turned up enough evidence to indict him. The matter is before the district attorney, and Mr. Arnold has been suspended immediately from teaching his class. The Sheriff was called the day after the board meeting by one of the parents whose boy was in the teacher's class last year. He read about your client's accusations in the local newspaper the following morning and called to say that his son has been also molested by Mr. Arnold, but they were too embarrassed to make an issue of it at that time."

Massey's eyes widened. He hadn't expected this fortuitous event. "I appreciate your passing the word on to me," he said. "I will relay the news to my clients so their boy can go back to class."

He hung up and grinned, then told Helen to get Leola Langley on the phone.

When she heard the news, Leola gasped. "I knew the good Lord would watch over us," she said. "Thank you, thank you. I can hardly wait to tell Sam. He hasn't slept for nights. Well, I'm going to get Billy off to school. Bless you, Mr. Massey."

▼

When Massey arrived at his office the next day, fog had rolled into the Bay Area from the Pacific Ocean and blanketed the valley. *Not nearly as nice a day as yesterday, but by ten it should burn off,* Massey thought to himself. At 9 a.m. when Massey arrived at the office, Helen rang the buzzer and announced, "You had a call from a Mr. Paul Jones a few minutes ago. He wants you to call him back right away." Massey picked up the phone and dialed the number.

The first words out of school board president's mouth confirmed the uneasy feeling that had suddenly come over Massey. "I hope you and your clients are satisfied, Massey," announced Jones. "Mr. Arnold blew his brains out at six-thirty this morning."

# CHAPTER 2

Five months later, Skip Massey's white Porsche was sailing through the tall timbers of the Sierra Nevada. It had been six hours since he left behind the brilliant blue waters of the Pacific under the San Francisco Bay Bridge, sailed across the Central Valley and finally entered into the deep shadows of forest thick with Douglas fir so prevalent in the High Sierra mountain range that forms the backbone of California. The car was winding down into a deep valley on the eastern slopes of the Sierras when he spotted the sign he had been looking for: "Susanville, population 10,382." His shoulders ached, and he tensed his fingers around the steering wheel and leaned back in the seat, stretching his cramped legs. He slowed the car down and drove onto the narrow road leading into town.

Massey looked around at the scenic vista. Susanville, California, sat at the head of the Honey Lake Valley, flanked by the cliffs of the Susan River Canyon. Low-slung white stucco houses and meadowlands dotted with wildflowers presented an idyllic image. That image, however, jarred jaggedly with the incredible news that brought him here.

Each time the subject entered his mind, he shook his head. *Why had his housekeeper, Leola Langley, a God-fearing, mild-mannered woman with a loving husband and two children, been arrested here, 300 miles from her home, for shooting and killing a complete stranger?*

An idea would nudge its way into his mind, but he considered it preposterous and he'd shrug it away. He repeated the ritual once more and focused on the shops and houses along Main Street. After a few minutes, he found the building he was looking for. It was made of

17

gray granite and sat on the right-hand side. He pulled the Porsche into a vacant spot in front. The curved marker above massive double doors proclaimed, "Lassen County Jail, 1928."

Massey eased his six-foot-two, 200-pound frame out of the car and walked up the cement steps to the broad veranda. A little light seeped out under the doors, but there were no windows facing the street. He turned the brass handle, pushed open the heavy door and stepped inside.

A man was seated behind a square oak table just across the corridor. He lowered his newspaper and glanced silently at the intruder, his eyes wary, scanning Massey from the top of his brown, wavy hair, to the dark blue Armani suit, to the gleaming black Florsheims. Apparently satisfied that he posed no threat, the man put the newspaper down and leaned back in the slatted wooden chair.

Massey walked across the stone floor to the table and read the nameplate perched on the edge, "Sergeant Tremont."

"Howdy, Sergeant," said Massey, giving what he hoped was a sincere, down-home smile.

The sergeant grunted. "What's your business, mister?"

"I represent Leola Langley, and I'd like to talk with her," Massey said, slipping a thick, white engraved business card onto the table directly in front of the man's clenched hands.

"Too late, mister, visiting hours ended at six o'clock," he said, running one hand through his greasy black hair.

"Sergeant Tremont, my client has been in custody for nearly seven hours without benefit of counsel. You know I can get a warrant to see her tonight. How do you think the judge will feel if I have to interrupt his favorite TV program because you wouldn't let me in?"

The man's face twitched, and he jangled the key ring on his belt. Then he picked up Skip Massey's business card and squinted at it. Finally, he stood up and said, "I guess it'd be all right. You ain't got a prayer in hell of gettin' her off. She went and shot a teacher named Stewart, then she signed a confession, all legal like," he said, locking eyes with Massey's. The sergeant was nearly as tall as the attorney, but rolls of fat challenged the rumpled brown uniform. "Follow me," he ordered as he brushed past Massey.

Massey followed the officer down a narrow cement hallway. On each side were rooms with steel doors. Through the small barred openings, Massey saw that most of the cells were empty and figured they must be filled with drunks on Saturday nights.

When they reached the room farthest along the corridor, Sergeant Tremont stopped and unclipped the key ring from his belt. He held the ring up high, tilting his head back to look at the numbers by the light of the fluorescent overhead. Then Massey heard the clinking of metal on metal as the officer turned the key in the lock. The sergeant opened the door, but his large frame blocked Massey's view of the room. He could smell disinfectant and the moldy odor of the bedding.

"You gotta visitor," the officer said in a gruff voice. Then he turned and bellied by Massey. "Ring this-here buzzer when you wanna leave." He pointed to a button by the door.

Massey stood just inside the doorway until his eyes adjusted to the lighting, which was even dimmer than in the corridor. The fluorescent tube flickered with a low glow, and a little light filtered through the small window on the opposite wall. When he could make out objects in the room, he grimaced. The cell was straight out of the 1920s. It had never been upgraded. A chipped, dirty porcelain commode stood in the corner next to a brown-stained washbasin. A small table with a chair was positioned under the window. Next to it was a twin-size cot. His eyes focused on the orange lump in the middle of the cot. He shuddered.

"My God, what has happened?" he said under his breath. He sat on the bottom edge of the cot. "Leola, it's Skip Massey. Can you talk to me?"

The orange lump stirred. He heard a muffled sound, then the figure unfolded, sat up and blinked at him. Her brown eyes were sunken in swollen, red-rimmed sockets, her face pale and blotched where she had lain on the crumpled blanket. Her brown hair was pinned back, but strands stuck out all over her head. Leola was about thirty-five, he guessed, but tonight she looked sixty.

She squinted at him for several seconds before a light came into her eyes and she grabbed his arms. "Mr. Massey. Mr. Massey. Thank God, you've come. Take me home. Take me back to Sam and the boys."

Massey took her hands in his and spoke slowly. "I can't take you home tonight. We have to talk about what happened. Then I'll see what I can do."

"I didn' do nothin'," she said in a thick Georgia drawl. "The police are trying to tell me I kilt somebody, somebody I never even heard of. Why would I go and do such a crazy thing? It don' make no sense. Please, you gotta take me back to my boys, to Sam." She started sobbing, her whole body shaking uncontrollably.

Massey let her cry for a good while. She was in no condition to explain what had happened. He squeezed her hands gently and said, "I'm going to get you some help, a criminal lawyer, first thing in the morning." He looked at his watch. It was just after nine. "Tonight, you try to get some rest. I'll be back tomorrow."

She looked up at him; trust mingled with anguish in her eyes. Then she moved back to the middle of the bed and huddled there, an orange lump on a gray woolen blanket. In the cold, dimly lit cell, she was the image of misery. Massey stood and backed toward the door. His hand shook slightly as he pushed the call buzzer. As he waited for Sergeant Tremont, feelings of bewilderment and sadness pressed down upon his shoulders like heavy sacks of sand.

Just as he heard the key work its way into the lock, he caught a different sound from the direction of the cot. He started to walk back, but as he moved closer, he stopped. The soft notes of a song punctuated by sobs rose from the orange mound. He recognized the strangled words of the hymn and shivered involuntarily. His mind traveled back to his youth, the day his sister had died. He'd passed by his mother's bedroom and heard her sobbing and singing the same hymn. "Rock of ages, cleft for me, let me hide myself in thee."

# CHAPTER 3

The arresting officer at the sheriff's department two blocks away wasn't in the mood to talk with any attorney about the murder. All he wanted to do was go home, go to sleep and quit thinking about the day's events. But he still had a pile of reports to finish. He had to give his investigative report to the district attorney the first thing next morning so the D.A. could file the murder charges. He had been bombarded all day with newspaper and TV reporters. It had been the worst day of his life. Sixteen years on the force, and never had he dealt with anything so traumatic.

But the man standing in front of him was stubborn about hearing all the details. Well, he'd gone over the story so many times, he figured once more wouldn't hurt. He fired out the facts in an emotionless, robotic manner.

"Well, Mr. Massey, I arrived at the scene of the crime shortly after noon today. Your client was standing over the body of a Mr. Edward Stewart, local schoolteacher. She was holding a 20-gauge shotgun in her hands. He was dying at her feet with a huge hole in his chest from a shotgun blast. I ordered the woman to put the gun on the ground, and she did. I told her to sit down on the grass away from the gun. She did that also without resistance. I then checked on Mr. Stewart, but I could find no pulse. The paramedics arrived and began working on the body. I then told your client she was under arrest and read her her rights. I immediately brought her to the station."

"Where she signed a confession?"

"Yes. We asked permission to tape-record her confession, and she agreed. No coercion, no bullying," he said, flicking at a fly buzzing near his ear. "Not only that, she stated she would do it all over again if she had the chance."

"Was she coherent from what you could tell, in a stable state of mind?"

"Yes. She was very calm."

"Did she tell you why she shot Mr. Stewart?"

"No. She kept repeating that he deserved to die and she was glad she was the one who had killed him. Take my word for it, big-city attorney or no, she's going to get the gas chamber."

Massey left the sheriff's office feeling depressed and exhausted. And he needed food. He hadn't had anything but a Big Mac on the drive up. That was hours ago. He headed for the hotel he'd passed earlier on Main Street. When he pulled into the circular driveway of the St. Francis, he saw it was getting a facelift. Ladders, buckets and other tools were scattered around the front. His heart sank. Just what he needed, to be awakened at dawn by jackhammers. He looked down the street but didn't see any other hotel signs. In frustration, he pulled the car into a guest parking space, took the briefcase off the seat next to him and got out of the car. He opened the trunk and removed the emergency overnight bag he always had packed and walked toward the entrance.

The three-story wooden building had stained glass windows and carved oak swinging doors, encrusted with panels of crimson and green crystal. *She must have been a queen in her day*, he thought as he pushed through the doors. He paused, startled by the unexpected elegance. An enormous gilded and crystal chandelier hung over the foot of the red-carpeted winding staircase. He had an overwhelming feeling, as he had at the jailhouse, that he had stepped back in time.

Massey walked over to an ornately framed oil painting above the stone fireplace. It depicted a beautiful young lady of the night, probably one of the famous madams who ran the place when Susanville was in her heyday during the California gold rush of 1849.

"May I help you, sir?" The deep voice startled Massey, and he turned toward the desk behind him to see a thin-faced, balding man in a western vest and bolo tie regarding him with a smile.

"Yes," answered Massey, walking over. "I got caught up in the atmosphere."

"First-time guests often do, sir," said the clerk. "We're in the process of turning the clock back a century here. There's a great demand for period facilities like ours," he explained. "We expect to be full every night when renovations are completed."

Massey listened politely for a few minutes about the hotel's plans, then asked for a room. After he finished registering, he looked around the lobby and inquired, "Do you have a bar?"

"The saloon is right down the hall, sir," said the clerk, handing him a room key. "Room 202. Corner room on the top floor. You shouldn't be disturbed by the construction."

Massey felt a surge of relief. "That's the first good news of the day," he said, and walked toward the saloon.

The room contained a polished mahogany bar with a brass rail. The only two other people in the room were sitting at a small table lit with a miner's lamp. Massey walked to the bar and slumped down on a stool. "A double Johnny Walker Black Label," he said to the buxom female bartender, dressed in a red velvet outfit with a plunging neckline. She handed him the drink, and he swirled the golden brown liquid in the tumbler before putting it to his lips. Then he downed the scotch in a single gulp.

"Mister, that's the way the old miners used to do it," the bartender said in a husky voice. "Want another double?"

"Nope, that's enough. What I need is food."

"The dining room's open, but it won't be serving the full menu this late." She leaned over the counter and revealed more of her buxom figure. "Be sure to come back for an after-dinner drink, honey."

Massey smiled as he pulled ten bucks out of his wallet, placed it on the bar and left.

"Thanks for the tip, mister," the woman called from behind.

It was nearly 11 p.m. and he was the only person in the dining room, which was decorated with mining gear and old photographs. He chose a table by the window that looked out on the few streetlights and a fantastic array of twinkling stars in the night sky.

A waiter dressed in Levi's jeans and a light brown western shirt with a bolo tie handed him a thick red menu, but warned him that only the sandwiches were available. Massey ordered a roast beef sandwich and a glass of merlot. When the waiter brought his order, he sipped the wine, nibbled at the sandwich and thought about Leola Langley.

What he knew for sure was that she had murdered a local schoolteacher. He couldn't discount the arresting officer's statement. She had signed a confession, even stating she would do it all over again.

He leaned forward and rested his head on his hands. "Leola murders a man she doesn't know, 300 miles away from her family. Signs a confession and then tells me she doesn't remember anything. Now she is counting on me to take her home to her family. How the hell did she get into this mess, and how the hell did I get involved? Christ, I only met the woman several months ago, and now I'm up to my ass in alligators."

"Pardon me?" asked the waiter, who had come up to the table quietly.

"Sorry. Just thinking aloud."

After finishing the sandwich, Massey dragged his tired body upstairs. The walls in his room had been freshly painted in a soft white, but the rest of the decor was from the 1960s. A picture of the planned restoration hung over the king-size bed. *Should be nice someday*, he thought as he undressed and threw his clothes on the chair in front of a shabby dresser.

He was too tired for a bath, so he took a hot steamy shower to help him unwind. When he finished, he put on his black boxers, crawled into bed and snapped off the light on the nightstand. His mind was still racing, but before long the double scotch and the glass of wine numbed his brain cells. He fell asleep.

▼

He was trying to yell as loud as he could for help, but he couldn't make any noise. He was clothed in jailhouse garb, and his cellmate was trying to cut his throat. He could see the glistening blade of the knife descending toward his jugular. Another second and his life would be over. He lashed out with his fist and hit the nightstand next to the bed. Abruptly Massey awoke from the nightmare, sweating profusely, and looked at the illuminated numbers on the clock which indicated 1:30 a.m.

He turned over and tried to go back to sleep, but his fatigued mind replayed the events surrounding his acquaintance with Leola Langley.

It was Susan Winters who had introduced him to Leola. That thought led him to more pleasant memories of Susan, the real reason he had dropped everything and raced up here.

Seven months ago he'd been sitting in the Superior Courthouse at the Palo Alto Annex during the closing moments of a fraud securities case against a major brokerage house and its dishonest broker. As he listened to the defense lawyer's boring closing argument, he looked back toward his clients in the front row.

Just then, the door in the back of the courtroom opened, and a gorgeous blond woman slipped quietly into the room. As she walked gracefully down the center aisle and sat across from his clients, Massey could see that she was petite, about thirty-five, and had a beautiful face with big blue eyes and full, rounded lips. She was dressed in a hot pink knit suit that revealed a knockout figure. Their eyes met, and she smiled and raised her hand in a brief acknowledgment. Massey stared for several seconds, wondering who she was.

Suddenly he recognized her. *Susan Winters. God, she's just as beautiful as she was, what, ten years ago,* he thought to himself, remembering the divorce case he had handled for her.

His fascination with her was abruptly interrupted by a bark from Judge Evans. "Mr. Massey, if you can take your eyes off that pretty woman in the first row, maybe I can get you to give your rebuttal to the jury. Mr. Finnegan has finished his closing argument."

Massey rose from the chair, sensing the warmth in his cheeks. "Sorry, Your Honor. I got so bored listening to Mr. Finnegan that I found my mind and, particularly, my eyes wandering." He looked over at the jury members who were chuckling with undisguised relief at the diversion.

About twenty minutes later, when the case had been handed over to the jurors, Massey went over to the woman in pink. "Susan Winters. You look stunning," he said.

"I'm sorry to bother you," she began. "I went to your office and your secretary, Helen, suggested I might talk with you here as soon as the case went to the jury. I hope you don't mind."

"Not at all. We'll go across the street for a cup of coffee while the jury is deliberating."

They selected a booth in the corner and slid onto the blue vinyl-covered seats opposite one another. Massey looked into Susan's eyes. "How have you been? I've often wondered how you recovered from that bitter divorce battle."

As Susan began talking, the waitress shouted at them from the kitchen door. "Massey, the bailiff just called. The jury has reached a decision."

Massey winced. "That's crazy," he said, mostly to himself. "They've only been out for fifteen minutes. Hardly enough time to pick a foreperson."

Then to Susan, "I've got to go back to court for the decision. If you've got time, come with me. Then after the verdict, we can go back to my office."

"I'm in no hurry," she replied. They left the coffee shop and hurried back across the street.

In the courtroom, Massey took his seat and waited for the judge to call the court in session. The jury filed out of the jury room and took their seats. The foreperson handed the verdict form to the bailiff, who handed it to the judge. As the judge unfolded the sheet of paper and looked at it, Massey saw the judge's jaw drop and his eyes bulge. He handed the verdict to the clerk, who read it aloud. "We the jury find the defendant liable to the plaintiff for the sum of eighty thousand dollars and levy punitive damages against the defendant . . ." There was a long pause followed by, "in the amount of three million dollars."

Massey leaped from his chair and ran over to his clients, who were crying and hugging each other. He put his arms around them, saying in a loud and happy voice, "We got those crooked bastards real good. They won't try that scam again soon."

After the chaos died down, he went over to Susan. "If you've got time, how about we move my office over to the bar at the President Hotel. We can sit in a booth, have a drink to celebrate the best win I've ever had, and talk about your problem for as long as you like."

Susan looked up. "You've got my vote, counselor."

They drove in separate cars to Michael's Bar and Grill at the President Hotel in downtown Palo Alto. Inside, they chose a table in a dark corner adjacent to a huge oak bar from the early 1900s. The large mirror behind the bar reflected the overhead Tiffany lamps.

A young waitress in a dark blue skirt and halter top took their order and returned shortly with a glass of white wine for Susan and a scotch and water for Massey. "Cheers to a great win," said Susan, raising her glass.

"Why, thank you. Now let's talk about you. I'm curious about why you came to see me."

Susan's blue eyes closed for a moment. When she looked up, he saw the moisture on her cheek. "I hate to ruin your party, Mr. Massey, but I feel like a total failure. I remarried four years ago. My husband is a college music teacher. He just left me and my daughter for one of his students."

"Oh, no," Massey said, taking her hands in his. "I'm so sorry."

She cried softly, and Massey took a handkerchief from his pocket and gave it to Susan. After she composed herself, they talked about her problems. Eventually they ordered dinner.

When Susan remembered to look at her watch, she was surprised. "I can't believe it's seven already. I've got to get home to my teenage daughter. She probably thinks her mother has been kidnapped." She rose and held out her hand to Massey. "Thanks, for dinner and a great conversation. I feel much better. Maybe there is life after death."

"I'll have my secretary call you tomorrow and we'll start down the ugly road of the divorce process. Thank you for celebrating my win."

▼

That conversation led to the beginning of a business relationship. And after that, a personal one. Massey was surprised at his attraction to Susan. He hadn't felt this way since his wife died four years ago. Susan made it clear that she was gun-shy of men and didn't want to get into a serious relationship. Even so, they dated frequently. Massey became so smitten with Susan that it wasn't long before he purchased a small condominium in Saratoga across from the Paul Masson Winery in order to be closer to her home.

Leola Langley's name first arose one Saturday evening shortly after he'd moved into his new condominium. Massey had invited Susan for dinner. A masterful cook, he had prepared beef Wellington with all the trimmings.

"What a fantastic meal," Susan told him. "You're a genie with many talents."

"If I were, I'd be able to snap my fingers and have the place cleaned," he joked. "What I really need is a housekeeper."

"I've got a great housekeeper," Susan said. "She's also a good friend. Practically raised my daughter. Her name is Leola Langley. Would you like to meet her?"

"Indeed," he had answered, smiling.

The following day, Leola Langley called Massey's office and agreed to clean his condo and do the wash each Thursday. She proved a very capable and dependable housekeeper. He trusted her enough to give her the key to the place so she could let herself in.

*That was five months ago,* he thought now. And those five months had been filled with tragedy. Since then, Massey had handled an ugly incident against the Los Gatos School Board involving a teacher who had molested Leola's son. *Now, the woman was in jail for murder and facing death in the gas chamber.*

# CHAPTER 4

Massey slept fitfully through the rest of the night. When he awoke the next morning, the sun was already pushing through the thin chintz curtains on the window. He looked at the clock. Seven o'clock. He got up and stretched. The sagging mattress had played havoc with his back, so he let the hot water from the shower massage his sore muscles for several minutes. By 7:40 he was in the restaurant ordering a hearty miner's breakfast.

He had carried his yellow legal pad with him. Massey knew that Leola's state of mind at the time of the murder would be a crucial element in her defense at trial. He knew of the devastating anguish she had undergone during the last two months and its toll on her mental stability. He wanted to have meticulous notes of her mental deterioration to give to the local criminal attorney who would defend Leola in Susanville.

Massey began making notes about the evening Leola and her husband Sam came to see him at Susan's house. It was late March, and he and Susan were having a glass of wine in her kitchen. The phone rang, and Susan frowned as she spoke to the caller. "Well, actually, Massey's here," she said. Then, "No, that would be fine. Please come right over."

"Sorry," she said as she set down the phone. "That was Leola. She and her husband, Sam, are coming over. They want to talk to you."

*Damn*, he thought to himself. *Another call at home from people asking for a professional freebie.*

"Leola sounded frantic," Susan said, as though she had read his thoughts. "I couldn't turn her down."

Within ten minutes, they heard a knock on the back door. Massey let Leola and her husband in. She wore a crumpled blue cotton dress with an apron streaked with spaghetti sauce tied around her waist. Her hands were trembling.

"Mr. Massey, this here's my husband, Sam," she said. Massey and the man shook hands. He was a wiry little guy, about five foot eight, 140 pounds, with ruddy skin and dark curly hair. He was dressed in grease-stained Levi's and a thin cotton T-shirt. His lips were pursed, his jaw clenched.

Susan came over and put one arm around Leola's shoulders. "Please, come into the living room," she said, leading them across the kitchen to a large room with beige carpeting and an off-white sofa, love seat and chair grouped together for conversation. "I'll make some tea," she said, and headed back to the kitchen, catching Massey's eye as she left.

Massey nodded his head slightly, as if to say, "Don't worry. I'll take care of them."

"What's the matter?" Massey directed the question to Sam. He could tell Leola was having a hard time holding back tears.

Sam stood up from the sofa, hesitated a moment, then took a deep breath. Slowly he began to talk, all the while gazing at the floor. "Last night when Leola and I were eating supper, a guy named Walker called us on the telephone. He said he was the daddy of Scotty Walker, one of our son's classmates. He told me that his boy's fifth-grade teacher put his damn hand down the back of his boy's pants at school, grabbed his bare butt and squeezed it. His boy told him our Billy and this here teacher had something goin' on."

Sam swallowed hard, fighting to keep his voice from cracking. He took a deep breath and was about to continue when Susan entered with a tray containing a pot of tea, cups, saucers and a box of tissues. She put the tray down on the coffee table and poured four cups of tea. Sam drank a little, cleared his throat and said, "His boy said the goldang teacher would call Billy out of class and take him down to the bathroom.

They'd come back to the class a little while later. He said they'd been doin' this for a couple months." Sam looked harder at the floor, unable to speak anymore.

Massey remained silent. He could tell Sam was basically shy and quiet, but tonight he was smoldering hot and about to erupt. Finally, the man looked up and met Massey's eyes. "I'm so dad-burned mad, I think I could kill the son-of-a-bitchin' teacher."

Sam paused and put his face in his hands, the only sound, his heavy breathing. "I need a break," he said. "I'm having a hard time gettin' it all out." Sam went to the sliding glass door leading to the back patio and stepped outside. He pulled out a cigarette, lit it and took a deep puff. Susan, Massey and Leola stared at him in silence.

Five minutes later, Sam snuffed out the cigarette and came back inside. Massey was the first to speak. "What did you do when you heard your son was being molested?"

"I went to my Billy's room and asked him if something was goin' on between him and his teacher. Billy refused to look me in the eye. He didn't say anything. Then my boy started bawling. Billy said he couldn't help it, that his teacher warned him not to say anything about his touching and kissing his wiener or else he would tell his mommy and daddy. Billy said he felt like killing hisself." Sam put his face in his hands and bellowed loudly. Leola got up and put her arms around him. They sobbed in unison.

Massey looked over at Susan on the love seat. She too was crying. He rose from his chair and sat down next to her, putting an arm around her and pulling her close.

Sam took several deep breaths. "I'm okay now," he said.

"What happened next?" asked Massey.

"The following morning, I went down to the principal's office and told him to get rid of that damn teacher because he was fooling around with my son. Y'all know what that idiot said?"

Sam looked Massey square in the eye. "He said Mr. Arnold's the best teacher in the school and my boy must be lying. I almost hit him on the spot. I got mad and said if he didn't get rid of the teacher, I'd have his sorry ass. He called for help and had me thrown out of the office. Can you believe that?" Sam sat down. He didn't say anything else.

Leola, wadding up several tissues in her hands, spoke in a trembling voice. "The next day we got in the car and went over to the superintendent's office. The secretary didn't even want to let us in the office, but Sam opened the door anyway, and we went in. Mr. Garrity, the superintendent, accused us of making up lies about the teacher. He treated us like white trash and walked out on us."

"Did Billy go to school today?" asked Massey.

"No," answered Leola, dropping onto the sofa beside her husband. "We're not lettin' him go back to that class until that sinnin' teacher is out of there."

She stopped speaking and the room got quiet again, the four of them sharing the emotional impact of the revelations.

"Mr. Massey, we need some lawyering," said Sam. "Ms. Susan tol' Leola how you were the best. I never seen my Leola like this, crying and carrying on. She's even spitting up blood."

Susan tapped Massey on the arm. "There's a school board meeting every Wednesday evening. That means one tomorrow night. Do you think we should go and report this to them? Maybe the board would take some action."

"Good idea," answered Massey. He turned to the couple huddled on the sofa. "Don't worry. We'll get this straightened out. Do you feel up to coming to the meeting?"

"We'll be there," said Sam. They all stood up and walked together into the kitchen.

As Sam and Leola left, Massey felt a chilling sensation run through his body, the same feeling he'd had many times before the start of a major case.

# CHAPTER    5

Massey was on his third cup of coffee in the hotel's restaurant, still making notes of the events leading up to the arrest of Leola Langley. He paused, remembering the news that Stanley Arnold had committed suicide. What happened next had been even more bizarre.

Three weeks after the suicide, he remembered taking Susan to his favorite restaurant retreat, Bellissimo, above Woodside on Skyline Boulevard, a narrow highway that runs from Saratoga to the Half Moon Bay highway, along the top of the Santa Cruz mountain range. One side looks down on the Bay Area Peninsula and San Francisco Bay, the other side on the Pacific Ocean. The view that evening was spectacular; lights from the cities and cars sparkled in the distance, and the ocean waters glistened as moonbeams struck the surface.

As he walked in with Susan, he smelled the pungent aroma of garlic and olive oil. The dining room was long and narrow, surrounded by glass so patrons could enjoy the spectacular view. Each table was covered with a red-and-white checkered cloth, and a bottle of Chianti wrapped in a straw basket sat in the middle. The walls were covered with prints of Italian seaport cities. Massey had often come to Bellissimo when he wanted to shed the cares of his law practice. Here, couples could engage in relaxing conversation.

They ordered martinis and after the waiter brought them, Susan turned to Massey. She appeared troubled by something. "Leola and I talked about Arnold's suicide this morning. She's been looking in the newspaper every day since the suicide, but there has been no mention of the death. I went down to the library and went through the *San Jose Mercury* and *San Francisco Chronicle*. Not a word. Isn't it surprising not to have some mention of the death of a popular teacher?"

"Perhaps the family requested the papers withhold any mention of the death," Massey responded.

"But Arnold has no family. I found that out when Amy was in his class. At a parent-teacher conference, he once told me that his wife and two children were burned to death in a fire at his apartment several years before. He was out of town at the time."

"I'll get a copy of the death certificate from the County Department of Vital Statistics tomorrow," said Massey, taking her hands in his.

Just then Domenico, owner of the restaurant, barged out of the kitchen and approached their table. Massey looked up at his old friend with dark brown, sun-parched skin, gray hair and a large Roman nose. Domenico was smiling and looking at Susan. "Ciao, mio amico. Who is this bella creature?"

"Susan, meet my old friend Domenico. He's from the isle of Capri." Massey smiled. "You've got to promise to stay away from him. He's got a passion for good-looking women."

Susan held her hand out and said, "Pleased to meet you, Domenico."

Domenico bent over and placed a big kiss on her fingertips. With a flourish and a bow, he announced, "Signora, your wish be my command."

Massey chimed in, "Give me a break, you old lecher. Go back to your kitchen, quit flirting with my girlfriend, and cook us up some of your great Italian cuisine with lots of garlic."

"For you and your lady, Signore Massey, I prepare a magnifico feast." He turned and strode back into the kitchen.

"What a charmer. Can he cook as well as he flirts?" Susan's eyes sparkled.

"He's awesome. You wait and see what the master creates."

Susan pursed her lips. "Leola tells me that Billy's classmates are calling him names. Worse than that, the bigger boys are beating him up, blaming him for the death of Mr. Arnold. At home, he stays in his room, eats very little and won't talk to his family. Leola thought at first that he would get over it, but now she is very concerned about Billy's physical and mental health."

Massey shook his head in sympathy. "It sounds like Billy and the family need help. I know a psychiatrist at the Children's Hospital at Stanford who deals with traumatized kids. I'll see if I can persuade him to do some pro bono work for Leola and Billy."

Out of the kitchen's swinging doors came Domenico carrying a tray loaded with bruchetta and his special appetizer, steamed mussels in garlic tomato sauce. After serving the dishes, he immediately turned, went to his wine cellar and brought back a very old bottle of Brunello Chianti from Tuscany. Soon to follow was the *prima piatti*, puttenesca, followed by the *secondo piatti*, osso buco. The meal was so delicious that Massey and Susan pushed the subject of the Langleys to the back of their minds. After they were finished, Domenico bid them goodbye. Susan told him, "This meal is the most wonderful meal I've ever had. Thank you so much, Domenico."

"I'ma glad you like it. Buona notte," he said, smiling and bowing. "Pleasa coma to my ristorante again."

The couple left the restaurant and slid into the Porsche. Massey turned on the CD player and Frank Sinatra's seductive "I've Got You Under My Skin" came on. Massey reached over and held Susan's hand. She responded by squeezing his hand.

"Susan, I totally enjoy your company," said Massey. "Ever since my wife died, I haven't been interested in dating, even though my friends want to introduce me to their 'perfect and gorgeous' single female friend. I must admit I'm now smitten with a beautiful woman whose eyes sparkle, and who is the most sensitive and intelligent person that I have ever met."

"Well, that is quite a compliment, Lawyer Massey. Are you often smitten with your clients?"

Massey looked over at her. "You devil, you're pulling my leg when I'm trying to be serious,"

Susan looked at him with her big blue eyes glistening. "I am truly flattered."

▼

When they arrived at Susan's home, Massey escorted her to the door. She looked up into his eyes. "Would you like to come in for a glass of port? My daughter is spending the weekend with her dad, so that jungle music she always plays won't be drowning out the conversation."

"Now, that's an invitation I can't refuse," replied Massey.

Once inside Susan turned to Massey. "If you don't mind, I'm going to put on something more comfortable. Why don't you light a fire in the fireplace? The port and the glasses are in the cupboard over the refrigerator," said Susan.

After lighting the fire, Massey dimmed the overhead lights in the living room. Susan entered wearing a soft, cream-colored fleece lounge outfit. The flames of the fire danced, and candles glowed next to two glasses of port on the coffee table. Massey turned around and saw Susan bathed in the candlelight. "You look like an angel."

She smiled back and their eyes held each other's. Susan walked over to him and he held her in his arms a long moment. Then they slipped down to the floor in front of the fireplace and listened to the soft background music of Kenny G that Massey had turned on. They toasted each other with the port. He set his glass down on the low table and put his hand behind Susan's neck and began massaging it.

"Umm, that feels good," said Susan.

They sat close to one another in silence for a long time gazing into the fire. Massey slid his hand lower and began massaging Susan's shoulders and back.

She sighed under the physical electricity of his touch. As his hands moved to her lower back, she rolled over and lay on her stomach. Massey's hands gently rubbed her buttocks. Susan turned on her side and murmured, "Just where are we headed here, Counselor?"

Massey reached over and folded her into his arms. They began kissing, long, slowly, passionately.

"God, I'm in love with you," whispered Massey.

"It think it's a two-way street," uttered Susan.

At that, they began undressing one another with the impatience and fervor of young lovers who know no bounds. Massey traced his fingers along the entire length of Susan's body and kissed each delicate and tender part of her. Susan began to utter soft moaning sounds against his chest as Massey entered slowly and softly. They passionately made love, both reaching a climax together as if they were one. They lay spent in each other's arms as the last embers of the fire died down.

# CHAPTER 6

As soon as Massey arrived at his office on Monday morning, he said to his secretary, Helen McGuiness, "Helen, go down to the county office complex in San Jose and get a copy of a Mr. Stanley Arnold's death certificate at the Department of Vital Statistics. He died on April second of this year."

An hour later Helen called from the county building, "Mr. Massey, the clerk can't find any death certificate for the entire year regarding a man named Stanley Arnold."

Puzzled, he called Sergeant Cardoza, the officer who investigated the Arnold case at the request of the school district. "Officer, this is Skip Massey. Are you sure Stanley Arnold committed suicide?"

"No question about it," was his reply. "On the morning of the suicide, I got a call from the superintendent. He said the body had been interred at a mortuary in San Mateo County. I couldn't get through to the coroner's office up there, so I called the owner of the mortuary who confirmed the death. I received a copy of the death certificate from them two weeks later."

Massey asked, "Did you ever see the body at the mortuary?"

"I was too busy. A copy of the death certificate was sufficient."

"San Mateo County, eh? Well, that explains why I couldn't locate the death certificate in Santa Clara County. Thanks, officer. Appreciate the information."

Massey thought it would be a good idea to get a certified copy of the death certificate and give it to Leola so she would be satisfied that Arnold had committed suicide. He wrote the Department of Vital Statistics in San Mateo County. Three days later, Massey received a call from Wendy Smythe, a clerk with the San Mateo County Department of Vital Statistics. "We don't have any record of the death of Stanley Arnold," she informed him.

"I don't understand what's going on," said Massey. "Sergeant Cardoza of the Santa Clara County Sheriff's Office has such a certificate. I'll have Officer Cardoza send you a copy." Massey hung up the telephone puzzled.

He called Officer Cardoza again and asked him to fax the copy of the death certificate. He received the fax within ten minutes. It looked official. Still, Massey called the clerk back. "I've got a copy of that death certificate and I'm going to fax you a copy. I would like to have a certified copy."

The clerk called back in about an hour after he faxed the certificate. "Mr. Massey, the death certificate you sent me is not authentic." Massey sat there stunned at the news. *What the hell is going on? This suicide is starting to smell like a rotten fish,* he said to himself.

Massey strode outside and hopped in his car. In minutes he arrived at the Sergeant's office. He barged in. Officer Cardoza was sitting at his desk in an office hardly big enough to house the desk, much less ten file cabinets full of documents. He was a large man of Portuguese heritage, with olive skin, black hair and big brown eyes. His tan gabardine uniform looked as if it had been rolled up into a ball all night. There were files and papers scattered all over the office.

"The document you sent me is a forgery. What the hell is going on? Let's see your original document."

"Hey, get off my back. It's valid. What makes you think it's forged?"

"Let me see the original," Massey insisted.

The Sergeant went to a cabinet and pulled a document out of a file. He sat down at his desk, cleared off a bunch of papers, and then reached down into a drawer and pulled out a magnifying glass. He looked at the document carefully for several minutes. Finally he looked up, surprise on his face. He pointed at the name "Stanley Arnold" and said, "Holy shit. Look closely through this. You can see where somebody whited out the original name on the death certificate and typed in Stanley Arnold's name. See the irregular spacing in the type, compared to the other type on the document? You're right, it is a forgery."

"The damn suicide was a hoax? Sergeant, what was the name of the mortuary you spoke with?"

A suddenly subdued Cardoza gave Massey the name of McClaren's Mortuary. Massey used the telephone on the desk and called the number. An answering machine responded. Massey left his name and office number.

No response came that afternoon. The next day Massey called the mortuary back. An operator said the line had been disconnected.

Massey dialed a lawyer friend of his, Alex Cochran, in San Mateo County. "Would you mind looking in the yellow pages of your phone book for the name McClaren's Mortuary?"

After a few moments, Alex responded, "Massey, no such animal exists, at least not in my telephone book."

Massey then called the telephone company and asked for the name of the person that subscribed for their services on behalf of the mortuary. The operator looked up the information on her computer and stated, "I have an address for McClaren's Mortuary at fifteen twenty-four El Camino Real in San Carlos. The subscriber is listed under the name of John McClaren at fifty-four forty-five Farley Drive, San Carlos."

Massey got in his car and drove to the business address of the supposed mortuary and then the listed home address of John McClaren in San Carlos. Both were nonexistent.

He telephoned Susan. "How about meeting me for a drink after work. I found out something really disturbing today. How about Victoria's Station, a little after five?"

"You're on. See you there."

Victoria's Station was located right across from De Anza College where Susan worked, on Stevens Creek Boulevard in Cupertino. Several years before, a couple of bright college grads had bought a bunch of railroad cars, painted them a rust color, welded them together to make a restaurant, and specialized in roast beef. The place became so popular that they started a chain. A few years later they sold the chain to a major corporation and walked away with a bundle of money.

This evening Massey was sitting in a booth in the caboose car when Susan sauntered in. "Over here, good-lookin'," Massey called to get her attention. She gave him a kiss on the cheek and sat down. She pulled out a pack of cigarettes from her purse, lit one and looked Massey in the eye. "Well, you've got my undivided attention. What's going on?"

Massey leaned over with his eyes locking onto her. "Arnold's suicide is a hoax. Somebody forged the death certificate. He must be alive and hiding out."

Susan sat upright, her jaw dropped and her eyes widened. "I'm in a state of shock. I can't believe it! A hoax? Arnold is not dead?"

"I'm afraid it's true," said Massey, telling her about the forged death certificate and the nonexistent mortuary.

"Did he pull it off to escape the arrest and humiliation? I wonder if he did this by himself, or was he helped by somebody else? Let's not tell Leola or Sam, because they'll go crazy."

"You may be right. Better not to say anything until we uncover all the facts."

# CHAPTER 7

Skip Massey looked at his watch; it was 9:45 a.m. He'd been at the hotel, taking notes on the events leading up to the arrest of Leola Langley, for over two hours. He was getting tired but also realized he needed to make a few phone calls to find an attorney to represent Leola.

He sat back in his chair, stretched his legs, raised his arms in the air and took a deep breath. He had a tremendous fatigue hangover from his lousy night's sleep. He wasn't looking forward to the rest of the day. His job was to find the best criminal attorney in town to defend Leola. He knew from past experience that in small communities, local lawyers have a great advantage over out-of-towners because everybody knows everybody, including the judge and the jurors. He knew he wasn't the right lawyer to defend Leola. Not only was he a foreigner in this small community, but he hadn't tried a criminal case in years.

His bladder was full from all the coffee he had consumed, so he got up and headed to the bathroom down the hall. On the way back to his table, he stopped at the telephone booth and called the county court clerk's office. He asked for the chief clerk. After a few moments, a woman's voice answered.

"Ma'am, I'm an out-of town attorney who needs to find the best criminal lawyer in town. Any suggestions?"

There was a momentary pause and then, "Let me have you talk to the bailiff for Judge Brandon. He sees all the cases, and maybe he'll be able to help you."

Massey held the phone while she switched the call

to another line. "Hello, Judge Brandon's chambers, Bailiff Henderson here."

"Officer, name's Skip Massey. I'm an attorney and an acquaintance of the woman arrested yesterday for shooting a local teacher. I need to find the best criminal attorney in town."

"Ed Ames and Jerry Kane are the ones you want to talk to. They are head and shoulders above the rest of the criminal lawyers in town. You'll need a good lawyer. Your client's in a heap of trouble."

Massey called the offices of the two attorneys but couldn't get in to see them until late that afternoon. He returned to the task of finishing his notes of the events leading up to Leola's arrest. Massey picked up his legal pad from the table and went to the lobby of the hotel, where he located an antique chair covered with red velvet in the far corner away from the front desk. It was quiet. He sat down and started writing about his search for Stanley Arnold.

The hunt for Arnold began the Tuesday morning after he and Susan had dinner at Victoria's Station. Massey remembered he woke up with a splitting headache. He staggered into the bathroom, turned on the cold water faucet and drenched his face. The coldness cleared the cobwebs. He took a good look at himself in the mirror and saw a couple of bloodshot eyes staring back. *Hey, you're getting too old for this late night drinking and romancing, my boy,* he said to himself, noticing the large bags under his eyes. He thought of the after-dinner drinks that he and Susan had consumed while talking late into the evening; his invitation to her to stop by his condominium for a nightcap. They eventually made love until the wee hours of the morning. *I'm having the time of my life with this lady. She may kill me off, but it's worth it.* A smile appeared in the mirror.

After dressing in a two-piece blue pin-striped suit, he headed for Los Encinos Elementary School to get information on Mr. Stanley Arnold. As he walked up the steps leading to the entrance, he took notice of the school building. Fairly new, single story, ranch style, with walls of windows to let sunlight into the classrooms.

Upon entering the building, he strolled down the quiet hallway toward the administration office. A secretary in a blue print dress sat at the front desk.

"Ma'am, my name is Skip Massey. I'm doing some investigative work concerning Mr. Stanley Arnold, who recently died. Do you have any information regarding his phone number and address?" Massey said as he handed her his business card. She looked at it and retreated to a side room.

In a few minutes she returned. "We don't have any address for Mr. Arnold, only his post office box number." She handed Massey a piece of paper with a post office box number in Los Gatos and a telephone number with a 415 area code and a 555 prefix. Massey knew the area code covered Palo Alto/Los Altos north to San Francisco.

He thanked her and left the office. On his way out of the building, Massey spotted a telephone booth and called the number on the paper. Arnold's phone had been disconnected.

He hopped into his car and headed for the sheriff's office where he hoped to catch Sergeant Cardoza. At the office, he was escorted by a woman officer into Cardoza's private office. It was as messy as before, with papers and files strewn all over the room. "Sergeant, now that we know the suicide is a fake, is your department trying to track Arnold down?"

"Certainly, we put out an All Points Bulletin yesterday. No results yet. I'm sure Arnold is laying low. We'll eventually pick him up. He can't hide forever."

Massey didn't have much confidence in the affable but disorganized officer. "What happens when the fugitive changes his looks and gets a new set of IDs?"

"Well, that can be troublesome. Guys have been known to elude us for years, but we eventually pick them up," the sergeant said, as he tossed a file on the floor.

"Are you going to assign any investigative officer to this case?"

"Sorry," Cardoza replied. "We just don't have the resources." He shuffled another stack of papers. "All of our people are tied up in a hunt for that serial killer stalking young women in the East San Jose area."

"Sergeant, in the meantime this pedophile is roaming the streets. How about a list of all of the Stanley Arnolds and their addresses from the State Department of Motor Vehicles in Santa Clara and San Mateo counties? I've got a real interest in tracking the bastard down before he molests another young victim."

The sergeant shrugged, "Wait here." He returned in five minutes and handed Massey a sheet of paper. It contained about twenty names and addresses. "Hot off the press. Any help would be appreciated. Unofficially, of course."

Massey walked toward his car scratching his head, wondering if Cardoza ever had time to solve anything. On his way up to his own office, he called information to learn what towns were covered by the (415) 555-prefix.

"Sir, it would be Palo Alto and Menlo Park."

Back in his office in Palo Alto, Massey had Helen bring him coffee. He sat down at his large oak desk and looked at the list of names on the DMV sheet Cardoza had given him. There were five names with addresses in the Palo Alto and Menlo Park area. He leaned over to his intercom. "Helen, any free time on my calendar late this afternoon?"

"You're free after four," she responded.

"Don't book any other appointments. I'm going hunting for a missing pedophile."

He left the office at 4:30 and headed over to the two addresses in Palo Alto, one on Seale Avenue and the other on Bryant. Both were upscale homes, too expensive for a teacher, but he checked them out anyway. No luck. He pointed the nose of the Porsche northwest and headed for Menlo Park.

The first address was located in a two-story apartment complex just off Alameda de las Pulgas, where many high-density apartment buildings were clustered. As Massey drove into the complex, he noticed the landscaping was fully matured and matched the green wood siding of the buildings. As he got out of his car, he spotted a sign indicating the manager's apartment.

When he knocked on the door, a gray-haired woman opened it partially. She poked her head out. She was wearing granny glasses and a plaid cotton dress. Massey looked down at the elderly woman. She couldn't have been more than four foot eight inches tall. Massey slipped her his card. "I'm looking for a Mr. Stanley Arnold," he told her. "I understand he lives here."

"Well, mister, I keep my nose out of my tenants' business. I don't divulge any information about them." She started to close the door.

Massey quickly put his foot in the door. "Ma'am, Mr. Arnold has inherited a great deal of money, and there is a small reward for information about his where-abouts."

The landlady looked up at Massey and said in a loud voice, "Bug off, mister. I won't fall for that old line. Out of here or I'll call the police."

Massey retreated as the old woman slammed the door. He thought this type of building would be suitable for a bachelor teacher. He would return with a subpoena for the old woman's records if he had to.

First, however, he checked out the other two locations. Both were high-end single family residences, once again out of the price range for a teacher. He knocked at the doors of both homes and was assured that Arnold had not lived there.

That evening at Susan's home, Massey fixed himself a martini and poured Susan a glass of wine. He sat on the living room sofa, took his shoes off, and lay back stretching and taking a deep breath. "Whew, did I get the old heave-ho today from the elderly landlady," he said to Susan. "I was trying to track down Arnold's residence, and this old gal refused to talk. She gave me the bum's rush."

Susan got out of her chair, strode over to Massey and cupped her hands around his cheeks. "Poor baby, you need to charm elderly ladies as much as you do me. I'll bet you an evening in San Francisco that I can get all the information you want out of her."

"Okay, wise guy, you're on," Massey said, raising his glass. "Here's to my new detective."

"Back at you, boss." Susan leaned over and kissed Massey on the cheek.

▼

The following day after work, Susan drove into the apartment complex in Menlo Park and parked in front of the manager's office. She got out of her blue Mazda sports coupe and rang the front doorbell. The gray-headed landlady opened the door a crack. "What's your business, young lady?"

"I'm looking for an apartment. I saw your 'For Rent' sign."

"Come in," said the little woman, opening the door fully. The manager went behind the counter, and Susan followed her to the front desk. "You're lucky, young lady, the one-bedroom unit was just vacated yesterday. They normally rent up right away. It'll be one thousand per month, a month's rent in advance, and five hundred dollars security deposit. Want to see the unit?"

Susan nodded.

"Follow me," said the little old woman, grabbing a set of keys from the key board on the wall. She walked out the door and headed toward the rear apartments. She led Susan up the stairs into a building at the very rear of the property and opened the door of unit 45.

Susan walked through a small living room over-looking the parking lot. Adjacent to the living room was a small kitchenette, and then straight ahead was a bedroom hardly large enough to hold a double bed. To the left was a small bathroom and a shower. The green shag carpeting was worn with noticeable soil stains, the wall hangings were faded and in need of repair, and the place was in need of a paint job.

"What a lovely unit, Miss . . . "

"Mrs. McKee, I'm the owner of these beautiful apartments."

That comment almost made Susan laugh out loud, but she contained herself and held out her hand. "I'm Susan Winters. I'm a teacher, and this looks like the place I need. It's close to my school. I used to date

48

a teacher in this complex a couple of years ago. I wonder if he's still here. I can't think of his name, but he always wore a mustache with a butch hair cut."

"We had a teacher move out just a couple of weeks ago, and he kind of fits your description. Could be the same man."

"That's too bad. He was a nice man. I'd love to look him up. Is he still in the area?" Susan said as she looked in the eyes of the little lady.

"I don't know. Actually, he didn't do the moving. His brother did it for him. Said his brother, Stanley, called and told him he'd been in a terrible accident, and needed help getting his furniture moved."

"That's it, Stanley Arnold was his name. I'm sorry to hear that news. By the way, I'll need to call a moving company to move my belongings. Who did Stanley's brother use? I might as well use the same company. Stanley always was a good businessman. He got good deals all the time."

The elderly woman thought for a moment. "The name on the movers' shirts was something to the effect of 'starving' or 'hungry' movers. They drove an old beat-up van. There were a couple of young kids and a huge fella who was the boss."

"I like the unit very much. I'm going to bring my sister back tomorrow and see if she agrees. Thanks so much for your time." They left the apartment and walked around the building.

"Hurry back before I rent the unit to somebody else," said the old lady as Susan opened her car door to leave.

On the way home, Susan called Massey on her car phone, "I'll meet you at Victoria's Station for a quick one."

Victoria's Station was the local singles hangout after work. When Susan arrived shortly after five, the place was already jam-packed and noisy with young, good-looking women and men, most of whom worked in the computer businesses located in the adjacent Cupertino Industrial Park.

Massey spotted Susan when she entered and weaved his way through the crowd to catch her. "Come on over here, I've got a table in the corner to get away from the roar."

When they sat down, Massey noticed a big grin on Susan's face. "You look like a Cheshire cat with a secret to tell."

"You owe me one, big boy. I know how to charm the old ladies, particularly gray-haired apartment managers in Menlo Park." Susan went into the details of her eventful afternoon.

"You're a winner. Let me go grab a phone book and see if we can find a moving company that fits the old lady's description." When Massey returned, he was carrying two phone books, one for Santa Clara County and the other for San Mateo County. In the Santa Clara County book they found an address for the Starving College Student Movers in southeast San Jose.

"Hot dog, young lady, you've earned a night out in San Francisco at a show and a great restaurant."

▼

The next morning Massey was up bright and early. He felt great after nine hour's sleep. He opened the curtains in the bedroom and looked out at the early morning fog. *Should burn off by noon and turn into another beautiful day,* he thought.

After a quick bowl of fruit and a cup of coffee, Massey set out for the Starving College Student Movers. He had vivid memories of southeast San Jose. As a teenager, he worked summers in the fruit-packing plants which flourished in the area before Silicon Valley's growth destroyed most of the beautiful fruit orchards. He remembered loading tons of tomato boxes onto boxcars. He'd go home with stinky tomato juice plastered all over his clothes. In those days, all he earned was fifty cents an hour for that back-breaking work.

Massey headed down Highway 17. He turned south at the 101 interchange and then east on Alum Rock Road. *God, driving the Porsche makes me feel like a college kid again,* he thought as he looked into the rearview mirror, in search of a highway patrol who might spot his speeding vehicle. It wasn't long before he spotted an old fruit-packing plant with a hand-lettered sign: "Starving College Student Movers, keep us fed and we'll move your bed."

As he parked in front of the building, he cast a puzzled eye at the new, dark gray Mercedes Benz parked outside the main door. He entered the dark hallway, and his shoes crunched on the paper and rubbish littering the floor. Seeing nobody around, he shouted, "Anybody home?"

A female's voice answered down the hallway, "I'm in here." As Massey entered the room where the voice came from, he saw a well-endowed young blond in a tight powder-blue sweater and a short black skirt. Her curly head turned around, and after she cracked her bubble gum, she said with an infectious smile, "Can I help ya?"

"I'd like to see the owner," he said.

"You're talking to her."

Massey's mouth opened and he uttered "Ahh . . . "

"Don't look so surprised. My husband and I have owned the business for five years. I'm Gladys. We needed cash to get ourselves through college, so we came up with this gimmick. Pretty good, huh?"

"With ideas like that, you'll both be millionaires in no time flat."

"Well, even though we're finished with school, the biz has been so good, we're planning on expanding. Who knows, maybe we'll make it."

"Well, if that's your Mercedes out there, I'd say you and your husband are well on your way."

"You like it? Chuck gave it to me for my birthday last month. Our business has really taken off. He thought we ought to live it up a little."

Massey shook his head. Amazing, she couldn't have been more than twenty-five years of age.

"You want to be one of our customers and have us move some of your furniture?" she said as she cracked her gum again, chomping up and down on the big pink wad in her mouth.

"Well, I'm Skip Massey, a lawyer representing an estate called the Estate of Arnold. I'm trying to track down some of the assets. You see, Mr. Arnold committed suicide. Somebody posing as his representative went to his apartment in Menlo Park and removed all of his personal belongings and furniture without permission. I'm trying to locate the furniture."

"An attorney?" She fluttered her eyes and cocked her head to the side. "Attorneys are getting cuter every day," she said, cracking the gum again. "Let me find the invoice and shipping order." She rose from her chair and wiggled across the room in her skirt, which barely hid her derriere. She pulled open a file cabinet, turned and saw Massey goggling at her. She smiled as if to acknowledge his good taste. Then she pulled out the invoice. "Oh, I remember this move. A guy called and asked us to move his furniture and personal belongings. We took the load over to one of those mini-storage warehouses in Cupertino, right off of Highway 280 and Stevens Creek."

"Did you ever see the fellow who ordered the move?"

"No, but my husband helped on the job himself." She got up and opened the door and shouted, "Chuck, come in here a minute, will ya." Before long, a burly guy about six foot five inches tall and weighing at least 250 pounds, wearing worn-out Levi's and a white T-shirt, came ambling up.

"Honey, this is Mr. Massey. He says he represents the estate of the guy we did the move for a couple of weeks ago in Menlo Park." She looked down at the invoice. "The guy's name was Stanley Arnold."

The big guy put his paw out to shake hands, and his hand was so large he could have wrapped his fingers around Massey's hand twice. "What can I do for ya?" he said as he grasped Massey's hand so hard his knees almost buckled. Massey had to flex his hand repeatedly in order to get the blood flowing again.

"Just a couple of questions?"

The big guy nodded his head and waited.

"Was anybody in the apartment when you went to pick up the furniture?"

"Let me think a minute. Yeh, a guy was there when we arrived. He opened the door for us."

"What did he look like?"

"Brown hair, glasses, kind of heavy. Oh, he had a limp when he walked. Said he was the brother of the tenant. Paid me in cash." The burly man shrugged his shoulders.

"Did he sign for the job?"

"Sure. It's right here, honey," said Gladys as she pulled out a pink sheet and handed it to Massey.

Massey looked at a signature that he couldn't read. He looked at Chuck. "Did he ever use a name?

"Not that I remember, mister."

"You've both been very helpful." Massey started out the door but stopped and turned toward them. "Great name for a business."

Massey headed down Highway 280 for the Cupertino Mini-Max Storage. When he arrived, he spotted an old guy in a red plaid flannel shirt and Levi's sitting in a black wooden chair in front of the manager's office. Massey parked and walked over to the man, noticing that the old geezer hadn't shaved in days. He looked at Massey and spoke through the few teeth he had remaining in his mouth, "What can I do for ya, mister?"

"Do you know where I can find the manager?"

"You're lookin' at him, sonny," he said slowly, squinting at him suspiciously out of the corner of his eye. "What's your business?"

"I'm Skip Massey, an attorney for the Estate of Stanley Arnold. I'd like to ask you some questions about the whereabouts of some furniture."

"You got a court order?" The old geezer spit out a wad of tobacco.

"No, but here's my card," Massey said.

The old boy, still sitting in the chair, looked at the card, then up at Massey. He shook his head. "This ain't enough."

Massey reached in his back pocket, pulled out his wallet, grabbed a hundred dollar bill and held it out to him. "Maybe this will be enough."

The manager looked at the size of the bill, his eyes widened and he winced. "Well, that's mighty kind of you, mister. Come right on in the office with me," he said as he rose from his chair, took the money out of Massey's hand, and proceeded to the door of the office.

"I'm looking for furniture stored under the name of Stanley Arnold," Massey said.

The manager looked through his records for several minutes, then said, "No Stanley Arnold, but how about a George Arnold?"

"That may be the right one," said Massey, keeping his voice calm. "Is the furniture still stored here?"

"No, that guy, George Arnold, and another fellow brought a truck two days ago and took all of the stuff out of here."

"Can you tell me what the two men looked like?"

The manager scratched his head. Massey was hoping the elderly man didn't have an early case of Alzheimer's. Finally he said, "Well, the best I can recollect is that both men were in their late forties or early fifties. The fellow that signed the application under the name of George Arnold had a limp, the other guy had a crew cut and a mustache. That's about all that I can remember about them."

"Did they fill out an application?"

"Sure, the guy George did when he first leased the space," the old man replied. He reached down in a file drawer in the desk and pulled out a card and showed it to Massey. He copied down the address and phone number, thanked him and left.

Once in his car, Massey dialed the number given for George Arnold and found the line had been disconnected. He drove over to the address on the card, nonexistent. *Where the hell do I go from here?* he thought.

While Massey was out tracking down Arnold's furniture at the movers and then the mini-storage, Susan left a message at his office requesting the pleasure of his company at dinner.

It was 6:30 p.m. when he arrived at Susan's house. Susan opened the door with an apron covering her skirt and gave him a quick kiss on the cheek. "Come in, I'm just finishing with the potatoes." He could smell the roast beef. He looked at the dining table. It was set for two, with a bottle of Groth cabernet sauvignon decanted and breathing. Massey took a seat on the living room sofa and relaxed at the sound of Frank Sinatra emanating from the speakers.

After a few moments, Susan entered with two martinis. She sat on the sofa next to him and ran her fingers through his hair. "Massey, you look exhausted. Any leads on the whereabouts of Mr. Arnold?"

"A little progress, but I'm pooped." He looked up at Susan with a frown on his face. "Today was interesting, but there's still not much to go on." He described his frustrating search for Arnold at both storage facilities. "The only lead I got was from the old manager who said the brother's name was George and the accompanying man had a crew cut and a mustache."

"Bingo," exclaimed Susan as she stood up, nearly knocking over her martini glass. "The guy with the mustache and crew cut is Stanley Arnold."

"You've got to be kidding. Arnold must have been hiding out somewhere away from the Peninsula since the fake suicide. What a stupid move on his part to show his face around here. It looks like he's giving us just enough rope to hang him. We'll find the dirty creep," Massey said with a grin.

Susan moved over to Massey and put her arm around his neck and looked him in the eye. "I think you ought to turn this information over to the police and let them find Arnold. It's too dangerous for you to continue this hunt alone."

"You're probably right, but Officer Cardoza and the rest of the police force are up to their necks in hunting down a serial killer. If we quit now, Arnold will be gone forever. Right now his tracks are fresh."

Susan replied with the same stern look on her face, "I still think it's dangerous, but I'll go along. What can I do, since I'm the reason you're involved. Look, Brother George is a phony. I know that Arnold had no relatives."

"Let's try to figure out who George is. He has to be a close buddy of Arnold's. My guess is he's probably connected in some way with the school system," responded Massey.

"My Amy was in Arnold's class five years ago. I met him occasionally on parent's night. He seemed shy and reserved, not the kind of man who would have many friends."

"He's got to have at least one damn good friend who's running the risk of a felony criminal charge of aiding and abetting a fugitive from justice. If he is as reclusive as you seem to think and his only contact was with his fellow teachers, he probably struck up a friendship with one of the teachers at the school," said Massey.

"That makes a lot of sense. You should have been a private investigator. Who knows, you could be as famous as Inspector Clouseau," Susan kidded.

Massey thought out loud for a moment. "I won't get to first base if I try to interview the principal. I'm persona non grata with the school district after my fight with the school board. How about you? Think you could use your charm again and get some information about which teacher was friendly with Arnold, or if he ever brought a male friend to a school function?"

"Not so fast. If I start asking questions about Arnold's friends and relatives, it wouldn't take a first grader long to figure out that I'm part of an investigation. The principal will clam up real fast if he knows Arnold faked the suicide."

Massey was quiet for a few moments and then said, "I've got an idea. Why don't you talk to Leola about requesting a transfer for Billy. You told me the kids are beating him up and he won't eat or go to school. Get him out of that school. Tell Leola you'll handle everything for her. That line will at least get you into the principal's office without suspicion."

▼

On Monday, Susan made an appointment with the principal of Los Encinos Elementary School, Mr. Street, to discuss Leola's son Billy. She arrived at the administrative offices around 9 a.m. and was ushered into Principal William Street's office. He rose and shook

Susan's hand. "Ms. Winters, I understand you are here concerning the Langley boy. Where is the mother?"

"I'm sure you understand. After the discovery that her boy had been molested by his teacher and then the teacher's suicide, she's so distraught over the incident she can hardly function."

"I didn't realize the incident impacted Mrs. Langley that way."

"Oh, it's taking a terrible toll on the family. She's so distraught that she asked me to intercede on her behalf. In case you're not aware of the situation, her son's class-mates blame Billy for the death of Mr. Arnold. They pick on him unmercifully during recess. His mother reports that he has come home with bruises all over his body. He has become withdrawn and is eating very little."

The principal seemed uncomfortable at Susan's description of the situation and replied, "Why hasn't the mother reported this? I have heard there was some trouble in the schoolyard, but not to the extent you are describing. How can I help?"

Susan answered, "The mother is requesting that you sign an inter-school transfer, so that her son can attend another elementary school in the district."

The principal looked up in surprise. "I had no idea. Now that I'm aware of the circumstances, perhaps we can monitor things better."

"No, that's unsatisfactory. The boy has been severely damaged psychologically. He needs a fresh start with classmates unaware of the past," Susan said with firmness in her voice.

"Let me call the principal at Pinehurst Elementary," said Principal Street, and he buzzed his secretary to make the call. He was soon connected. After several minutes of telephone conversation, Street hung up and turned to Susan. "They will take the boy at Pinehurst. I'll process the request so he can start classes on Monday."

"Thank you so much. I know his mother will be relieved. Out of curiosity, did Mr. Arnold have any close friends or relatives? My daughter was in his class several years ago, and he was her favorite teacher. She wanted to send the family a short note."

"Stanley was pretty much of a loner. He didn't socialize, and as far as I know didn't have any relatives."

Susan pressed him further. "Well, didn't he ever bring anyone to functions like the Christmas party or the faculty barbecue?"

"I don't think he ever did, Ms. Winters. As I said, he was a loner. Didn't talk about himself much. He was into his teaching. We all considered him to be one of the best. Thanks for your efforts." He turned his back and went to his seat.

Susan stood there a moment, but decided she'd gotten what she came for.

When Susan exited the building, she stopped at a pay phone in the parking lot. She wanted to talk to the superintendent, Garrity. She knew that he had been the principal of Los Encinos Elementary for a number of years while Stanley Arnold was teaching there and would probably know more about Arnold than Street. She checked in the phone book and dialed the number. When Garrity's secretary answered, Susan asked for an appointment.

The secretary asked her to hold, then clicked back on the line. "I'm sorry. Mr. Garrity says you'll have to go through proper channels. He says to have Mr. Massey contact our lawyer."

Susan knew Garrity must have recognized her name as Massey's accomplice who served the board members with the complaint the night of the blowup. She would get nowhere with him. She thanked the secretary, hung up and dialed Massey's office.

It was 4 p.m. when Massey's phone rang. As he picked up the receiver, he thought to himself, *Christ, this is the fortieth time this damn phone has rung today. It's taking the fun out of the practice of law.* His attitude suddenly changed when he heard Susan's voice on the other end.

"How about meeting me at Vega's for a drink. I ran into a stone wall today. I think I've failed as your detective."

"It'll be a relief to get away from this telephone and see your pretty face. Shortly after five?"

"You're on."

# CHAPTER 8

Vega's was a little dive off of Saratoga-Sunnyvale Road. The owner, Jake Cook, had regular customers who gathered around the bar in the early afternoon, stayed until after supper, and then went home smashed. Jake was a character, a big humorous man with a large gut acquired from sipping beer while tending bar. His face was a muddle of red blotches from broken blood vessels caused by his heavy drinking.

As Massey entered Vega's, he smelled stale beer and looked up at a smoke haze above the bar where the regulars were watching the Giants game on the TV. Jake was pouring tap beers. The rest of the restaurant was empty. Massey waved hello to Jake and went over to a table in the corner where he could have some privacy when Susan arrived. The place was dimly lit and his table was covered with a red-and-white checkered tablecloth. Massey liked the quiet privacy of the place, nothing fancy. Jake came over to get his order. "I'll have a Miller on tap while I'm waiting for my girlfriend."

Moments later, Massey saw Susan coming through the back door from the parking lot.

"Sorry I'm late," she greeted him. "I went to the elementary school this morning and talked to Street. I didn't get back to my office until after lunch, just in time to be greeted by a lecherous district auditor. He took all the time in the world to go through the books. I think he's got a crush on me, and likes to stay as long as he can on these monthly audit reviews. I've tried to give him the 'get lost' look, but he doesn't get it."

"Who can blame the guy. Just don't give me that message."

After Susan ordered a glass of wine, she reached over and squeezed Massey's hand. "How was your day?"

"Lousy. All I did was talk on the telephone. I left the office with twenty-five unanswered calls. The law business is beginning to drive me nuts. There's never any peace and quiet. I guess that's why I love being alone with you where the world gets put into proper perspective."

"Before too long, we've got to take some time off and visit some romantic hideaway where we can be alone together. This Langley case is taking too much of our free time together," said Susan, gazing into Massey's eyes.

"That's a great solution, but I have a better one. I can't stand being away from you. Is there a possibility that we might share the same roof every night?"

"Is that a marriage proposal or what the younger set calls an LTA, a living-together arrangement?" said a surprised Susan.

"It's your choice. I just know that I want to be with you as much as possible. I'm deliriously in love," said Massey. His face felt hot.

Susan was silent for a moment and then reached out and held both of his hands in hers. She looked into his eyes. "I need more time before I get so involved. I love you dearly, but I'm scared. When my husband left me for a nineteen-year-old student, I was left with about as much self-esteem as my golden retriever, who is afraid of everybody. I swore off men because I didn't want to get hurt again. I must admit that being with you is wonderful and exciting, but I need more healing time. I am so afraid of being vulnerable. I hope you understand, because I love your company and I love you. I must admit I'm lonely when I don't get to see you. If you can wait until my daughter graduates next year, I will seriously consider your wonderful offer."

"Well, that's not a bad beginning," Massey said with a tone of disappointment in his voice. "I'll give you all the space you need, but I'm a persistent cuss."

"I appreciate that," Susan replied, and smiled into his eyes.

Jake arrived with a beer and glass of white wine and placed them on the table. Susan said after taking a sip of her wine, "My afternoon of playing detective didn't turn out so well. Street told me that Arnold was a loner and had no friends or relatives. I tried to get an appointment with Superintendent Garrity, but he recognized my name and I got stonewalled. Told me to go through you."

"Well, we'll just follow his advice. We're both getting stonewalled. We've got Arnold hiding out after feigning suicide in order to avoid being prosecuted for sexually molesting Billy Langley. On top of that, Billy is going into a psychological tailspin. I want to get to the bottom of this case and locate Arnold. I think the next step to pry information out of these people is to go the legal route. The good news is that the Langleys still have the suit pending against the school district for damages. I'll just fire up some subpoenas for the deposition of Mr. Garrity. We'll get the information out of him. In addition to Garrity, I think I'll subpoena Jones, the board president, Gary Fillmore, the testy guy on the board, and Principal Street, who may have more information than he gave you."

# CHAPTER 9

Massey called Dave Barnie, an attorney in Santa Clara, who represented the school district. After Arnold's suicide, Massey had granted an open extension to answer the civil complaint because the Langleys were unsure about whether or not they would pursue damages. Massey had known Barnie a long time. A good lawyer, tough as hell, and a bit on the irascible side. He was an avid Old Blue, a University of California graduate. Each year before the Stanford-Cal Big Game, Massey and Barnie would bet twenty-five bucks with a zero point spread. Massey had collected the bet three out of the last four years, and the other game had ended in a tie. Barnie hated to lose. He was so frustrated after the last year's loss, he'd gone into a blue funk for a month.

Despite the man's feisty nature, Massey always liked Barnie. He had played linebacker for the California Golden Bears in the mid-fifties and was honest as hell, but a tenacious street fighter. His word was his bond, a straight arrow, no bullshit, no time-waster, a lawyer who got to the heart of the issues real quick.

"Hey Dave, Skip Massey here. I'm going to crank up the Langley case against the school district. Want to set up depositions of some of the administrators and members of the school board. How about sometime next week?"

"Christ, Massey, what the hell's the rush? I haven't even answered the complaint," Barnie retorted.

"The kid's mentally going downhill, not to mention his family. They need money to pay doctor bills, so I have to speed up the process. Why don't you pay me a couple of million and save everybody the time and energy. I'll even pay you back the twenty-five bucks you lost last year," Massey said, knowing the needle would raise his hackles.

"You demeaning son of a bitch. You'll have to work your butt off to win a nickel in this two-bit case. You must like working for free. Tell me whose depos you want, and I'll contact them. Give me thirty days to answer the complaint."

"I need the depos of Street, Garrity, Jones and Fillmore. By the way, bring your old football helmet along. You and I are going to butt heads in this case. Give me a call when you've lined up your players."

"You're on, wise ass."

That afternoon, Helen informed Massey that the depositions would be held on Monday, May 27, at 9 a.m. They would start with the principal, Mr. Street, followed by Fillmore, then superintendent Garrity, and lastly Paul Jones, the board president. Massey told her to call Barnie and tell him that he needed a half day with each deponent.

▼

The following Sunday at 3 a.m., Massey was in a deep sleep at his condominium after his late night with Susan. He returned home exhausted after the late night coupled with his hectic schedule the previous week.

All of a sudden, Massey was jolted by a thunderous noise that sounded like a huge explosion. "What the hell?" he cried as he jumped out of bed, turned the lights on, and looked out the window. Lights in the other units were being turned on.

He grabbed a robe and stepped into his slippers, then opened the front door to see where the blast had come from. At once he saw a glow spreading out over the top of the unit located in front of him. He rushed down the path toward the parking area. Smoke was billowing from a blazing fire. He started running to the area. Several people were shouting. His heart was pounding as he came upon the area where he had parked his car.

"Oh no." He could hardly breathe. His beloved 1987 Porsche had been completely blown apart.

Someone yelled, "Call 911!"

A voice answered, "The police and fire departments are on the way."

Massey stood still in stunned disbelief. "Who the hell did this? Is some son of a bitch trying to send me a message?"

Sirens screamed in the distance and soon a fire engine and several police cars slammed on their brakes. The police immediately cleared the area of people and the firefighters doused the blaze in several minutes. It was still smoking when a police officer started asking him questions. After answering, Massey returned dejectedly to his condominium.

Back in the room, he picked up the telephone. "Susan," he whispered, his voice shaken, "Sorry to awaken you. You were right about the danger in pursuing Arnold. Some bastard just blew up my Porsche."

"Oh, I'm so sorry for getting you into this mess. Let's quit now and get on with our lives. Please, honey?"

"Whoever is behind this bombing just got my dander up. Scheduling depositions must have triggered this bombing, warning me to lay off. No way. My father's Cherokee grandmother gave me enough heritage to start beating the war drums. I'm on the warpath."

Massey was still smarting from the previous night's violence when he arose the next morning. He called a cab and was driven to the Porsche dealership in Cupertino. It wasn't long before he was driving to work down Highway 101 in a new black Porsche Carrera.

He arrived at his office twenty minutes late for the deposition of Principal Street. When he entered the conference room, he apologized to Dave Barnie and added, "Some SOB blew my car up last night. I had to get some new wheels in order to get here."

"What's made you so popular?" his friend chided, but concern showed in his voice.

"I've got a hunch. I may know more in the next two days," he said as he looked in Street's direction for any sign of guilt.

Massey's conference room doubled as a law library. Books were stacked in shelves all the way around the room from floor to ceiling. In the center was an eight-foot-long mahogany table Massey had purchased from a real estate broker when the man retired. It was a beauty. The court reporter was already seated in her chair and had her stenographic machine loaded with paper, ready to go.

Barnie was wearing his usual rumpled brown tweed suit with his blue and gold tie at half mast, hanging loosely around his neck. His worn leather briefcase sat in front of him on the table. About six foot two, with blond scraggly hair, Barnie weighed about 220, of which at least 20 pounds were nestled in his protruding belly. Fifteen years of working fourteen hours a day in the law business, together with his chain smoking and nightly martinis, had taken their toll on this former linebacker. He looked ten years older than his forty years of age.

Principal Street sat next to Barnie wearing brown slacks and a light brown starched shirt. He was in his early forties, tall, brown hair, with horn-rimmed glasses. After everybody was settled, Street was sworn in by the court reporter. He stated under oath that he would "tell the whole truth, nothing but the truth, so help me God."

Massey started off with a few background questions and then went to the subject of Arnold. "Mr. Street, how much do you know about the personal life of Mr. Stanley Arnold?"

"I only came to the school district as principal at the beginning of last school year. We never socialized. I know a little bit of his background from our occasional coffee breaks. Mr. Arnold said he used to be an officer in the Marine Corps. I must admit that surprised me. He said he served in Vietnam. He told me he still had vivid memories and nightmares about the war. After the war, he married and settled in Santa Clara and had two children. However, tragedy struck six years ago. When he was out of town visiting his parents, his apartment caught fire and burned to the ground, killing his wife and children."

Massey hesitated, taken aback by the principal's remarks. Then he regained his poise. "Did Arnold exhibit any abnormal behavior during the time that you knew him?"

"No, not as far as I was able to observe. Arnold was probably the best instructor in the school. He took his job very seriously. He was a tough disciplinarian."

"Did Arnold ever exhibit any signs of behavior that indicated he was sexually motivated toward children?"

"Wait a minute, Massey," piped up Barnie, "this witness is no psychiatrist, and anyway what do you mean by 'sexually motivated'?"

Massey didn't flinch. "Mr. Street, do you understand my question?

"I think so."

"Mr. Barnie, your objection is noted for the record. Do you remember the question, Mr. Street, and if so, what is your answer?"

Street leaned over to Barnie and looked at him. Barnie nodded, knowing his objection was probably not valid.

"The answer is, absolutely not."

"Do you know if Mr. Arnold had any friends or relatives?"

"I don't know of any outside friends or relatives. As far as I know, Mr. Arnold never brought any guests to school functions."

"Did you ever hear Mr. Arnold state that he had a brother named George?"

"No."

"When did you first learn of the alleged sexual molestation by Mr. Arnold of one or more of his pupils?"

"About a month ago Mr. Walker, whose son, Scotty, was in Mr. Arnold's class, called me to say that Mr. Arnold had put his hand down the rear of his boy's trousers. The next day the Langley father came to see me, stating that he thought Mr. Arnold was sexually molesting his son Billy. I was stunned by the charges. Mr. Langley created a scene, yelling and shouting.

He demanded the teacher be fired or suspended from teaching his son's class. I had to call the police and have the man escorted out of the office. I felt his accusations against Arnold were totally out of line. I didn't believe them."

"What did you do next?"

"I reported the matter to the superintendent. He too was stunned and angry about the accusations. The superintendent told me that he had been in the district when Arnold was originally hired. In fact, he was the principal at Los Encinos Elementary School for twelve years while Arnold was teaching. He said he knew a lot about Arnold, and there was no way Arnold could be involved in any such activity."

"Did you and superintendent Garrity discuss the subject of calling in the police to investigate?"

"Because Mr. Langley had been so angry, I asked the superintendent if we should start an investigation. He told me in no uncertain terms that the district was not going to ruin a man's reputation on the basis of accusations by two fifth graders."

"What occurred next?"

"The superintendent called me the next day and said that Mr. Langley had barged into his office unannounced and began screaming and yelling, asking for the teacher's suspension and demanding an investigation. Mr. Garrity told me that he had no choice but to notify the school board of the accusations. However, he wasn't going to recommend an investigation at that time."

Massey asked a few more questions, but it became evident he had obtained all the information he was going to get out of Street. Massey ended the deposition. Principal Street appeared relieved when the questioning ended.

It was around lunch time, and after the principal left, Massey looked at Barnie. "Come on, I'll roll you for lunch."

"You're on. I've got revenge on my mind after you fleeced the Big Game bet out of me with no points. What a pigeon I was."

After lunch, Massey returned to the conference room to continue the depositions. He looked over at the witness chair where Gary Fillmore was glowering at him. *If looks could kill,* Massey thought, *I would be dead.* Fillmore's curly hairdo looked as if he had just walked out of a hairdresser's salon. He was dressed in a light blue Italian silk suit with a dark blue ascot tie and sported a set of white loafers on his feet. He oozed the cockiness of a bantam rooster.

As Massey took his seat, he ignored Fillmore and said, "Madam Reporter, please swear in the next witness."

"Mr. Fillmore, did your attorney explain to you the nature of a deposition?"

"Yes," he answered in a sharp tone, indicating his displeasure at having to waste his valuable time.

"Do you understand that I'm going to ask you questions regarding this case? If you don't understand the question, ask me to rephrase it. Answer the question audibly rather than nodding your head. Lastly, you may consult your attorney at any time during the deposition. Fair enough?"

"What do you think I am, stupid?" he responded.

"Mr. Fillmore, let's get one thing straight right off the bat. I'm the one who asks the questions, not you. Now would you mind answering the last question?"

Fillmore didn't say a thing.

"Would you like the reporter to read the question back?"

Fillmore said nothing.

Barnie scowled at his witness. "Mr. Fillmore, that's a proper question. Answer the question!"

Fillmore just sat there stoically.

Massey could see that Barnie was reaching his boiling point. After about ten seconds of silence from Fillmore, Barnie got up from his chair and looked sternly at his client. "Let's go off the record. The witness and I are going to go outside and have a little talk." Massey agreed and chuckled at the scene that was unfolding. He thought, *Barnie is no time-waster. He'll read the riot act to Fillmore and take this egomaniac down a couple of notches.*

When Fillmore and Barnie returned after a few minutes, Fillmore appeared rather subdued. Massey could tell that Barnie had laid the wood to him in no uncertain terms. Massey resumed the questioning, and reluctantly Fillmore began answering, but his answers were short, without much detail. When Massey asked him to expand on his answers, he would lean over and ask Barnie if it was necessary, and Barnie would nod his head.

When Massey asked him if he was married, Fillmore answered in the affirmative. When Massey asked if he had been divorced and how many times, Fillmore blew, "It's none of your damn business!"

Massey responded quickly, "Look, Mr. Fillmore, if you don't answer my questions, then we'll have a little talk with Judge Silver at a contempt hearing. The good judge has been known to give belligerent witnesses substantial fines and sometimes jail. Now, Madam Reporter, please read the last question back to Mr. Fillmore?"

Fillmore was silent.

"Mr. Barnie," Massey said, rising from his chair. "I'm suspending the deposition and filing a motion for contempt. This witness has no intention of cooperating this afternoon. I intend to ask the court to levy a hefty fine against Mr. Fillmore. Madam Reporter, could I please have the transcript by this evening to attach to my motion."

Massey rose from his chair and was about to walk out of the conference room when Barnie stood up and glared at his client. "Let's go off the record so Mr. Fillmore and I can have a few words about our relationship. Mr. Fillmore, you're getting your ass in a sling. Judge Silver is one tough judge and will have no mercy on you. Quit the tough guy act. I don't care how much you dislike the other lawyer, you are hurting the school district's case. If you won't cooperate, you hire your own lawyer and pay for your own legal expenses. The district doesn't represent jerks. Understand?"

Fillmore shifted in his seat, paused and then nodded.

Massey motioned the reporter to go back on the record. "Mr. Fillmore, since you indicated you are willing to cooperate, let me ask again. Now, how many times have you been married?"

Fillmore curtly responded, "Four times."

"Did you know Mr. Stanley Arnold?"

"Only by reputation."

"How did you become aware that there were sexual molestation allegations made against Mr. Arnold?"

"President Jones had called a special closed meeting of the board and told the members that a couple of fathers of fifth-grade students accused Mr. Arnold of sexually molesting their sons. Mr. Jones asked us if we would consent to having the county sheriff's department initiate an investigation. We all agreed, over the objection of the superintendent."

"Was there any discussion about suspending Mr. Arnold pending the investigation?"

"One of the board members, I can't remember which one, asked about suspending Arnold while the investigation was being conducted. President Jones said the superintendent was dead set against it, because he believed suspension would give credence to the allegations. This time the board went along with the superintendent's recommendation."

Massey finished his questions. As Fillmore was heading toward the exit, Massey couldn't resist sinking a needle into the witness and said, "I want to thank you, Mr. Fillmore, for being cooperative and answering my questions."

Fillmore turned toward Massey. His lips twitched, but he just nodded, and gave Massey a look as if to say, *Just wait, one day I'll punch your lights out, mister.*

After Fillmore was out of the room, Barnie looked at Massey. "That SOB doesn't like you, Massey. How come?"

"That bastard almost got into a fistfight with me at the board meeting. There's no love lost between us. He's my leading suspect for the destruction of my beloved Porsche, but I can't imagine his motivation."

The next morning was set for the deposition of Superintendent Roland Garrity. Massey arrived at the conference room a little late as a result of a lengthy telephone call. Mr. Garrity and Barnie had already arrived and were seated. The reporter was ready, so Massey asked her to swear in the witness.

Massey looked at Garrity, fifties, a little portly, brown hair, and casually dressed in a dark brown sweater, light brown slacks and loafers. Massey hadn't seen him since the school board meeting when he blew his cork at Massey's accusations against the teacher. He didn't seem very subdued considering the fact that the accusations turned out to be true. On the other hand, Massey's first impression was that Mr. Garrity was a pompous ass. He was probably caught up in his self-importance at being the superintendent.

Massey started off by asking a few background questions. Garrity stated he was single, had been a bachelor all his life, no children, and no present girl-friend. He was first employed by the district in 1965 after getting his teaching credential. His first position was at Los Gatos High School as a mathematics teacher. In 1978, he became the principal at the Los Encinos Elementary School. Twelve years later he was appointed to the position of superintendent of Los Gatos School District.

Massey asked, "When did you become acquainted with Mr. Stanley Arnold?"

"A little over twelve years ago, when I became principal of the Los Encinos Elementary School. He was already teaching mathematics."

"How well did you know Mr. Arnold?"

"Not well. He was a fairly private person. After his wife and children were killed, it took a year before he would talk about it. Then, he would occasionally open up and discuss his pain."

"Do you know if he had any friends?"

"I don't think Arnold had any close friends. At least I never saw him with anybody other than a teacher or two at lunch. As I said, he was a private person who poured his energy into his classroom."

71

"How would you categorize Mr. Arnold as a teacher?"

"In my opinion, Mr. Arnold was far and away the best teacher in the district."

"How did you hear about Mr. Arnold's sexual molestation involvement?"

Dave Barnie barked, "Objection, counsel, you're assuming a fact not in evidence. There is only an allegation of sexual molestation. That's an improper question, and I'll instruct my witness not to answer the question."

Massey rephrased the question. "Mr. Garrity, how did you learn that Mr. Arnold was alleged to have had a sexual involvement with one of his students?"

"I received a call from Mr. Street, the principal at Los Encinos, telling me that the fathers of two of Arnold's young male students made accusations of sexual misconduct against Mr. Arnold. He said one of the parents, a Mr. Langley, came to his office demanding the teacher be fired or suspended. The father became so belligerent he had to call the police. Mr. Street told me he didn't believe the accusations and thought the two boys had a vendetta against Arnold."

"What did you instruct Mr. Street to do about the situation?"

"Keep abreast of the situation and report any suspicious circumstances," replied the superintendent.

"Why didn't you start an investigation into the allegations right away?"

"Because I trusted Mr. Street's judgment that this was a hoax. After all, this teacher had been teaching for more than ten years without incident and was recognized as one of the best in the business. I don't go chasing windmills."

"What happened next?"

"The next day one of the fathers, Mr. Langley, barged into my office without permission and began shouting and hollering about his son's being sexually abused. He was hysterical and demanded that I fire or remove Mr. Arnold from the classroom immediately. Mr. Langley was so abusive that I told him I didn't have time to talk. I walked out of the office."

"Did you do anything in connection with the matter after the meeting with Mr. Langley?"

"Yes, I thought it best to consult the board in a closed session. That evening I called them together for an emergency meeting. I told them about the incident and the events that I just related. The board asked for my recommendation. I told them that I was dead set against any investigation or suspension of Arnold. When the word got out into the community, a suspension would be tantamount to the confirmation of the allegations and would ruin the man's excellent reputation."

"And what action, if any, was taken?"

"The board, however, decided to have me contact the Sheriff's Department and ask for an investigation."

"What happened next?"

"I called the Sheriff's Department and was placed in contact with a Sergeant Cardoza. I told him what I've told you today, and he said he would initiate an investigation. I didn't hear from the officer until two days after the regular board meeting where you served the board with a complaint. The sergeant said that he had gathered sufficient evidence about the charges and that the district attorney was going to indict Mr. Arnold. I was totally shocked. I called Mr. Arnold and told him of my conversation with the police. Either that evening or the next morning, Mr. Arnold committed suicide."

"Did you go to Mr. Arnold's funeral?"

"No, I think his relatives had private services, because I never received any notice."

"Have you had any contact with any of his relatives?"

"Yes, I was contacted by a brother, George, several days after Mr. Arnold's death. He asked me if Mr. Arnold had any back pay due him, and if so, to send the balance to Mr. Arnold's post office box in the name of the Estate of Arnold. He said he had the key to the box. I checked with the accounting office and had them send him the pay that was due."

"Did you ever meet the brother or get his phone number and address?"

"No."

Massey elicited a few more answers which weren't really probative and thanked the superintendent for his testimony.

While Massey was putting his notes in his briefcase, he glanced up as Garrity was leaving the room. Roland Garrity had a distinct limp.

Massey quickly said, "Dave, I do have one more question for Mr. Garrity, would you mind?"

"Christ, it's ten after twelve and I'm starving. One more, okay?"

The court reporter unpacked her stenographic machine, loaded it with paper, and said she was ready. "Mr. Garrity, I notice you have a limp. May I ask you what causes your limp?" Both Garrity and Barnie seemed startled, probably puzzled about the relevancy of the question, but Barnie told his client to answer so he could get to lunch.

Garrity curtly answered, "I served in Vietnam and stepped on a land mine. The army doctors saved my leg but not my foot. I have an artificial left foot."

Massey asked him if he knew Arnold in the service, and he said, "No."

"I forgot to ask you, did the brother, George, ever contact you again?'

"No."

"Do you know if Mr. Arnold had any other relatives?"

Barnie interrupted, "You said one more question and now you're asking the fourth question. This one is the last and then Adios!"

Garrity replied, "No."

With that answer, Barnie jumped out of his seat, stuffed his notes into his tired briefcase and walked out the door with Garrity limping behind. As Garrity walked out of the room, Massey stared at him, wondering if that could be was the culprit who blew up his car.

Massey had purposely not asked Garrity about his role in the Arnold furniture move. He didn't want to tip him off that he knew Arnold was not dead. Had he done so, Garrity would have contacted Arnold, who would run for cover. Massey had in mind other ways for ascertaining the whereabouts of Mr. Stanley Arnold.

Massey took only about twenty minutes deposing the president of the board, Paul Jones. It didn't take long to find out that Jones didn't know much more about Arnold than Fillmore.

# CHAPTER 10

Now that Massey had a pretty good clue that Superintendent Roland Garrity was in on the Arnold getaway, he decided to turn to his old friend, Mike O'Malley. Big Mike was a private investigator who had pulled many a rabbit out of a hat.

Massey had used several private eyes during his career. Some were better with the camera, others were more aggressive and took risks to get the evidence they wanted, but none was better than Big Mike O'Malley. Mike wasn't much to look at. He stood five foot ten inches and weighed 325 pounds. He was just plain fat, particularly in the hips, and when he walked, he waddled like a duck with the jelly fat bouncing in all directions. Mike's problem was genetic as his mother, father, two brothers and sister were all huge. Not a one weighed less than 300 pounds. But, when it came to brains, Mike O'Malley stood at the front of the line, head and shoulders above the rest of the investigators.

When Massey made the decision to get Mike involved, he acted at once. "Mike, Skip Massey on the line."

"Massey, I haven't heard from you in quite a while. You're not using some other broken-down private eye, are you?"

"No sir. You're the best in the business. Right now, I've got a real puzzle for you to solve. My housekeeper's boy was sexually molested by his fifth-grade teacher. When the police were about to arrest the teacher, he feigned suicide and skipped town. I spent some time trying to track him down and found out that the superintendent of the school district is probably his accomplice. I'm sure he knows the teacher's whereabouts. I'd like you to track down this pedophile so I can have the police salt him away before he gets to any more young kids."

"Sounds interesting. I'll come right down to get the details." Twenty minutes later Mike waddled into Massey's office. They met for an hour while Massey briefed him about all of the information he had gathered. Mike shoved his usual $1,000 retainer fee into his wallet and told Massey he would get back to him as soon as he found the suspect.

▼

It wasn't until late Friday, June 21, that Mike stopped by Massey's office unannounced. He plunked down a complete investigative report plus several photographs and a videotape. Massey looked up at Mike. His brown hair was in its usual mess. He had a big smile on his puffy face and his body was wringing with sweat. "There's a lot more to this case, Massey, than just Arnold. Wait until you read the report. It'll knock your socks off. I've got to run. I'm late for a dinner date with a big New York steak." He turned and waddled out of the office with the fat in his hips jiggling up and down in unison with his gait.

Massey picked up the report and ruffled the sheets of paper. He pressed the intercom button. "Helen, hold my calls for the next half hour." Then Massey sat back in his chair and began to read the lengthy report.

DATE OF REPORT: Friday, June 21, 1991,
Palo Alto, California.

INVESTIGATIVE REPORT PREPARED FOR:
Attorney Skip Massey

Wednesday, June 5, 1991
This investigator located Mr. Garrity's address in the phone book at 221 Peabody Drive, San Jose, and at approximately 2 p.m. proceeded to the location.

Nobody appeared to be home, so your investigator entered the home by unlocking the front door with a plastic card.

*Nothing like a little criminal trespass,* Massey thought to himself, then continued to read.

After searching the inside of the house, the investigator came upon a drawer in the den full of pictures of young children with no clothes on and in various sexual positions. After further surveillance of the home, he couldn't find any addresses, telephone numbers, or other information bearing on the whereabouts of Mr. Stanley Arnold. Before leaving the residence, he placed a receptor in Mr. Garrity's telephone and placed hidden cameras in the kitchen, den, living room and bedroom.

"Why the hell is the superintendent of schools collecting porno pictures of little kids?" Massey said out loud in utter amazement.

Wednesday, June 12, 1991
Your investigator arrived at the subject's residence at approximately 6 p.m. At 6:30 p.m. the subject exited his residence and left in his automobile. The suspect was followed to San Francisco, where the suspect parked his vehicle on Mission Street between Third and Fourth streets. As the suspect exited from his car, your investigator was able to take several good photographs of him. The suspect walked easterly down Mission Street to the Adam and Eve Porno Shop where he stayed for about two hours. The suspect left about 11 p.m. and the investigator followed him as he headed south down Highway 101, presumably for his residence in San Jose.

After fifteen minutes, your investigator returned to the porn shop and found a large room displaying various films, pictures and sexual paraphernalia. Mostly, however, the shop featured scenes of young children. He then approached a young man behind the display counter and pulled out Garrity's photograph, taken earlier. The investigator flashed his fake IRS identification card and asked the clerk if he had ever seen the man in the picture. The clerk looked startled, and then said he didn't recognize the individual.

When your investigator arrived home, he checked the wiretap on the suspect's telephone. At 12:37 a.m. the suspect received a call from a male. The voice on the line sounded like the clerk that your investigator confronted at the porn shop. The man on the telephone called the suspect by the name of "Boss" and reported that an IRS agent had approached him asking him to identify the suspect.

Massey's eyes opened wide when he read the word "boss."

Thursday, June 13, 1991
Your investigator drove to San Francisco City Hall and entered the business licensing department. He asked the clerk if she could obtain a copy of the business license for Adam and Eve Porno Shop. After a few minutes, the clerk came back with a copy of a license for Adam and Eve Porno Shop. Your investigator studied the photocopy and saw that the address of the owners was 221 Peabody, San Jose, which is Garrity's address.

That evening your investigator checked the wiretap and picked up a call that Mr. Garrity made to Susanville, California. He addressed the man on the other end of the line as Edward and told him that some IRS agent came into Adam and Eve Porno Shop. Garrity asked Edward if he was sure that they had paid all of the taxes on the business.

Friday, June 14, 1991
Your investigator proceeded to the regional telephone office and looked at a reverse telephone directory for the City of Susanville. He easily found

that the number that Garrity had dialed was listed under the name E. Stewart. However, there was no street address listed.

Monday, June 17, 1991
Your investigator drove up to Susanville, California. He asked several business owners if they knew an E. Stewart. None did. At dinner, however, he was waited upon by a young mother who said that Mr. Stewart was her daughter's fifth-grade teacher.

Tuesday, June 18, 1991
At 9:30 a.m. your investigator proceeded to the school to locate Mr. E. Stewart. After obtaining information about the location of his class, he took three pictures of him with the telephoto lens during a recess. After school he spotted Stewart walking to a 1985 Honda Accord. Your investigator followed him to a residence located at 775 Old Mill Road and took several more pictures as Stewart exited his vehicle and headed for the door of the residence. He observed that the teacher had a mustache and short brown hair.

Wednesday, June 19, 1991
Your investigator proceeded to Los Encinos Elementary School in Los Gatos. He asked the secretary for fifth-grade class photos taken in 1990. She handed your investigator the photo and he identified the suspect. The secretary identified the man as Mr. Stanley Arnold. He then took out his camera and snapped a picture of the fifth-grade class of 1990 and its teacher. The investigator went back to his van and compared the picture that he just taken with the picture of the teacher in Susanville. No question, the same person appears in each photo.

Submitted by Mike O'Malley
Private Investigator

Massey sat in his chair stunned, trying to absorb what he had just read. The superintendent and one of his teachers not only were involved in a scheme to feign suicide and then secrete Arnold to another location, but also, the two participated as partners in a San Francisco porn shop business heavily weighted in child pornography. *What in the world motivated these two respected men to engage in such an illicit activity?* he thought to himself, dumbfounded by the astonishing revelations of the investigator's report.

Massey picked up his phone and dialed Susan. "How about dinner at my place tonight? I've got a stick of dynamite to show you. I just received my investigator's report on Arnold. He's found Arnold. You won't believe the tangled web we've uncovered."

"I'll be there a little after six. I can hardly wait to see the report."

▼

Susan arrived at Massey's condo at 6:10 p.m. The smell of Massey's rosemary roasted chicken was permeating the air. Massey, wearing his cooking apron, came over and gave her a big hug. "Well, my good-looking girlfriend, I'm not going to tell you about the report. It would ruin the suspense. Take it in the living room while I finish getting dinner ready." He handed her the report.

"How about a glass of wine? I've had a horrible day," Susan said, as she tilted her head back and walked toward the living room. "That auditor I told you about. He's getting real pushy. The jerk is married, but he insists on flirting with me. I told him today to get lost, but he just kept coming on like a bull in heat."

"Why don't you tell your boss that you're being sexually harassed? That will cool him off in a hurry."

"Good idea, Massey. I'll get my nerve up tomorrow and tell Kim, my supervisor."

"I can't blame the guy for chasing a beautiful broad like you, but one more mention of him harassing you, and I'll polish him off," said Massey, coming out of the kitchen with the wine for Susan.

Susan sat down in Massey's dark green leather sofa, took her shoes off, stretched out and began reading the report. After five minutes, she exclaimed in a voice loud enough for Massey to hear in the kitchen, "I'm shocked beyond belief. The superintendent involved in a porn business?"

"Read on, it gets even more unbelievable," Massey shouted back.

After ten minutes, Massey came out of the kitchen with his apron off. He was dressed in shorts, a Hawaiian shirt, and sandals. "Let's have dinner on the patio. I'll set the table. Are you finished with the report?"

"Just about. I'm stunned," Susan said, and shook her head. A few minutes later she finished the last page, closed the report and put it on the coffee table. She leaned back with her hands on her temples, her head cocked back, and took a deep breath to restore her senses. "These two, Garrity and Arnold, ought to be in jail for the rest of their lives. I wonder how many other youngsters they've abused. Those porn prints of the young children are disgusting. By the way, what's on the videotape that the investigator gave you?"

"I don't know, but it's undoubtedly a porn movie. We'll have to look at it, but not tonight. Dinner is ready. Let's eat."

Susan was silent for a few moments, obviously thinking about what she had just read. "Massey, what do you think makes a man so sick that he gets his kicks out of looking at porn photos and flicks of little kids? And what's worse, a grown man who gets a thrill out of fondling scared little kids?"

Massey responded, "Well, I got curious about the same questions after I read Mike's report and stopped by the library. I dug around the medical science section. In most cases these youngsters, who later become pedophiles, had a trusted adult, most often a parent, sexually stimulate them. At first the child is repulsed, but after a while, the need for sexual stimulation magnifies."

Massey continued his explanation of the information he had gathered at the library. "Eventually the child is overwhelmed by the sexual stimulation. When the sexually abused child becomes an adult, he is reluctant at first, but his inner child's urge for stimulation is so great that he cannot help himself from preying on a young child. Once that sexual inner drive has been acted out, the child molester is internally coerced to repeat the act with the same child or others. A child molester is driven by a madness that excites his sexuality. The molester is not the master of his own fate and is almost always untreatable."

"How about another glass of wine to calm my nerves? My mind is reeling. Your explanation is telling."

Massey returned with a refill and handed it to Susan. He looked at her. Her forehead was furrowed. He worried about having shared this unseemly business with her.

Susan remarked, "I don't think we should tell Leola about this report right now. She is so upset over Billy, I don't think she can handle much more. She told me today that she had seen Dr. Tishman last night. He wants to have Billy hospitalized because he hasn't been eating for the past two weeks. He's lost twenty pounds. She says the doctor thinks the boy is suffering from anorexia and will starve himself to death if not treated."

"Young children, after they are abused, take a big hit psychologically. I hope Dr. Tishman can turn Billy around."

"I do too. All of this is madness. Leola is the sweetest person I know. She didn't deserve all of this turmoil," Susan said with tears welling in her eyes.

Massey put his arm around Susan's shoulders. He knew how sensitive she was. He knew this episode with Arnold was affecting a lot of people, including himself and Susan. "Take it easy. We're doing the best we can. I'd just like to see these two men brought to justice."

Susan wiped away her tears and said, "Leola gave me permission to call Dr. Tishman. He told me the situation in the Langley family is really serious. Billy is blaming himself for the suicide of Arnold. Somehow the word got out, and now even the kids in his new school are harassing him about the teacher's suicide."

"The poor kid. He can't seem to escape the torture."

Susan continued, "The doctor says Billy is very depressed. On top of everything else, Sam has gone into denial about the episode. He hardly comes home when Billy is awake. When he does come home, he's usually drunk. He refuses to talk to Billy, and Billy naturally feels he is being rejected. This whole incident with Arnold is affecting the marriage, and Billy feels responsible. The doctor said that Billy is in such a state of depression that starving himself to death is his solution to ending the family misery. Skip, Leola is about ready to burst at the seams."

Massey was silent for a few moments, thinking about the next course of action. "Probably the best way to bring these two men to justice is to contact Sergeant Cardoza so that he can gather more evidence to substantiate what Mike has found. If he can verify this information, then he will go to the district attorney. Then he will probably go to the grand jury and seek indictments against Garrity and Arnold. Maybe the Langley family will stabilize if Garrity and Arnold are behind bars."

"God, I hope you're right."

"Let me fetch dinner and join you with a glass of wine. Maybe the wine and a good meal will lift our spirits."

The evening was warm while Susan and Massey sat on the outside patio eating dinner. They got off the morbid subject of the Arnold case and began to relax. Susan took a sip of her wine, then set it down, came over to Massey, sat on his lap, and commenced rubbing his neck. Looking directly into his eyes, she whispered, "Skip, I enjoy your company. We're becoming quite an item. As a matter of fact, at night when I'm home, I get very lonely. I think it's time that we share a roof over our heads."

"Are you saying what I think you're saying?" said an elated Skip Massey.

"I talked to Amy about our living together and she's all for it. She enjoys your company and thought it would be great to have a man around the house. I am getting over my hang-up with the man thing and want to be with you twenty-four hours a day."

"Now that is an offer I can't refuse. I'd love it. I'll pack my bags and be over this weekend."

Massey reached up and pulled her body close to his. He gave her a passionate kiss which lasted until Susan pulled away, took a deep breath and said, "Well, I have thought a lot about the situation. I am not ready to get married yet, because I don't want to make another mistake."

Massey responded, "I think we can get to know each other better if we live together. When you date, you don't let your guard down. People who date are always on their best behavior. If we live together, you'll get to know my strengths as well as my weaknesses, of which I have many."

"I'm afraid you'll see an ugly witch without any makeup when you awaken in the morning. That will be the test of your love, Mr. Massey," said Susan, kissing him again.

"Hardly. The thought of sharing the same bed with you each night is overwhelming. Once I get my foot in the door, you may have me forever."

"That's a plan," said a smiling Susan Winters.

"I think the sooner the better. We ought to get a little practice at togetherness tonight, and I'll pack my bags tomorrow and be at your doorstep after work. How's that for quick action?"

Susan leaned forward and whispered in his ear, "Now that sounds like an even better plan."

▼

At 221 Peabody Drive, Roland Garrity was seated in his living room enjoying an evening glass of wine, unaware that he had been under surveillance. He sat contemplating the events of the last several months and his involvement with Stanley Arnold. He smiled, raised his glass, and thought, *Boy, did I pull that off. Can't believe it went so well. When Stanley got into trouble* over the Langley boy, I was really worried that he would get arrested and our business together would be exposed. That would have just ruined me. I would have been fired as superintendent right on the spot and never been able to teach again.

I have to admit, my plan was a stroke of genius: a fake suicide, then a bogus death certificate, and finally getting Stanley a job way on the other side of California under an alias. Nobody will ever find him. I warned Stanley about fooling around with any more youngsters, and I think he learned his lesson with the Langley boy.

I know I shouldn't be in the porn business, a respected educator like myself. But ever since I was a kid, I've always liked to look at a young girl's body. I remember when I was about twelve years old, I noticed my sister's chest was starting to swell. My sister, who was fifteen at the time, caught me looking at her from under her bed when she was undressing. I admit I was curious about nudity then, still am. At first she got mad, and then about ten minutes later came to my room and said it was okay if I watched her undress. Whew, was that a thrill. First time I ever had a big hard on. About two weeks later she asked me to wash her back while she was bathing. Now that was a biggie. Not only did I soap down her back, she let me wash her tits. Talk about a hard on. Then she grabbed my hand and moved it down to her pussy. I just exploded. My crotch became all wet. First time I ever had an orgasm. She made me feel real special. Only problem was that she found a boyfriend about two weeks later and shut me off. I was really hurt and felt like she jilted me.

About two months later my mother ran away with another man and left us in the care of our father. I hardly ever saw her after that. Talk about feeling rejected. That really hurt me. I've never trusted women since and hardly ever dated. I like being a bachelor although I admit I always love to watch films and pictures of nude young women. That's probably why I got into business with Stanley.

Some 300 miles away, Stanley Arnold set aside the papers he had just finished correcting. It had been a good day at school. His thoughts turned to how lucky he was to be in this new environment. He had just escaped the public accusations and the threat of criminal charges that would have arisen had he stayed in Los Gatos. He thought to himself, *The guy's a genius. Who could have thought up this scheme. Only Roland Garrity.*

*When I got in trouble with that Langley boy, Roland was madder than hell. Said I ruined everything. Then when the police decided to arrest me, he came up with this suicide bit. It was masterful. I love my new job in Susanville teaching my class. I promised Roland I would never do such a thing again. I must admit, I was really scared when they discovered that I was involved with Billy Langley. However, he enjoyed it as much as me. I never harmed him. Most of the young boys don't have anybody show affection to them like I do. Many parents these days hardly pay attention to these youngsters. I'm not really a bad person. I give the kids hugs and rub their bodies to make them feel like they're loved.*

*I know exactly how they feel. I'll never forget when my uncle Don, my dad's younger brother, used to babysit me when I was Billy's age. He started giving me massages before I went to sleep. Soon he began stroking my penis. At first I didn't like it, but soon it felt so good. I'll never forget when I became overwhelmed with emotion. Was that ever a thrill. I've never forgotten. Two years later he was transferred to another state and I never saw him again, but I still have fond memories of our relationship. After a while, I began to date girls, then graduated from high school and joined the Marines. I was sent over to Vietnam and fought in that horrible war. When I returned I went to San Jose State and got my teaching credential, then married and had two lovely children. We were a very happy family. About six years ago, when I was at a teacher's convention down south, I got a call from the police. They said my house had burned, killing my wife and kids.*

*It took me several years to get over the grief. I decided not to date again because it brought back painful memories. I started helping little boys a couple of years ago. I knew it was wrong, but they enjoyed my care and loving. I could never forget the episode with my uncle and the pleasure he gave to me.*

# CHAPTER 11

Massey looked up from the chair in the St. Francis Hotel's lobby. He had finished his notes on the background of the murder Leola committed. He stood up, stretched his tired body, and looked at his watch. It was 3:45 in the afternoon, time to interview a couple of defense lawyers. His back hurt like hell from sitting hunched over for such a long period. He packed his notes in his briefcase and stopped at the front desk to ask directions to the office of attorney Ed Ames.

As Massey headed down the street, he couldn't help but wonder about all of the vital players in this murder. What motivated Leola Langley to suddenly transform from a mild-mannered, loving mother and avid Christian woman to a cold-blooded murderer? How about Sam Langley? Did he abandon his family in their time of need and contribute to this chaos? What the hell was Garrity the superintendent doing in the porn business with Arnold? And what prompted Arnold to become a pedophile after being a Marine and having a family? Nothing was adding up.

▼

Two days before Leola killed Stanley Arnold, she had arrived around nine at Skip Massey's condo in order to clean his unit. *I had a horrible night again last night. Sam didn' get home until afta I'd fallen asleep on the sofa. He was still passed out when I got up, so I sent my older boy off to school, Billy's in the hospital ya know, and then went to Mr. Massey's house to clean it like I do every week. I did the wash first and then started cleaning the unit. I stopped when the wash was done and folded the clothes and began putting them away. When I started to put his shorts away, I opened the top drawer of his chest and pushed aside a couple pairs of shorts to make room for the clean ones. Mah eye caught a folder. I thought the file didn' belong there so I pulled it out. I noticed the folder had the words "Investigative Report, The Whereabouts of Stanley Arnold." I saw a video underneath and I picked it up, too. The name was "Play Time." I remember shaking when I sat on the bed to look through the file. I wondered why was there a report on Mr. Arnold? He's dead. I began to read the report. As I read through it, I started to groan and cry. Is this all true? Oh God, he's alive. When I finished the report, I began to sob. I got curious 'bout the video and went out to Mr. Massey's video machine and put the tape in. After a while I recognized my poor Billy in the film dancin' around and then this evil man started playin' with him. I vomited and then felt dizzy, then I fainted.*

*When I woke up, I remembered all about mah childhood. I'd forgotten that for years. Now the pictures of mah childhood became clear as day. I was born in the small town of Abbieville, Georgia, one of two children, mahself and mah brother who was ten years older than me. Mah mother and father never finished high school. Mah father was a farmer, barely makin' any money. We was real poor. Our home was an old shack with a dirt floor on a one-acre plot two miles from Abbieville. Each school day me and mah brother would walk to and from the school. Every day when I got home from school, I had chores to do. Mah momma was always afraid of mah daddy. He was a serious man with a hot temper. I remember him beatin' on her when they got into a big fight. As me and mah brother got older, we all learned to be quiet so as not to create trouble. One bad incident and mah father would bring out the switch made out of a reed. He'd whip us until we cried and promised never to act badly again. I quickly decided I'd be daddy's good little girl.*

*I remember when I was seven. It was the first time. Mah daddy came into mah bedroom in the middle of the night, and placed his fingers in mah private parts. I was too scared to say anythin'. All of a sudden, he puts his penis in there. I never experienced such pain in all mah life. I kept quiet* though, 'cause I was scared of him. I didn' want to get him mad. Finally, mah daddy grunted, laid back on the bed, and then got up without saying a word and went to his room. I remember cryin' mahself to sleep. Mah daddy continued doin' this every week until I was fifteen. I was able to talk my parents into lettin' me stay with Aunty Rachel in town so my folks wouldn't have to haul me to mah new high school which was ten miles away in town.

One thing that bothered more than anythin' when I was growing up. I always wondered why mah momma never came to mah rescue when mah daddy was a rapin' me. That hurt more than the pain that I went through.

The next three years with mah Aunty were the happiest of mah life. I had no chores after school except to help with dishes, so I was able for the first time in mah life to make friends with mah classmates. For the first time, I began to think that I could have a happy life.

In the spring of mah last year of high school I met Sam Langley, and we'all began goin' steady. Sam was a Southern Baptist from a hardworkin' religious family. After Sam began takin' me to church on Sunday, I found that religion gave me hope I'd never known. It wasn't long before Sam proposed to me. I really wasn't ready to marry so soon, but I wasn't about to return to the family farm. We'all decided on the spur of the moment to drive down to New Orleans in Sam's 1956 Chevy the night after graduation and get married.

The night of the wedding, we stayed in a small and dirty motel room that cost five dollars. We'all had hardly kissed before this night and I was scared to death. Sam thought I was a virgin, and I know he was expectin' big things that night. As soon as we got into the motel room, Sam stripped his clothes off and stood there with a big penis. He reminded me of mah daddy and I started vomiting. He musta thought I was sick, but I was scared to death. I didn' want none of that. He just kinda groaned and we went to bed. We never did have much of a sex life. I guess mah daddy made me hate bein' close and huggin'.

As the painful memories of her childhood ran through her brain, she began to sob uncontrollably. Eventually Leola returned to her senses, got up

89

emotionless and headed out the door of Massey's condominium, looking very determined.

▼

Two days later, Leola was sitting in the back seat of a police car. She looked down at the handcuffs on her wrists, then out the window. The vehicle was traveling down the road in a town she didn't recognize, and she could see flashes of color in the passing store fronts caused by the whirling lights on top of the car.

She thought of what had just happened in a cold, indifferent way. She had been hiding behind a bush in front of a 1985 blue Honda, waiting for a man to come out of the school building, a despicable man. He had destroyed her family. Her son was in the hospital starving himself to death. Her husband was becoming a hopeless drunk. She would stop this man from hurting anyone else. She shot him dead. He was as evil as her father. She was a God-fearing Christian, and God would praise her for getting rid of a despicable devil.

A man's voice startled Leola. "Ma'am, I've asked you to get out of the vehicle three times already. You don't seem to hear me," said an officer wearing a blue uniform and a blue leather-rimmed hat. He had the door next to Leola open and was leaning into the back seat.

Leola suddenly looked up at the officer and realized that he was speaking to her. "Ma'am, come with me." He reached out, took her by the arm and led her out of the car and up the steps of the new county building, then into the booking room at the station headquarters. Leola was fingerprinted and led to an interrogation room. An hour later she was escorted out of the county building and taken to the Lassen County Jail three blocks away. She was given an orange inmate's jumpsuit and taken to a cell within the facility. The county jailer led her into the cell, then retreated and closed the steel door with a loud bang.

Leola sat on her hard bed staring at the stark white walls and began to think about her childhood again.

She really hadn't remembered those years. *I jus' can't believe I've forgotten those horrible things,* she thought to herself.

She lay in her cell gazing at her surroundings: cement floors, toilet in the corner, the thin cot she was sitting on, barren white walls, a dim lightbulb in the ceiling. Then she became enraged, her body started trembling, and she cried out, "That monster of a man has ruined my life and my family. He's going to rot in hell!" She started sobbing, laid on the cot and fell asleep in exhaustion.

Two hours later she awakened from a deep sleep. She looked up at her surroundings. She was startled at what she saw: a jail cell with steel bars, no windows, a small commode in the corner, and she was sitting on a hard cot. "Lordy, why am I dressed in this orange outfit? What am I doin' in this place? Help, help!" she shouted as loud as she could.

She could hear somebody running down the hall. A man opened the door. He was dressed in a tan uniform wearing a badge.

"Ma'am, are you all right?"

"What am I doin' in here?" Leola shouted.

"You're charged with the murder of a man."

"What? I didn' kill nobody. Where am I?"

"You're in the Lassen County Jail, ma'am."

"God, the Lord help me!" she cried out. With that she lay back on the cot and began weeping. Something was drastically wrong.

▼

Three days before the murder of Arnold, at one in the morning, Sam Langley errantly steered his Toyota into his garage, nearly hitting the rear wall. He got out and wobbled over to the kitchen door. After he opened it he noticed that all the lights in the house were off except for a small one in the living room. As he staggered into the living room, he noticed his wife asleep on the sofa. He just kept going and stumbled down the hallway where he threw himself on the master bed and passed out.

The next morning he woke up and walked around the house, not finding his wife or oldest boy at home. He assumed Leola had gone to work and the boy to school. He fixed himself a pot of coffee and sat down to ponder recent events. He was reeling with all of the frustrating emotions that erupted after Billy's incident. He began sizing up his situation:

*God, mah head hurts and I'm late for work. I knows I'm doin' wrong, but I jus' can't stand all the sobbin' around here. This place is like a tomb. All Leola does is cry and worry about the kid. I know he's in the hospital and all that, but what about me? I'm hurtin' too. She jus' doesn't pay no attention to me whatsoever. I can't help it if I stop by Pinky's on the way home from work. At least there's some happiness in there. Now you take Sally, that cute little barmaid. Man, has she got big tits and is she friendly. Ya know, I never did get much lovin' at home from Leola. We had trouble right from the start. It took years before I could even touch the woman. Even after we had those two kids, I could hardly touch her. I guess lovin' was jus' not high on her list. Well, this little Sally, man, she's a firecracker. She's the most lovin' gal I ever met. You want a roll in the hay, you oughta try Sally. Those big tits shakin' all over when she's on top.*

*I know I'm drinkin' and foolin' around. Never done this before. But all this stuff 'bout Billy and Leola just got me down. Maybe when Billy gets well, Leola and me will get back together like the old times.*

# CHAPTER 12

Massey walked down Main Street for three blocks looking for the office of Ed Ames. He came upon an old Victorian home, painted in various shades of blue. Out in front was a sign, "Ed Ames, Attorney at Law."

Wooden stairs led to the veranda and an antique oak door. As Massey opened the door, he entered a waiting room decorated with early 1900s furniture with velveteen coverings and a three-foot brass scale of justice sitting in the corner. He went over and pressed a bell ringer on the counter. Soon a large man with black hair, about six foot four inches tall and 230 pounds, emerged from the side door off the foyer. He had on an expensive dark suit, silk tie and black leather shoes. It was obvious from his office furnishings and clothes that Mr. Ames was doing quite well in this small town.

"Hi, I'm Ed Ames. My secretary is off to the post office. You must be my 4 p.m. appointment. I read about the murder in the paper. Big news for this small town."

"Skip Massey's the name. I'm impressed with your decor," he said, as he shook hands with the large lawyer.

"I'm a history buff," said Ames. "I refurbished the place based on an office of a San Francisco friend of mine who did a smashing early-1900s remodel. Come on into my office."

As they entered the office, Ames pointed to a cushioned leather chair in front of a large, beautiful oak desk. Massey took his seat and Ames ambled to the chair behind the desk. This man with large brown eyes and a dark complexion looked like a rugged individual who could defend himself in a street fight. "Now, what's the order of business?"

"There's a lot more to this killing than meets the eye," Massey began. "The woman in jail is my housekeeper, Leola Langley. She lives in Los Gatos. The teacher who was killed used to be her son's fifth-grade teacher. Five months ago, he was about to be arrested for sexual abuse of her son. When the teacher got wind of the pending arrest, he feigned suicide. Everybody figured he was dead, but a few loose ends didn't come together. I started looking into his death, found him with the help of a smart private investigator, and tracked him here."

"Fascinating story. I could use a good investigator. There are none around these parts. Sorry to interrupt. Please continue."

"The mother told me last night in jail that she doesn't remember killing anybody, and can't understand why she is in jail. Whoever is going to defend her needs to get a psychiatrist up here right away to see if there is an insanity defense."

"Undoubtedly, but why are you interested in talking to me?" Ames responded.

"I learned early in my practice that if you want to find the best lawyer in town, you call either the bailiff or the clerk, because they've seen all of the attorneys in action. Judge Brandon's clerk said you and Jerry Kane were the best around."

"Jerry's my old partner. He's damn good, but so am I. He's been having a few problems lately, however. About five years ago, he tried a murder case, lost it, and his client was sentenced to death. He never got over the loss and started hitting the bottle. That's when we parted company. I understand he has been recovering from his problem. He's a good man, big heart, and thinks he can win everything. He's also a sore loser. Tell me more about the background of your client?"

For the next half hour, Massey told Ames all he knew about the case and then handed him a copy of the notes he had just written. Ames said, "Give me a while to review these. Help yourself to some coffee in the kitchen in back."

After twenty minutes Ames put the notes down and looked at Massey. "Let me give you a frank opinion. I don't think your client has a prayer of beating a murder one rap unless she's totally insane and the judge and jury buy her story. I know you're banking on sympathy, but the people up here are red-necked as hell. This is a law-and-order community, the district attorney is tougher than hell and very popular with the community. My advice is to plea bargain and see if you can plead her to murder two."

"I'll consider your advice," Massey responded, getting up. Before leaving, Massey asked Ames about his fee.

"In murder cases, I charge twenty thousand dollars up front. Assuming we can't get the district attorney to plea bargain, and the case goes to trial, the total fee would be about fifty thousand. As I said, this will be one tough case and take a ton of preparation," said Ames.

"Mr. Ames, thanks so much for your time. I've got an appointment with Jerry Kane now, and I will be in touch with you shortly. By the way, tell me how to get to his office, if you don't mind."

"Say hello to my old partner, will you?" Ames said as he rose and shook Massey's hand.

Kane's office was just around the corner. Massey noticed it was located in a multi-office, tilt-up cement building, not nearly as posh as Ames' quarters. But Massey knew that the opulence of the office doesn't always reveal the quality of the lawyer.

After walking up the two flights of stairs, he noticed a dilapidated door with a printed sign on it, "Gerry Kane, Attorney at Law." Massey entered and faced a scene completely different from that in the office of Ed Ames. Here the furniture was worn and shabby, the carpeting faded and soiled. There was a counter at the end of the foyer with nobody there. He called out, "Anybody home?"

After a moment, a man with a slight build emerged. He had a full head of curly gray hair, huge bushy salt-and-pepper eyebrows, blue eyes, a ruddy complexion and a rough red nose. When he extended his hand, his blue eyes twinkled. "Hi, I'm Jerry Kane. Are you the lawyer who called about the gal in jail charged with the murder of the teacher?"

"That's me. Name's Skip Massey," Massey said as he held out his hand to shake Kane's hand.

"Come on into my office and sit in that tattered chair across from my desk. Mind if I puff on my bad habit while we talk?"

Massey shook his head, "Not at all. Gave up the damn habit myself ten years ago. It's been a struggle ever since."

Kane sat down in an oak swivel chair behind his desk, pulled out a pack of Marlboros, lit one and inhaled deeply, blowing out a huge ring of smoke. "I can't lick the habit. Whenever I try, I'm back at 'em in a couple of weeks."

Massey couldn't help but notice the huge pile of files and mounds of papers piled on the desk before Kane. Massey had been in many a lawyer's office and had seen similar desks. Each of these messy lawyers knew exactly where each file or shred of paper was located. It was one of the seven wonders of the world.

"Now, tell me where are you from, and how come you know this suspect way up here in the sticks?"

Massey explained that he was a lawyer in Palo Alto and that Leola was his housekeeper.

Kane looked sharply at Massey. "Since you're a lawyer, why aren't you going to defend her?"

"Good question. Well, two reasons. First, I haven't tried a major criminal case in fifteen years. Secondly, about fifteen years ago, I learned the hard way about trying a lawsuit in a rural county against a local lawyer. I walked into the courtroom in a little cowpoke town in the San Joaquin Valley. Nobody was there except the bailiff. After waiting with my client for thirty minutes, I asked the bailiff where the judge was. He smiled and said, 'Counselor, opposing counsel and the judge are planning a pack trip into the Sierras together.' Needless to say, I lost before the trial even started."

"You're a smart lawyer, Massey. There's been plenty of big-city lawyers who come up here with their forty-page briefs and several associates, thinking they are going to intimidate the judges with all of their sophistication and eloquence. Country judges don't cotton to those boys."

"I've made some background notes on the case," said Massey as he handed his papers to Kane.

Fifteen minutes later, Kane looked up from the notes and said, "Let me be straight with you, Mr. Massey. I lost my last murder case. But I think there is a decent chance of getting her off on a manslaughter count."

"How do you reach that conclusion, in light of the fact that she has already confessed to the murder and was lying in wait for the man she shot? Your former partner, Mr. Ames, thought it was a murder one or two conviction because of the premeditation involved."

Kane shook his head thoughtfully. "It's the human factor. After reading your notes, I think she has a very sympathetic story to tell. She will draw a lot of emotion from the jury, particularly mothers. I'm not a defense lawyer who relishes putting the defendant on the stand, but if we can get strong enough medical testimony that tells her history and tends to support her irrational actions, I think a jury up here would hate what the pedophile did much more than what your client did. I don't think they would want her locked up for a long time, much less give her the death penalty."

Massey knew he had found the lawyer to defend Leola. Kane was smart and had a great sense of humor, but the quality that most impressed Massey was Kane's ability to connect with another person, a trait that Massey deemed as the most important in a good trial lawyer. This man didn't talk down to you, and Massey realized the average juror would be able to relate to him.

Kane continued, "I charge a ten thousand dollar retainer fee, and I bill at the rate of one hundred per hour."

"Let me use your phone for a minute and I'll call her husband."

Massey was directed to the foyer where there was a phone on the table. He was able to find Sam at home. "Sam, Skip Massey here. I just finished interviewing two lawyers up here who were recommended as the best around. I've selected one that is very smart and he thinks she has a chance of getting a reduced count of murder, which would mean a short stay in jail. He wants a retainer fee of ten thousand dollars and charges one hundred bucks per hour, which by comparison to Bay Area lawyers' fees is very good." Massey spent the next ten minutes with Sam, talking over the total fee and other expenses he might have to bear, such as bail bond amounts.

When Massey returned to Kane's office, he said, "You're hired."

Kane nodded and asked, "Are you going to be around tomorrow morning? I'd like to meet with you and go over the case in more depth. Since you're a lawyer, I'd be more than happy to have your assistance in preparing and trying this case. Two heads are always better than one."

"I'm okay for tomorrow morning," Massey responded, "but I have a horrendous schedule for the next couple of months. I can help on weekends and occasionally on weekdays."

After shaking hands with Kane, Massey left his office and headed for the hotel.

The two attorneys met at 8 a.m. the next morning to go over the case. When Massey arrived, Kane had a big pot of coffee brewing and poured a cup when they sat down in the library / conference room.

Massey started off, "What's the procedure up here regarding setting bail for Leola?"

"Let me call Judge Brandon's clerk and get the earliest date I can for her arraignment and bail hearing. Right now, bail is arbitrarily set by the judge at a million bucks. At the bail hearing, I can make a motion for a lower amount, but it's going to be tough to get much of a reduction in a capital case," answered Kane.

Massey spoke up. "I don't think Leola can take much more jail time. I think she'll have a total break-down. I'm sure her husband can use their home as collateral for bail in the quarter of a million range. Any more than that, and she'll have to stay in jail until we can get this case to trial. But she'll be a real nut case by then."

Kane looked at Massey with a frown on his face. "That's a very tall order. I'll try for that amount, but don't bet your last dollar on it. I was thinking last night that we ought to line up our medical expert as soon as possible and have him interview Leola so that he can testify as to her state of mind close to the time of the killing. I read in your report that Mrs. Langley was being treated by a psychologist in the area. We ought to get in touch with him right away."

"For the last couple of months, she's been treated by a friend of mine at Stanford Medical Center, Dr. Stan Tishman. I think he has a pretty good read on her. Let's get him up here to interview her. What I don't understand is why she doesn't remember killing anybody. There must be a medical explanation."

"I'm not sure any jury is going to buy that scenario. Even if your doctor comes up with a damn good explanation, I think we will have a hard time selling that story to our country folk. It's worth a try, however. At any rate, let's get him up here pronto. What I'd like to see right away is that confession she signed right after the murder."

Despite Kane's enthusiasm, Massey became silent as the seriousness of Leola's chances for getting a lengthy jail sentence or the death penalty began to sink in. Massey placed a call to Dr. Tishman at Stanford Hospital. Fortunately, the doctor was in and doing his rounds. The nurses were able to locate him and he came to the phone. "Stan, Skip Massey. Leola Langley has been charged with the murder of the teacher who molested her son. It looks like the state may have a good case for the gas chamber."

"Wow! I thought the teacher committed suicide."

"After the so-called suicide occurred, Leola was suspicious that he was still alive because there was never an obituary about him in the newspaper. I hired an investigator and tracked him down in Susanville. How Leola learned his whereabouts is still a mystery to me. Anyway, she came up here two days ago and shot him to death with a 20-gauge shotgun. I saw her the night of the murder, and she said she didn't have any recollection of killing anybody and didn't know why she was in jail. Funny thing, I believe she was telling me the truth. I need you to get up here as soon as possible and figure out what the hell is going on. I know that the mind can act pretty weird at times, but this one takes the cake. Your medical testimony on her mental condition at the time of the killing will be vital to her defense," Massey pressed.

"I'm busy as hell, but I'll see if I can rearrange my schedule. Wednesday is probably my best day. I'll let you know tomorrow. By the way, when I last saw her, which was Wednesday, July 10, she disassociated," said the doctor.

"Hey, that's the day before the murder. That testimony will be extremely valuable. The sooner you interview before and after the date of the killing, the more credible your testimony will be regarding her state of mind at the time of the killing."

Massey put the phone down and turned to Kane. "Great news! The doctor saw her the day before the killing and said she was disassociated. His testimony is going to be a beaut. He thinks he can make it up here on Wednesday. I'll fly him up. Can you make arrangements with the district attorney to have the doctor see her around ten in the morning? After the doc's interview, we'll interview him."

"Sounds good to me. I'll make the arrangements with the district attorney. In addition, I'll see if I can get a copy of her confession out of him," said Kane.

"Let's hope that confession isn't as damaging as I think it is. I'll head back home now and be back on Wednesday. I'll have my staff brief the applicable law regarding diminished capacity and insanity with all the up-to-date cases. Hopefully, we can find a defense based on mental incapacity where she could get a manslaughter conviction and a short jail sentence."

After Massey checked out of the hotel, he climbed into his Porsche and roared down the highway, headed for home.

# CHAPTER 13

On Wednesday Massey was able to borrow a plane and a pilot from his old friend, Stan Levitt. He and Dr. Tishman took off early in the morning from the San Jose Airport in a twin-engine Cessna. The plane touched down at the Susanville Airport two hours later, and Jerry Kane was there to meet them in his red Ford Bronco.

Massey introduced the two men, and Kane looked over Dr. Tishman after shaking his hand. The doctor was tall, thin, with lots of red hair and freckles, about forty, and wore small gold-rimmed glasses. Massey read Kane's mind immediately. He basically feared this highly educated doctor would talk over the heads of these country jurors and lose them.

"Nice to meet you, doctor. I've got you an appointment at the jail with Mrs. Langley at ten." The three men climbed into Kane's Bronco and headed for the county jail.

Once there, they walked up the steps and were greeted by the slovenly Sergeant Tremont. "What'cha all here for?"

Kane explained, "When I talked to the district attorney on Monday, he told me he'd arrange for an interview between Mrs. Langley and her doctor this morning at ten."

"Lemme look at the notes here." The sergeant shuffled through a bunch of papers on a clipboard. "Here it is. Note from the district attorney. Says to let her doctor see her this mornin'. You can use the visiting room over there." He pointed to a door down the hall about thirty feet away. "I'll go get the prisoner and bring her down here. Once inside, I'm gonna lock you all in. When you want out, just rap on the door."

After a few moments, Massey looked up at the dim hallway where Leola's cell was located and saw her being escorted down the hallway in paper sandals and orange jail garb, with shackles on both her ankles and wrists. Her hair was a mess and she didn't wear any makeup. Massey noticed huge bags under her eyes. As she approached the three men, she looked down at the ground. Massey spoke kindly to her, "Hi Leola, I brought Dr. Tishman to see you." She looked up at Dr. Tishman, briefly smiled, and then looked down again at the floor, seemingly embarrassed to be seen in these surroundings.

Sergeant Tremont turned and looked at Massey with scorn. "No talking or touching the prisoner until I get her in the visiting room." He led her to the door and unlocked it, leading Leola inside a screened cage that would separate the prisoner from her visitors. The surly sergeant then turned to the men outside. "You all can come in here now. I'm going to stand outside this window and make sure nobody tries to slip the prisoner anything."

"Mr. Kane and I are only going to say hello to Mrs. Langley. Then we'll leave the doctor to interview her for an hour or so," Massey responded.

"Well, be quick about it," snapped the grumpy sergeant.

When Leola saw the three men entering the room, tears welled up in her eyes. Massey spoke gently, saying "Leola, this is Mr. Kane. He's a local lawyer, the best in town, and he is going to help us work on the case so we can get you back home with your family. We're going to leave for a short while. Dr. Tishman wants to talk to you alone."

As they were about to leave, Massey told Tishman, "Jerry and I are going down to the St. Francis Hotel for coffee. Call us when you're through and we'll come and get you."

▼

Two hours later the three men were sitting in Kane's conference room. Dr. Tishman looked up. "She's not well. She's a psychological mess. She ought to be in the hospital, receiving care for a severe case of depression."

Massey said, "Do you have any idea what the devil motivated Leola to kill Arnold? It's so out of character for her."

"In my opinion, all the pain associated with her son built up an emotional response that caused her to explode into an irrational state of mind—or more technically, 'an altered state of mind'—which resulted in a killing that, in reality, she never intended. I think when Billy was hospitalized for anorexia, it caused her to snap, caused a severe and sudden change in her personality."

Jerry Kane asked, "Does she still deny any recollection of killing her victim?"

"She has absolutely no memory of the murder or any events surrounding it."

"How's that possible?" asked a quizzical Kane.

"There's a syndrome that we shrinks call the Repressed Memory Syndrome. A severe traumatic event can cause a memory lapse for a short period of time. Sometimes the trauma may be so severe that the loss of memory extends for a lengthy period of time. For example, many severely abused children cannot even recall their childhood. I really think that Mrs. Langley was so severely traumatized, not only by the Arnold incident, but also by the hospitalization of her son and destruction of her family, that she snapped, started hallucinating, became divorced from reality, and then killed the victim. The act of killing, by itself, was also very traumatic for her. She just stuffed the memory of the killing into the deep recesses of her mind. As a result, she doesn't have the faintest notion that she murdered someone."

"That's explosive testimony. It is going to be crucial for the defense, if we can just get it into evidence," responded an excited Skip Massey. "Do you think that she can mentally hold up if we don't get her out of jail on bail?"

"I don't think she can hold herself together until trial, which I assume would be in the next several months. She needs extensive medical treatment. If you can get her released on bail, I will see that she is hospitalized and receives proper treatment. If not, then I expect she will deteriorate rapidly and probably not be in any condition to go to trial."

Massey turned to Kane. "Did you get that hearing date for the reduction in bail?"

"The hearing is set for this Friday at nine. I think we should get an affidavit from the doctor about Leola's condition. It should help us get Judge Brandon to lower the bail. Anyway, Massey, did you get a chance to have your staff prepare that research memo on possible defenses in our case?"

Massey dug into his briefcase, pulled out a legal memo and handed it to Kane. "The doc and I'll go grab some sandwiches and soft drinks for the three of us while you stay here and read the memo. When we get back, we can put together the doctor's affidavit and go over the case law that my staff dug out."

After the two headed out for food, Kane reached in his top drawer for a cigar. After lighting it, he leaned back in his swivel chair, put his feet on his desk, and began puffing on his cigar while reading Massey's legal memo.

Memo Re: Diminished Mental Capacity
    as a Defense to Murder

For: Skip Massey
From: Dave Hult, Senior Law Research Attorney

I. Diminished Capacity Can No Longer
Be Used As A Defense To Murder.
In 1981, the state legislature abolished 'diminished capacity' as a defense to murder and made other significant changes in the criminal code regarding the charge of murder. The elimination of the diminished capacity or irresistible impulse defense was a direct result of the acquittal of Dan White, a San Francisco policeman, who shot

to death San Francisco supervisor Harvey Milk in 1978. White was fiercely anti-gay and his lawyers successfully used the irresistible impulse defense, which in a nutshell was a defense that was used when the killer mentally couldn't control himself from killing the object of his hate. At the same time, the legislature split criminal murder trials involving intentional acts into two phases, the guilt phase and then the penalty phase. Evidence of diminished capacity can only be introduced at the penalty phase of the trial and would have no bearing on whether the defendant is guilty of any of the murder counts. This type of evidence is strictly heard for the basis of determining the length of the sentence of the convicted person.

2. The Issue Of Mental Capacity
Is Admissible To Show No Premeditation.
Penal Code Section 28 allows evidence of mental disease, mental defect or mental disorder on the issue of whether or not the accused actually formed a required specific intent, premeditated, deliberate, or malice aforethought when the suspect is charged with murder.

3. Recent Cases Do Not Allow Evidence
Of Mental Disorder Where The Accused Knew
The Nature Of His Act.
*People v. Leever*, App. 1 Dist, 173 CA.3d 853 (1985) Evidence of mental illness was not admissible when the court found that the defendant by pointing the gun at his victim knew that harm would occur and hence understood the nature of his act.

4. Post-Traumatic Stress Syndrome Defense.
This defense (termed the PTSD defense, for post-traumatic stress disorder) is used in cases of war veterans who have flashbacks to battle and believe that they are in a war zone. During the

flashback, the killer believes the person he is accused of killing is actually about to kill him on the battlefield. This defense is only allowed in cases where there is strong medical testimony that the veteran, during the war in which he served, suffered severe emotional trauma which ultimately manifested in the individual a severe reaction, and the veteran has a flashback of his war experiences. There may be some similarity between our client's mental condition and that of a war veteran.

5. Battered Wife Syndrome Defense.
   There are two cases on appeal where the defense lawyers used this defense when two wives killed their spouses, based on the same flashback theory. Several states allow this defense, but to date, the California courts have not. A decision by the appellate courts on these two cases should come fairly soon. This defense is one step removed from our client's situation, and if the appellate courts allow the defense, we would be in a position to argue the similarity of the situation.

The brief continued, mentioning other cases. Kane, while puffing on his stogie, finished reading it, set it down and looked at the ceiling. He found the memo most fascinating. He looked at his cigar and realized that he had almost smoked it down to the stub. Instead of throwing the butt of the cigar away, Kane began chewing and sucking on it.

When Massey and Tishman returned with lunch, Kane said, with the stub end of the cigar still in his mouth, "Before we work on the doctor's affidavit, let's go over your staff's legal memo while I still have it fresh in my mind. I want to see if we can come up with a solid defense theory."

All three sat down at Kane's conference table. Kane began, "Let me give you copies of our client's confession, which I didn't receive until late yesterday afternoon.

I don't like what I read at all. As you'll soon see, it becomes evident that she recalled all the events of the killing when she gave the confession. I certainly don't like her statement that she would kill him again if she had the chance."

The room was silent for a couple of minutes while Massey and the doctor read the confession. Finally, Massey looked up. "Whew, this statement that she hid behind a bush before killing him and her statement that she would kill him again are the most damaging pieces of evidence against Leola. She might have been mentally ill when she killed Arnold, but her acts certainly confirmed her ability to distinguish the wrongful nature of her act. I'm sure the district attorney's office thinks it has an open-and-shut case for murder in the first degree, what with this confession and several eyewitnesses."

"I don't like it either," said Kane. "Doctor, how are you going to get around this confession?"

The red-headed doctor looked through his specs and peered quizzically at Kane. "It's not so very different from the Vietnam veteran who has a flashback. Seconds before the flashback is triggered, he can be as normal as you and I, but when the flashback trigger is pulled, the veteran is a totally different personality, a killer, absolutely intent on killing his victim because he thinks the attacker is trying to kill him."

Kane challenged the doctor, "Well, that may be true for the veteran, but our gal hasn't been through a war. How are you going to convince a jury that whatever triggered her personality change caused her to hop in her car and, twenty-four hours later, lay in wait behind a bush to kill a teacher as he was going to his automobile. I don't see the parallel situation."

Tishman pulled out his pipe, lit it, and then looked at the two lawyers. "I'm troubled myself by the stretch, but I don't think I know all about Leola's background. I think there's a lot more to learn about Leola Langley, something that led her to react so violently. That apparently cold-blooded killer is the antithesis of her normal personality: loving mother and a Christian woman who leads an exemplary life."

Massey added, "Even if we can explain her flash-back, the trigger, and the irrational behavior, I think we have an uphill battle getting a judge to allow the post-traumatic stress syndrome theory. The courts so far have limited the use of the defense to war veterans only."

Kane remarked, "I think our only defense has to be that she was so mentally ill that she couldn't form an intent to kill. I know the district attorney will beat us to death with that confession, but I believe we need to focus on facts that will allow us to utilize that approach."

"Doc, can you help us with that theory?" asked Massey.

Dr. Tishman thought for a while and took a couple of puffs on his pipe, blowing smoke rings in the air as he thought about the question. "Let me try this on you. There is no question in my mind that she was in a hallucinatory state of mind when she killed the teacher. Basically she wasn't Leola Langley, she was another person. Leola Langley's mind never intended to kill anybody; the other person took over and formulated the intent to kill."

"Nice try," said Kane, "but that damn *Leever* case cited in Massey's legal brief says that the killer has the requisite intent if he knew at the time of the killing the nature of the consequences of his act, even if he is hallucinating or under the influence of drugs or alcohol. I pulled that case out and read it while you two were out getting lunch."

Massey then spoke, "I think we face a real uphill battle on that theory. I thought of the heat of passion defense, which would give us a chance for manslaughter and a minimum sentence. But the courts have limited the use of this defense and require the passion and murder to be so connected in time that there is no cooling-off period. The best example is that they allow the defense when a husband or wife finds the spouse in bed with someone else, and immediately the killer goes into a rage and kills the spouse, the other party, or both."

Massey continued, "Doctor, you told me that you last saw Leola on the day before the murder and she was disassociated. My guess is that she had already discovered Arnold was alive when she saw you. That's a day before the killing. That's a substantial cooling-off period. I don't think there's a snowball's chance in hell of getting a judge to buy the heat of passion defense."

"I agree with you," responded Kane.

Massey then leaned back in his chair, looked up in the air, stretched his arms. "Gentlemen, I think our only chance is the post-traumatic stress syndrome defense. I know the judge will probably not allow that defense, but if we can get the evidence in for the purpose of appeal—the evidence of these two pedophiles, their porn business, the abuse of the son, the tearing apart of the family—all this shocking evidence will inflame a jury, and I believe they will be sympathetic and look for any loophole."

Kane responded, "Good thought. Let's go for it."

"Doctor, have you ever testified in a post-traumatic stress syndrome case before? Because the courts insist that the expert have prior experience in this area."

"I'm afraid not," responded the doctor.

Kane chomped on his cigar butt, stuck it in the left side of his mouth and then stated, "Well, we are going to have to find somebody with experience in this area. Doctor, we will need you, obviously, to testify on her state of mind before and after the shooting, but we will have to hire a doctor with experience in this field who will testify, if he can, that she had a horrific experience similar to the veterans, so significant that the experience of her son's trauma caused a flashback. I've used a local doctor here who is a Vietnam veteran. Massey, you ought to interview him and see what you think."

"How soon can I get in to see him?" asked Massey.

Kane put his cigar butt in the ashtray, picked up the telephone on the table and dialed the phone. While waiting for the doctor to answer, he said, "God, I love these Cuban cigars." Then he spoke into the phone, "Scott, Kane here. I'm defending the gal who shot the teacher last week. I think we've got a situation similar to the area that you're familiar with, the flash-back defense. Any chance my co-counsel from Palo Alto can get into see you right away? Great, I'll send him right over. Hold on a second. Let me see if it's okay with him."

Kane looked at Massey. "He can see you right now."

Massey then turned to Dr. Tishman. "The interview will take no more than forty-five minutes. Is that okay? I know you're on a tight schedule." Tishman nodded his head.

Kane then spoke into the telephone, "Scott, he'll be right over. Name's Skip Massey."

Massey only had to walk down Main Street to the end of the small business district to find Dr. Scott Smith's office. On the way over, he thought about how tough it is to find a psychiatric medical expert with good forensic skills. It was like trying to find a needle in a haystack.

The office was located at the fringe of the business district in one of a series of old residences that had been converted to office use. This particular building hadn't been remodeled except for the new paint job in two tones of dark green on the outside and an off-white color on the inside. Massey walked into the former living room, which was nicely furnished with a couch and a couple of chairs, magazines on the coffee table, and a few early-California gold mining pictures on the walls. Massey was expecting to find a neat and tidy shrink, dressed up and ready to do business.

Massey spotted a sign on the coffee table, "Be seated, the doctor will be with you in a few minutes." He waited for several minutes and then said in a loud voice, "Anybody home?" A few seconds later, out walked a guy wearing a pair of sandals, blue jeans and a white T-shirt, with stringy blond hair, looking like a 1960s hippie. His looks took Massey by surprise.

"You don't like the looks?" said the doctor, walking up to Massey with his hand extended, ready to shake Massey's hand. "I'm Dr. Smith. You must be Mr. Massey, the lawyer from the big city?"

Massey shook his hand half-heartedly. "I'm not impressed," he said.

"So much for a cordial introduction," Smith replied. He turned and led Massey to his office, which obviously was a former bedroom. Inside the doctor seated himself in a massive Naugahyde reclining chair while Massey took a seat on a small sofa.

The cool exchange between the two had made for an awkward situation. Massey said, "Sorry about the remark. Your looks didn't match my expectations. I should have remembered that the cover of a book is no gauge of the quality of the story."

"Apology accepted. Big-city folks have a difficult time accepting country garb. I understand from Mr. Kane that you two are going to defend the woman who shot the teacher. I think you've got an uphill battle on your hands from what I've read in the papers."

"If there is one thing in life I've learned practicing law, it's don't prejudge a case until you've heard all of the evidence. I've been fooled many times. Some people are good storytellers and lie with a straight face, yet others can't look you in the eye when they're telling a true story. You think they're lying when they are absolutely telling the truth."

The doctor replied, "Well, I guess I owe you a reciprocal apology. What you said is true. I see good storytellers skate free while innocent defendants, who get nervous and appear to be lying, get convicted."

After their initial rocky start, Massey realized the ice was beginning to thaw. "Jerry Kane recommended you as having experience in treating Vietnam veterans with post-traumatic stress syndrome. Jerry also said that you had recently been involved with the PTSD defense in the Sacramento area."

Dr. Smith picked up a pencil and twirled it in his hands. Then he set it down and looked Massey in the eye. "I served in Vietnam as a foot soldier, got shot up, and when I returned, I saw a lot of my buddies having severe emotional problems. As a result, I decided to become a psychiatrist. I have treated many vets and have testified regarding the PTSD defense in five prior cases. Recently in a Sacramento case, the jury didn't buy my flashback testimony."

"My research staff indicates the defense is fairly new and not fully accepted by the courts, much less juries. I know how difficult it would be even if the defendant was a veteran, which our defendant is not," Massey replied.

"You're right. The average juror can't really understand how these men can have a disassociated flashback in which they lose touch with current reality. The most common flashback is an anxiety reaction which produces a flight response. If flight is not an option, the person experiencing the flashback will fight whoever is threatening. I've seen flashbacks occur in these men many times. Fortunately, only a few ever wind up killing a person. But, how does this defense apply in your client's case? She's no vet."

Massey gave him the background of Leola, her son, and the suffering that she and her family went through after the Arnold incident. He also told him about the son's hospitalization for anorexia. "What I would suggest is you call Dr. Tishman. He'll give you a far more complete story of the family turmoil and the mental condition of Leola than I can."

"I may go visit him."

"At a minimum, I want to get into evidence some PTSD testimony from you for appeal purposes. More importantly, however, if the judge allows this type of evidence, then we can get into what caused her to go into orbit, and that testimony will inflame the hell out of the jury. Maybe they'll even shift the blame from the defendant to the victim," Massey said wishfully.

"Very good point, although it would certainly be a long shot," replied Dr. Smith.

Massey then asked, "If your life were on the line, who would you use to testify as to the mental state of mind of the defendant in this case?"

"Me," Dr. Smith said without hesitation. "I'm the best around. Not only that, I'm a local. Bring in a flat-lander and you'll never win the case. The locals can't stand the big-city folks, particularly doctors and lawyers."

"So far, I'm impressed with your credentials. But let me tell you my experience with psychiatrists as expert witnesses," Massey started.

The doctor interrupted, "Let me guess. I'll bet most

of them are afraid to take the stand and render a definite conclusion. They always leave an opening."

"You're right again. In addition, too many in your profession are arrogant, talk over the heads of the jurors without painting the big picture, and then when it comes to cross-examination, are not flexible enough to handle tricky questions that threaten their conclusions."

"Don't forget that most of these doctors are normally sheltered from the real world. It's easy to play God when you're telling people how to act in a psychological treatment format. As a result, most of them think they're better than the ordinary person and really don't connect with the jurors. You'll find out that my war experiences took a lot of that cockiness out of me," said Dr. Smith.

Massey continued, "What's worse is that they often can't handle adversity because they've never experienced hardship. They often become flustered and freeze when hit with a question that threatens the integrity of their direct examination. What I mainly look for in an expert witness is someone who speaks with authority, in a humble sort of way, and most importantly, a witness who can handle a fierce cross-examination by the other side."

The doctor got up from his chair and pulled out a drawer of the cabinet behind him. He searched for a second, then drew out a manila folder. "Here, this file contains a list of cases that I've testified in. Call these lawyers and have them tell you what kind of witness I am."

"Can I borrow your telephone in the front foyer to call a couple of the lawyers right now?"

"Be my guest."

All the lawyers Massey called gave Smith good marks, stating he had the ability to establish a great degree of credibility with the jury, and that he was an accomplished expert witness. Massey got up from the chair where he had been making the calls and knocked on the door to the doctor's office. The doctor opened it. "Well, did I pass muster?" he asked.

"With flying colors. One thing, however. How about getting a haircut, change those jeans and T-shirt, and get a regular pair of dress shoes when you testify?"

Dr. Smith looked at Skip Massey with a half smile. "You are an insulting son of a bitch, aren't you? You don't like our local garb?"

"It's not whether I like it or not. It's whether the jury will like it."

"How stupid do you think I am? I always put on a pair of slacks, a sweater, and get my curls clipped a bit. That's about what everybody, including the judge, is used to around these parts of the country. I won't be out of place."

"I guess I can't get used to country living," Massey said with a smile.

"Well, stick around a few months and you'll get in the swing of it. We might even have you in curls."

"Not on your life, Doc," Massey told him. "I'll be in touch with you shortly to get into the specifics of the case, and then make arrangements to have you interview the defendant, Leola Langley."

"You forgot the most important part," said the good doctor as Massey stood up, preparing to leave. "I charge three hundred dollars per hour."

"That's pretty high-priced for a local hick," Massey said, and then he added with a grin, "Sounds reasonable, though, for a smart hick."

"You've got a deal." They shook hands, and Massey left with a good feeling about their PTSD expert.

Massey walked back to Kane's office to tell him he had hired Dr. Smith. Kane then drove Massey and Dr. Tishman back to the airport. As Massey was boarding the plane, he shouted back to Kane, "Call me after the arraignment on Friday, and let me know if you were able to get bail reduced."

Kane gave Massey the high sign, the door closed, and the plane's engines started. The plane sped down the runway, then up in the air, and headed for San Jose.

# CHAPTER 14

Jerry Kane carried his worn-out briefcase up the granite steps leading to the Lassen County Courthouse. The granite building was erected in 1891 from the massive amounts of granite stone that permeate the Sierra Nevada. The courthouse, a few blocks from Main Street, rests on a hill overlooking the town. It is a majestic edifice that stands as the symbol of justice in the small community. There was only one Superior Court Judge in the County of Lassen, Judge Brandon, who had been appointed by Governor Reagan.

Kane liked Judge Brandon a lot. He was a tiny little guy, totally bald, but had a quick mind, was smart, fair, and didn't tolerate time-wasters. He would cut lawyers off at the pass if they started rambling. When faced with a young lawyer delivering a lengthy dissertation, the judge would bang his gavel in mid-sentence, peer down at the lawyer and announce, "Well, young man, you're the only one in this courtroom who's enjoying your rambling discourse. I'll give you sixty seconds to finish your argument." Kane used to smile as the lawyer would redden and become so tongue-tied he couldn't finish his argument.

Come unprepared to court, and the judge would go into orbit. "Don't waste my time. You're obviously not prepared. Go home. Do your homework and come back here in two weeks." Kane recalled receiving that tongue-lashing when he first started practice in Susanville. He had been up all night drinking and didn't have time to prepare his oral argument. Kane never forgot the humiliation, and rest assured, it never happened again.

Now Kane walked into Judge Brandon's courtroom. The court was crowded with twenty or so lawyers, waiting to present their law and motion arguments to the judge. Kane took a seat in the jury box where most of the experienced lawyers sat. They all knew each other, and Kane waved to a couple of old friends. He looked up at the massive courtroom ceiling, forty feet high at least. He turned and saw the familiar massive oak bench, closed in the front with oak paneling, where the judge would be sitting in a few moments. It was elevated at least six feet above the main floor. Kane recalled many times while arguing his case, the judge would peer down and look directly into his eyes, scaring the hell out of him.

"Hear ye, hear ye. Please rise. The Superior Court of Lassen County in and for the State of California is now in session, Judge Carl A. Brandon presiding. Please be seated," shouted the bailiff, Ed Henderson, at the top of his lungs.

The judge entered the courtroom wearing his black robe and looking very stern. He took his seat behind the massive bench, looked over at the local lawyers in the jury box, and said, "Good morning, ladies and gentlemen. Let's begin with this morning's calendar, Madame Clerk."

The judge's clerk, Anna Quigley, announced in a loud voice, "Case #60349, People versus John A. Selby." The district attorney, Steve Aaron, was already seated at the counsel table, and a lawyer rose from the audience and seated himself at the table for opposing counsel. The lawyers began their arguments, which would last several minutes before the judge made his decision.

Kane saw that his motion for bail was next. The arraignment hearing for Leola had been set for 2 p.m. that afternoon before a municipal court judge on the second floor. While the other lawyers were arguing the first case, Kane was thinking about Leola, and the fact that she had been incarcerated for ten days now. When he saw her two days ago, there was no doubt that she was mentally deteriorating by the day. Her spirits had sagged to the point that she no longer cared about living.

116

Kane had requested the sheriff to put a twenty-four hour watch on her until she stabilized.

Kane remembered going to the judge's chambers yesterday at the end of the day, to chat with him about the case and give him some of the background. When he asked the bailiff, Deputy Ed Henderson, to see the judge, Henderson told him, "Jerry, you wouldn't want to see the judge today anyway. He is in a terrible mood."

"Why's that? Some smart-aleck lawyer tried to talk back this afternoon and he blew?" Kane surmised.

"Oh, that never ruffles him. But about three weeks ago, he asked the State Supreme Court chief justice for a judge to be temporarily assigned up here, to help out during a trial which has already lasted six weeks. The judge is frazzled. Since he's the only Superior Court judge in the county, he has to handle the whole load by himself. He is fighting a losing battle, you know, probate, law and motion, everything. He just received the news that his request was denied. He's fit to be tied."

"No wonder. I'll be in his courtroom tomorrow morning. I hope he's cooled off. Last couple of times I've seen him, he's looked tired as hell," Kane told the bailiff.

Kane became focused on the task before him when he heard the clerk call his case. He rose and took his seat at the counsel table opposite the district attorney. The district attorney stood up and gave a spiel about what a heinous crime Leola had committed, and what a threat she would be to the community if she were freed pending the trial.

Kane stood up to speak, but had hardly gotten a word out of his mouth, when the judge interrupted him. "There is no way I am going to let a cold-blooded murderer out on bail without a million-dollar bail bond being posted. Motion denied. Next case, Madame Clerk." It was obvious to Kane that the judge, after talking with the district attorney, knew that raising a million-dollar bond was out of the question for Leola and her husband. No bail bondsman would risk that sum on an out-of-towner with no resources.

Kane called Massey after the hearing. "Massey, the judge was grumpy as hell and refused to budge on the bail. Million bucks. He wouldn't even let me get a word in edgewise. I'm going to slip into his chambers early next week and bend his ear a little on this case. I think I can reason with him and get the bail reduced. I'll call you afterwards."

Jerry caught the judge the following Monday in his chambers before the jury trial was scheduled to begin. The judge stood and shook hands with Kane. "I'm sorry I bit your head off on Friday about the bail for that gal who killed the teacher," he said. "That damn chief justice thinks we don't have anything to do up here in these mountain counties. Her highness has a great big legal staff, while we have a skeleton staff. When we get over-loaded and ask for help, she turns her back on us. I'll tell you now that when she is up for reelection, she isn't about to get my vote. What can I do for you, Jerry?" The judge slumped back in his chair.

Kane noticed black circles around the judge's eyes and said, "Judge, you look overworked and underpaid."

"There are times when I wish I could walk away from this rat race. I can't let my hair down in the community because I've always got to be the perfect role model. I can't get too close to any attorney or I'm accused of being prejudiced in his favor. It is a pretty lonely life. Right now I wish I could hit a bar, have six martinis and go on a fling. I'd be the happiest man alive."

Kane looked closely at Judge Brandon. In his early sixties, small but well built, he was a man who used to be in good shape but now was beginning to show his age faster than most. His hectic pace of life had etched so many wrinkles in his face that Massey was reminded of a blond beauty who spent her life sunning herself, only to wind up with wrinkled and leathery skin. Also, the muscles in the judge's chest had retreated to his belly through inertia. A little gruff, but down deep, a good human being.

"Well, you probably want to tell me about this gal who shot the teacher, right?"

"It's a real interesting story. I'll keep it short. My client, Leola Langley, is a housewife with two young children. She lives in Los Gatos. Her youngest boy was molested in the Bay Area by the same teacher she allegedly killed. Please keep that fact confidential."

"What the hell's the teacher doing up here?" the judge asked.

"That's the interesting part. After the parents requested that the school administration investigate the molestation charges, he faked suicide the day before the sheriff was to arrest him. Damned if the superintendent didn't send him up here incognito."

"You've got to be kidding!"

"I'm not. The woman's kid went downhill and had to be hospitalized, and when she found out the teacher was still alive, she went berserk and allegedly came up here and blew him apart."

"What's her background, Jerry?" asked the judge, listening intently to Kane's story.

"She is a very religious person, Southern Baptist, married to a hardworking husband for the last fifteen years, no past criminal record. She isn't a threat to anyone. I have a lawyer from the Bay Area helping me out in this case because he is a friend of hers, and he says she is honest and would not run," said Kane.

"Religious, eh? I thought one of the Ten Commandments says, Thou shall not kill. I guess she didn't remember that one."

"She was following the oldest instinct in the world, a mother's instinct to protect her young. The problem now is that she is dangerously depressed. Her doctor thinks she's going downhill fast. He says unless she gets immediate mental care, she won't be able to stand trial. If we can get her out on bail, he's going to place her in the Santa Clara County Hospital."

The judge thought for a moment and then looked at Kane. "What amount of bail do you feel is reasonable?"

"Two hundred thousand," said Jerry.

"Okay. We'll set up a hearing for Wednesday on a new motion for a bail reduction," replied the judge.

Two days later, Judge Brandon reduced the bail, and Leola was released the following day. Sam took her straight to the Santa Clara County Hospital for around-the-clock mental health care.

The following Saturday, Massey was sitting in Stan Levitt's Cessna preparing for landing at the Susanville airport. It was now a little more than four weeks after the murder. Every weekend since the killing, he'd been flying up to help Kane prepare for the trial. Massey liked Kane's low-key style of lawyering. While Massey had observed that Kane was a heavy drinker in the evening, during working hours he would put the bottle aside.

During lunch breaks, Kane and Massey usually wandered over to a small downtown restaurant called Effie's. Shirley Effie, the owner, was one hell of a cook. Most of the townspeople frequented her restaurant. On the last occasion that the two had lunch at Effie's, Kane started to talk about his personal life for the first time. "My wife and I had three children right after I finished law school."

"You went to Boalt Hall, didn't you? Damn good school."

"Yeh, it was tough, but I made it with flying colors. After I got out, I was hired by one of those large San Francisco firms, not knowing that they expected young lawyers to work nights and weekends. I wasn't home much, and my wife and I became complete strangers. After five years of marriage, my wife realized she was living alone and raising the kids by herself. She told me she was leaving me for another man because the law business demanded so much of my time that I didn't have any left to raise a family, much less time to care for her. I really loved her, but I'm the first to admit the law business turned out to be too much like a jealous mistress."

Massey could see tears well up in the eyes of the Irishman. Kane looked down at his plate to hide them. "After the divorce, I quit the firm and fled to Susanville," he continued. "I got a golden retriever, set up a law office, and proceeded to practice law in this small community. It was tough at first, but with my background at the big firm, I prepared my cases more thoroughly than the local attorneys. Soon I began winning most of my cases. Word traveled, and now

I'm beginning to build a fairly good business. Still can't get over my wife. That's probably why I've never remarried or even dated."

At lunch they decided they needed to set the deposition schedule. Mr. Roland Garrity, the superintendent of schools, the co-conspirator, was to be the first in order. Because Massey had filed the civil action against the school district in Los Gatos, they had the advantage of taking a deposition in the civil case without having to notify the Susanville district attorney. This was a tremendous advantage to the defense, because the criminal prosecution wouldn't know where the defense was headed.

Massey thought for a moment and then looked at Kane. "Garrity will probably bring a criminal attorney along to the deposition since he's in hot water."

"What did happen to the superintendent?"

"About three weeks after the supposed suicide, I went to the sheriff's office to see Sergeant Cardoza, who did the preliminary investigation on Arnold. I told him we suspected he feigned his suicide, but he seemed little interested in pursuing the matter. Said his office was too busy. Three months later when I walked into the sergeant's office with a copy of Mike O'Malley's investigative report, I threw it on his desk. I told him if he had a moment to spare, why didn't he glance at the report? I added he might find it very interesting. Then I waited for his reaction when he read it."

Massey paused, recalling the scene. "At first he just scowled at me, then he picked up the report and glanced at it. All of sudden he started reading intensely. When he got to the porno shop section, his eyes widened and he muttered, 'Jesus Christ!' After he read Arnold was not dead, he looked up in disbelief and uttered that he couldn't believe it. I told him, 'You'd better believe it, as there is an even more tragic sequel to the story. Somehow, Mrs. Langley learned the whereabouts of Stanley Arnold, went up to Susanville and shot him to death. She is now charged with the first degree murder of Arnold.' He just sat stunned and in a state of disbelief." Massey paused again before he went on.

121

"Finally, the asshole says, 'Holy shit, this story is unbelievable! I can't believe that Superintendent Garrity is up to his ass in the cover-up and the porno operation. When this news breaks, shit is going to hit the fan.' Then he announces with great renewed interest that he is going to check out my investigator's report and visit Susanville to verify the death of Arnold. I told him it was about time he took this case seriously, turned around and left," continued Massey. "A week later I picked up the morning newspaper. The headlines read that the superintendent was indicted for aiding and abetting a fugitive of justice. A week later the whole school board resigned. I guess they were too humiliated by their inaction to the pleas of the Langleys."

"Great story, after the way the board treated you and the Langleys at the meeting. A fitting obituary," said Kane.

When they finished lunch, Massey left for Palo Alto as he had a ton of work to catch up on. As he parted, he told Kane that he would arrange the deposition of Garrity sometime in the next two weeks.

# CHAPTER 15

Massey had his secretary arrange for the deposition of Garrity, but because of the criminal indictment against the superintendent, Massey foresaw Garrity's criminal attorney telling his client to exercise his right to refuse to testify under the Fifth Amendment of the Constitution rather than answer most questions. Rather than wasting time filing motions to compel the witness to answer legitimate questions, Massey got the lawyers to agree to have retired Judge William Amelia attend the deposition so he could make immediate rulings.

The judge was sitting at Massey's conference table with a cup of coffee when Massey walked in two weeks later to start the deposition. "Good Morning, Your Honor. I haven't seen you for several months. I trust that your golf game is as good as it's always been. I'm still smarting over the five bucks you fleeced from me the last time we played."

The judge smiled. "I hope your law practice is better than your putting, Mr. Massey. I'm ready for a rematch anytime."

Promptly at 10 a.m. Garrity's two lawyers walked into the conference, followed by Garrity who limped into the room, his head down and eyes on the floor. As he sat down in the witness chair, Massey glanced at him. It was five months since Massey had seen the arrogant superintendent at the school board meeting loudly chastise him for his accusations against Arnold, and only a month since Garrity's first deposition. Now when Massey looked up at Garrity and studied his face, he was astonished. He looked like death warmed over, hollow and sunken eyes with large bags underneath, a contorted face with wrinkled skin. Massey thought he looked ten years older than when he last saw him.

Massey refocused on the task at hand, the deposition of Roland Garrity. The court reporter swore Garrity in. "Mr. Garrity, this is a continuation of your previous deposition. I won't go over questions already asked, but wish to go into new areas of discovery. My first question is, Were you ever in business with Mr. Arnold?"

Garrity became white as a sheet. "Objection," shouted Archie Finnegan.

"What's the basis for the objection, counsel?" said Judge Amelia.

"What is the relevancy of this question regarding the civil suit?" demanded Garrity's lawyer.

"Counsel for the plaintiff, what's your reply?" asked the judge.

Massey responded, "Your Honor, the civil case is for damages to my clients and their son for failure of the school district to take proper action to remove and/or investigate a teacher, Mr. Stanley Arnold, when they had knowledge that the teacher was sexually molesting the child. I want to bring out evidence that Mr. Garrity and Mr. Arnold had a business relationship, and that because of this association, Superintendent Garrity had a bias in favor of his business partner. It was for this reason that the school district did nothing about this matter until the lawsuit was filed."

"I think that's a proper question," ruled the judge.

"My client is going to take the Fifth, then, Your Honor," retorted the lawyer.

"On what basis?" inquired the judge.

"My client has been criminally charged with obstructing justice and harboring a felon. This evidence will bear on those issues."

"May I respond, Your Honor?" Massey said. The judge nodded. "Being in business with Mr. Arnold is no crime. The question addresses the motive of the witness if in fact they were business partners."

The judge was quick to reply to Garrity's lawyer, "Your client, counselor, has not been charged with any crime in connection with his business activities. Instruct your client to answer the question."

Garrity's lawyer had no comment and told him to answer the question.

"Once again, were you ever in business with Mr. Arnold?"

"No," was Garrity's nervous reply.

"Let me show you the business license for the Adam and Eve Porno Shop, which bears a residential address in San Jose and has the names and signatures of John Smythe and Karl Paulsen listed as co-owners of the business." Massey looked at Garrity, who was visibly shaken. He went on, "Now, do you recognize the residential address listed on that license, namely, two twenty-one Peabody, San Jose, California?"

There was a long pause. Garrity was now red as a beet and twitching. In a voice barely audible, he said "Yes."

"And whose address is that?"

"It's mine."

"Now, Mr. Garrity, the names of the owners on that business license are fictitious, aren't they?

"Yes," he replied, his head bowed.

"You and Mr. Arnold were the co-owners of the porn shop, weren't you, Mr. Garrity?"

"Yes."

"And that's your handwriting of those two fictitious names, isn't it?"

"Yes."

With that answer, a fuming Judge Amelia sternly said in a commanding voice, "Mr. Garrity, you are under oath to tell the truth in this deposition, and if I hear any more bald-faced lies from you, I'll see to it that you are charged with perjury, and that you spend time in jail. You understand?" Garrity raised his head and nodded.

Garrity now began to answer the questions. Massey found out that he and Arnold purchased the business five years ago, that they were making a small profit, and that Garrity was responsible for running the business while Arnold kept the financial records.

Massey told Garrity that his investigator noticed that they had more child pornographic videos than most stores, but Garrity said he didn't think so. Massey then asked him who owned the company named Youth Fantasies Productions, Inc. Garrity said he didn't know.

"Mr. Garrity, let me turn to another subject. Subsequent to Mr. Arnold's feigned suicide, my investigator discovered that Mr. Arnold was residing in Susanville, California, and teaching in the local elementary school. My first question is, Did you ever talk to Mr. Arnold while he lived in Susanville?"

"Objection," shouted Garrity's lawyer, Finnegan. "My client is charged with the crimes of obstruction of justice and harboring a fugitive, and this questions Mr. Garrity's knowledge of the whereabouts of the fugitive, which is one of the key elements in Mr. Garrity's criminal case."

Judge Amelia answered, "I agree, counsel, the question bears on the criminal charges now pending against Mr. Garrity. He does not have to answer that question nor any other question related to his role in Mr. Arnold's disappearance, and that includes his knowledge of the whereabouts of Mr. Arnold."

Since this line of questioning was now blocked, Massey quickly brought the deposition to an end.

Massey was disappointed, but knew he could get proof of Garrity's knowledge of Arnold's whereabouts by subpoenaing Garrity's telephone bills. They would show the calls to Arnold in Susanville. Furthermore, he could prove Garrity's involvement with the scheme to feign suicide and relocate Arnold to another area by subpoenaing the owner of the Starving College Student Movers. Now with the confirmation that Garrity and Arnold owned the porn shop, Massey could put before the jury the role these two men took in this sordid affair.

After the deposition, Massey called Susan to see if she wanted him to pick up anything at the grocery store for dinner. "Let's just have leftovers. I'm not really hungry," she responded half-heartedly. Massey thought it was unusual for Susan not to be her old chipper self. He wondered why.

# CHAPTER 16

For the past several months, Massey had found it necessary to be out of town on weekends while he flew up to help Kane with Leola's case. On weekdays he had been going to work early in the morning and arriving home after eight. There had been little time left for Susan and Massey to spend together.

One Friday evening, the day before he was to fly up to Susanville, Susan said to him with exasperation in her voice, "Massey, we need to take some time off work and be alone."

"I agree. It's been a grind. Let's go to the Ventana Inn down on the Big Sur coastline. It's a great hideaway and a beautiful resort. We can spend the weekend, soaking up the peace and serenity. They have small bungalows nestled amid redwood, oak and bay trees. It's so quiet, all you hear is an occasional cawing of a crow."

"Sounds perfect." Susan took his hand. "I'm sorry to be so impatient. My nerves are frazzled with Leola's trial looming on the horizon."

"It's settled. Next weekend, we'll head for Big Sur." He rose and held Susan for a long moment, caressing her until he was interrupted by the shrill ring of the telephone. "Sorry, I've been expecting a call from my researcher. He's stayed late looking for a couple of cases that might help us out before I take off for Susanville early tomorrow."

Skip couldn't help but notice Susan's look of disappointment.

▼

The following Friday, Susan and Massey climbed into his new Porsche and zoomed down Highway 101 to Salinas, then to the beautiful but twisty Highway 1. As they traveled down the coast, Massey exclaimed, "Smell that ocean air. It's exhilarating."

"The ocean views are breathtaking," added Susan.

Massey pointed out, "Look out there, where the surf is crashing over those large rock outcroppings. They say that this coastline is more beautiful than the Amalfi coast in Italy."

After a while Susan became unusually quiet.

"Anything bothering you, Susan?"

Susan shook her head, but said nothing.

It was 6 p.m. when they checked in at the main desk of the Ventana Inn. They sipped wine in front of a roaring blaze in the massive stone fireplace in the main lobby. After finishing, they walked up the trail to their unit, perched on a knoll with panoramic views of the majestic Pacific Ocean.

Fireplace wood had been stacked at the front door, so Massey grabbed a couple of logs. Susan held the front door open for him. When Massey saw the beautiful views of the ocean through the floor-to-ceiling windows, he exclaimed, "Now that's a showstopper! I feel like we're floating in the sky. Heaven can't get much better."

Susan didn't respond as Massey placed the logs and kindling in the fireplace. "The first order of business is to build a fire." After lighting the fire, he opened the sliding glass doors. "Smell that air. You can really smell the bay and oak trees. God, I love this place, it's almost as beautiful as you."

Susan was in the bedroom unpacking her clothes and didn't respond. She returned in a white bathrobe which had been hanging in the bathroom closet. Massey went over to the bar and fixed a martini for each of them and then turned on background music. "That ought to relax us."

"Well, stranger, what have you been up to these

128

days?" said Susan rather hesitantly as they sat down with their drinks in front of the fire.

"Your name is Susan, isn't it?" Massey retorted with a laugh.

"I was wondering if you remembered."

"Am I beginning to get some bad vibes?"

Susan sighed, "I'm wondering what it would be like to leave the rat race in the Bay Area and move down to a place of such beauty and serenity. Where we could have some time alone."

"Try me," Massey replied.

"You couldn't sit still for a minute. The peace and calm would drive you crazy. I am beginning to think you are a workaholic."

They sat and listened to the music for a few moments, then Massey rose. "I'll open this great bottle of 1984 Jordan cabernet sauvignon and let it breathe. What do you have in that picnic basket you brought?"

"I fixed a dinner of braised quail in a red wine sauce, marinated green beans with feta cheese, and pasta with chanterelle mushrooms," she said, rising and going to the kitchen to unpack the contents of the basket.

"That sounds awesome. If you lose your job, open a restaurant. You'd be a smashing success. Where did you learn to cook so well?"

Susan replied, "It's in my blood. My mother's of Italian descent and my father is French. They're both great chefs and started teaching me when I was very young."

Soon Susan had unwrapped the food and arranged things on serving plates. She brought the plates and the utensils to a table that Massey had moved in front of the fireplace. Massey in the meantime had gone to the bedroom and changed into the remaining bathrobe. Upon returning to the living room, he dimmed the lights and the shadows of the flames began dancing on the walls.

He gazed at Susan, sitting at the table with the glow of the flames behind her. "Pretty romantic, eh?"

She didn't respond. They ate dinner with Massey doing most of the talking while Susan listened. As they were about to finish dinner, Massey said, "Honey, the weekends in Susanville are getting to be old hat. I long to be with you."

"I'm afraid I'm a contributor to your stress, getting you involved in Leola's case. I'm beginning to think I created a monster problem."

"I'd do anything for you. Did I tell you that I am madly in love with you? Will you marry me?" he pleaded.

Susan was quiet for a moment, then turned to Massey and looked at him wistfully. "Skip, I'm so sorry, but I can't under the present circumstances. I've been doing a lot of thinking recently about the direction of our lives. We seem to be getting into a familiar rut, where you go about your business and I go about mine. It's like we've become strangers in our household. I love you, Skip, but I'm scared. I don't want to fail again, and I see clouds looming on the horizon. Your law business is like the jealous mistress who just won't let go. I'm beginning to think that you and she have more in common than you and I."

"I'm dumbfounded," said Massey, rising and going to the sofa. "I'm crushed by your answer." Massey sat quietly back on the sofa. "I guess I understand where you're coming from. I know I've been spending a large amount of time on Leola's case, particularly on the weekends. But I was putting all this time and effort into her case because I love you, and I know Leola means a lot to you. I guess I let it get away from me and forgot the big picture."

"I'm sorry to ruin our party," she said, stroking his face. "I feel guilty about the state of our relationship, because I helped to create it. Try to understand me. I was madly in love with you. Right now, I'm not sure. I need to live alone for a while so I can sort out my feelings." Tears welled up in her eyes. Massey put his arms around her and held her for a long time. She wept quietly.

Massey realized Susan was serious and no words were going to ease her pain. They went to bed that evening hardly saying a word. Massey stayed awake most of the night, worrying about their future. He had never met a person like Susan before. He found that when he was with her, he could talk about his innermost feelings, something he had never done with anyone before. They could talk for hours about their lives, dreams, and aspirations. He vowed that night to change the direction of his life. He didn't want to lose this beautiful creature.

They checked out of the inn the next morning and silently rode out of paradise toward home. When they arrived at Susan's home in Los Gatos, Massey packed his clothes and belongings, and said a brief goodbye to Susan's daughter Amy. As he backed out of her driveway, he saw Susan crying as she waved to him. Massey had tears in his own eyes and a knot in the pit of his stomach.

▼

When Massey arrived at his office that Monday, he found a legal brief on his desk concerning the use of the post-traumatic stress syndrome defense in other states. After pouring himself a cup of coffee, he tried to focus on the brief, but his mind kept shifting back to Susan. He wanted to pick up the phone, call her, and beg her to take him back. He thought to himself, *Dumb idea.* Massey decided the best course of action was to allow her some space, go slow, but most importantly convince her through action that the law business would take second place in their lives.

Massey sat back in his chair and lay the brief down on the desk, deep in thought. He heard the telephone ring. It was Jerry Kane. "How are we doing, Jerry?"

"Not so good. I received our notice of trial in this morning's mail. It's set for Monday, October 21, at nine in the morning. Christ, that's less than a month. We've got a ton of preparation to do."

"I'll be up this weekend. The love of my life just gave me the boot for working too hard so I've got no engagements. I'll be up early Saturday morning. Right now, I'm reviewing a research brief on the PTSD defense. I'll bring it with me when I come up. See you

Saturday," Massey replied, then hung up.

Massey went back to the brief. The research staff had scoured the case law in all fifty states and found no cases similar to Leola's circumstances, in which the killer was not a veteran. They also researched the battered woman syndrome defense and pointed out that some states allow this defense, but this type of defense would be doubtful when applied to a nonspousal relationship. Massey knew that while each state has the right to enact its own set of laws, court decisions made in other states, contrary to California laws, are certainly not binding on California judges. However, lawyers often argue the merit of these out-of-state decisions and sometimes influence a "forward" thinking judge, or more specifically, a liberal judge who thinks he is a legislator.

After finishing the brief, Massey was curious to know where the two battered wife syndrome cases were in their progression through the California appellate system. Massey buzzed the intercom to his research department. "Dave Hult, you there?"

"Yes siree, what can I do for you?"

"Call the respective clerks of each of the appellate courts handling the battered wife cases, and find out if any one of the cases is going to be decided within the next couple of weeks. Hopefully, we can get a favorable appellate decision before Leola Langley's case comes to trial. It's now set for October 21. If any of the appellate cases come out in favor of the plaintiffs, we could argue that the judge should incorporate the same altered state-of-mind theory used in the defense of these battered wives."

Hult got back to Massey in a few hours. "Mr. Massey, one of the battered wife syndrome cases was orally argued in the first appellate district in San Francisco several weeks ago, and the court is in the process of writing the opinion. It should be published fairly soon."

"That's great news. That district court is so liberal, they'll bend over backward for the battered wife. Keep on it, Dave. I need a positive decision."

When Massey landed at the Susanville Airport early Saturday morning, he was surprised that Jerry Kane wasn't there to meet him. He called Jerry's office and home phones. Getting no answer, Massey called a cab and went to Kane's office. When Massey rapped on the office door, he heard a voice inside holler, "Come on in."

When Massey walked into Kane's office, he saw the ghost of the man he had left only a week ago. Kane's eyes were bloodshot and watery, his clothes disheveled, and he smelled as though he hadn't taken a bath in a week. He had at least an inch-long beard and could hardly hold his head up.

"Jesus Christ, what's happened?" Massey said, shocked at what he saw.

Kane mumbled in a slurred voice, "Oh, I'm jus' celebratin' my fiftieth birthday. We had a hell of a party."

"Let me drive you home and get you to bed. Tomorrow, I'll call you first thing, and we'll go down to the office and start preparing this case. We've only got three weeks left." Massey took him home, undressed him, and threw his smelly body into the shower. He then got him into bed and told him, "Get a good night's sleep, and stay the hell away from the bottle."

The next morning at six, Massey knocked on Kane's door, waking him from a sound sleep. Kane opened the door and peeked out from behind it. He looked like hell warmed over, but at least it appeared he hadn't been on the sauce. Kane didn't remember a thing about the previous day or even how he got home to bed. Massey put a pot of coffee on, and after it was ready, poured the local attorney a cup of stiff black coffee as he was getting dressed.

"So what's the problem?" Massey asked as Kane came into the kitchen.

"I just celebrated my fiftieth, that's all," he responded.

Massey put his hand on Kane's shoulder, looked him in the eyes and said, "How long has it been since you've fallen off the wagon to this extent?"

Jerry looked down as he replied, "I don't know. With this trial coming on, I've been getting nervous. You see, I haven't tried a murder case in five years. The last one I tried, I lost. It was the first time I ever lost a murder case. It's been grating on my conscience ever since."

"Hell, we all lose cases. That's nothing to go over the deep end about."

"Well, that's easy for you to say, but my poor client is on death row, and I think about him and the trial all the time. I blame myself. I made a bad decision and put him on the stand. The prosecution just killed him on cross-examination. I thought he would do well, but he froze. They had him so confused that he was saying stuff that wasn't even true. He just hung himself. The poor bastard didn't deserve the death penalty."

"What did the defendant do?" asked Massey.

Kane had his elbows on the kitchen table and his hands on his cheeks, holding up his head. Sadly he said, "He was out drinking, the party got out of hand, and he hit a guy who was making a pass at his girlfriend. He hit him so hard, he broke his neck and killed him. That's not death penalty stuff. A rookie lawyer could have gotten him off, but I didn't. Let me tell you, booze is about the only thing that helps me forget about this case. For weeks I've been lying awake at night thinking about Leola's case. I've had nightmares about losing the case and sending her to the gas chamber. Massey, I don't know if I can go through with this case."

"Look, you can't take the blame. This is the law business. You try your damnedest, and you let the chips fall where they may. I know each of us figures that when we go to trial, we can beat the other side because of our talents. And when we lose, we think that we could have won if we had only chosen a different strategy or made a different closing argument. There isn't a trial lawyer alive who doesn't believe that."

"I just can't forget that case," Kane said, shaking his head.

"I know the losses are remembered and the wins easily forgotten, but you can't blame yourself if you've prepared the case and done the best you could do," Massey responded, trying to cheer him up.

Jerry stayed sober that Sunday, and they accomplished a lot. They plotted their strategy. Massey told him that he would bring Leola up next weekend so that they could prep her for trial. They were both mindful of the dangers of calling the defendant to the stand to plead for her own defense. Massey, however, thought they needed her to testify about her son's abuse and the effect it had on her family in order to evoke as much sympathy as possible from a jury.

Kane told Massey, "I'm very much against putting her on the stand. The last time I saw her, she was *non compos mentis* and there's no telling what she'll say."

"Her husband says she's recovering nicely and is out of the hospital. Our psychiatrists probably can get the facts before the court, but the presentation would be much more dramatic if Leola could tell her own story. I'll bring her up here next weekend. Let's see how she performs."

As Massey left late Sunday afternoon, his parting shot was, "Jerry, stay off the goddamn booze. I need you, and Leola Langley really needs you."

# CHAPTER 17

Massey flew Leola up to Susanville the following Saturday so he and Kane could go over her preliminary testimony. Jerry met them at the airport. Massey noticed that Jerry looked better and was apparently on the wagon. Massey thought, *In his mind, maybe he's beginning to rationalize if something goes wrong, he can blame part of it on me, and not be the sole person at fault.*

During their flight to Susanville, Massey noticed that Leola looked rested and calm. She had restored life in her eyes rather than the zombie gaze she had after she was arrested. After conversing with her, he thought she seemed to understand his questions and gave rational answers. She had lost about twenty pounds during her stay in the hospital and physically looked much better. After seeing the change in her looks, Massey felt better about using her as a witness. He wondered, however, how much of the past her mind had suppressed.

At Kane's office, Jerry seemed rested and eager to get the trial prepared. When they sat down in the conference room, Massey told Leola, "What we're going to do is to prepare you to testify in your own defense. You can explain what happened to your boy and your family. The purpose for putting you on the stand will be to evoke sympathy from the jurors. Right now we haven't decided to definitely put you on the stand. The ultimate decision will be made after the prosecution rests its case."

Jerry added, "Leola, you have a constitutional right not to testify. I personally am very reluctant to put a defendant on the stand. But it may be the only way to avoid conviction."

Massey had prepared a general list of subjects that he thought Jerry might ask Leola, leaving him to frame the particular questions. Nothing is worse than a lawyer and his witness who memorize the script. All emotion is lost and the jurors suspect that the client's lawyers have prepared and fabricated the witness's answers. Massey had a credo: Trying a case is like producing a good play. It's got to flow with emotion in order to get the desired results.

Jerry reviewed Massey's questions for Leola, made a few additions and told her, "The cardinal rule is to listen carefully to the question, take time to think before giving the answer, and then look at the jury and give the answer."

After asking her some initial questions and giving her tips on how to improve her presentation, Jerry started asking Leola about her background. When he started into the line of questions regarding the specifics about Billy's involvement with his teacher, Leola became fidgety and reluctant about giving answers.

Kane noticed Leola's sudden change from her former calm attitude and said, "Ma'am, I know all of this is difficult for you, but unless we give the jury a rational explanation of what triggered you to kill the teacher, I'm afraid you'll be spending the rest of your life in jail."

Leola suddenly looked startled, and then a sad expression appeared on her face. Massey thought Jerry's last statement had probably hit her like a bolt of lightening and pulled her out of denial, into the world of reality. She suddenly started trembling. She was no doubt thinking about what it would be like to spend the rest of her life locked up without her family.

It was obvious that Kane's comments upset her, so Massey said, "Let's hold it a moment while I get Leola a glass of water and an aspirin to calm her down." In a few seconds Massey returned from the kitchen to the rear of Jerry's office and handed the aspirin to Leola, who promptly swallowed the pill.

After a few short minutes, Jerry asked her if she was ready to proceed. She nodded once again. Jerry then asked in a soft voice, "What impact did the teacher's sexual abuse of your son have on him?"

After the question sank in, Leola broke down and wept uncontrollably. After a few minutes, she looked up though bloodshot eyes which were pleading with Massey, "I can't go on. It's too painful. I don't have the stomach for this. I jus' can't go over all the hurt I feel for poor Billy and my family. I'm so sorry, Mr. Massey."

The lawyers decided to end the session, and Massey escorted Leola to the waiting room and then returned to Kane's office. "Jerry, I'll work with her at home. Hopefully, she'll be able to handle direct examination at trial."

"I wouldn't bet on it, my friend," said a dubious Kane.

▼

Back in Los Gatos, Massey met with Leola the following Tuesday, and the session was again a washout. When Massey got into the vital areas regarding Billy, Leola just couldn't verbalize the events. Massey still believed her testimony was crucial to her case. He tried to figure a way to get her over the hump.

That night Massey called Susan. "I need your help with Leola. I've been trying to prep her for cross-examination, and she breaks down every time I ask her questions about Billy. I really need to have her get control of her emotions so that she will be a good witness at trial. Her testimony could save her life. Since the two of you are such good friends, maybe you could spend the next session with us and give her the boost she needs to get over this hurdle."

"Well, with Leola's life on the line, I'll be more than happy to help. Where and when?"

"10 a.m. this Thursday at my office?"

"I'll be there," she responded.

▼

On Thursday in Massey's conference room, Susan sat next to Leola with her arm around her. Leola got through the testimony fairly well. There were a few episodes of tears, but Susan calmed her down and Leola would finish her answer to the question. After a couple of hours, Massey was satisfied that they had made substantial headway. "Leola, we're finished for now, but we'll have a go at the questioning several times before trial, particularly in front of Kane."

Massey and Susan walked outside to the parking lot and watched Leola's car pull away. Massey turned to her and said, "This session went much better than I expected, after our blowout with her in Susanville. I now think she can help her case substantially if she can testify. However, a key ingredient to her success is going to be your continued presence with her. I don't think she has the constitution to do it alone."

"Let me talk to my boss. I'll try to be with her during those sessions and trial. I'll get back to you shortly. Incidentally, I'm hungry. If you don't have anything planned for lunch, I'm buying. I owe you so much for helping out my friend. I feel so guilty about the whole mess. Here I get you involved, then tell you to take a hike."

They walked over to Il Fornaio on Cowper Street in downtown Palo Alto, just a block from the office. The upscale restaurant served fabulous Italian food. They sat outside in the courtyard on the crisp fall day. Massey and Susan both ordered the chicken salad with bacon and Parmesan cheese. "Great minds think alike," Massey said to Susan after they ordered. Massey, however, kept his distance and asked questions about Amy, Susan's job and her parents.

After lunch, as they walked back to the office, Susan took Massey's hand and looked at him. "Massey, that was a nice lunch. I enjoyed it."

"So did I. I'll call you tomorrow and give you a couple of dates when we'd like you to accompany Leola for another prep session. Also, see if you can clear your calendar for the trial, which is set for October 21. You wouldn't have to be there the whole time, just when she testifies."

As they parted company, Massey gave her a little peck on the cheek and said, "That's for old times."

Massey waved goodbye to Susan as she drove out of the parking lot. He thought he noticed tears in her eyes.

▼

Massey called her three days later. "Are you a gambler?" he asked.

"What do you have up your sleeve, Mr. Massey?"

"Well, you got burned by your former husband and still carry scars, and I'm now gun-shy as hell. Do you have any time next weekend to spend a couple of days with me in Cabo San Lucas? One of my friends has a cabana on the beach. We could just enjoy the sights and each other's company."

Susan replied, "A wise friend of mine once told me, 'Nothing ventured, nothing gained.' Besides, I like your company."

On Friday afternoon, Susan and Massey boarded Mexicana Airlines and flew three hours to Cabo. The cabana turned out to be a lovely condo on the beach about one mile north of town.

That evening Massey and Susan dined at a romantic restaurant known as Señor Pepe's on the side of the mountain above the town. From their outside table, they looked down at the town's sparkling lights. Close by on the deck of the restaurant was a handsome Mexican with a guitar, strolling from table to table singing beautiful Mexican ballads. They both ordered margaritas before dinner. Massey could tell Susan was enjoying the evening. He looked into her sparkling eyes and without thinking said, "God, I miss you, you beautiful creature."

Susan reached across the table and held his hands. "I can't tell you how much I've missed you. I think about what life would be like with you full time."

"Let me tell you about the lessons I learned at the Circle." She looked at him with raised eyebrows. "The Circle was a patch of grass that divided a street where I grew up in Palo Alto," he explained. "All the neighborhood kids gathered there to play tackle football. Every time I got tackled by the older kids, I knew I had to get up and try harder. I learned that if a guy just keeps trying and never gives up, he can succeed at just about anything he puts his mind to. At Ventana, you gave me a message that I deserved. From now on, you are my first priority and always will be. I promise, I won't forget."

Susan had tears in her eyes. "Skip, when we were at Ventana, it was the hardest moment of my life. You proposed to me, and I turned you down. I felt awful about that, but I thought the issue was so big that it would be a matter of survival of the relationship. I'm so sorry I hurt you. These last several weeks have been the worst of my life. I missed you so much, I could hardly keep myself from calling you and begging you to come back."

After dinner, Susan stood in her nightgown on the veranda outside of their bedroom. Moonbeams danced on the ocean waters. Latin mood music played softly from the stereo. As Massey came out of the bathroom in his shorts, he noticed the silhouette of her body beneath the thin gown. He came up behind her, put his hands around her waist and gave her a kiss on the nape of her neck.

"God, I've missed the wonderful smell of your body and the feel of your smooth skin." His hands reached around her waist and he caressed her firm breasts.

"I didn't know if we would ever have a moment like this again. I was so worried I'd lost you," she sighed as she turned and put her arms around his waist, pulling him close.

They embraced each other, rocking back and forth for several minutes to the rhythm of the music. He could hear Susan's heavy breathing as they swayed in unison in the stillness of night, the dark shadows broken only by the distant glow of the stars and moon. He lifted her into his arms and gently laid her on the bed. They lay listening to the sounds of the lapping waves on the shoreline.

Massey whispered, "Will you marry me?"

"Yes, I'll never let you get away again."

That night they slept in each other's arms, making love and listening to the waves crashing outside their cabana.

# CHAPTER 18

Judge Brandon's clerk called Jerry Kane during the first part of October, telling him the judge had set a pretrial and settlement conference for October 14, a week before the trial, at 9 a.m.

When Massey and Kane arrived at the courthouse, the bailiff escorted them to Judge Brandon's chambers. As they entered, Massey looked at the judge sitting behind his desk. His appearance was much different from the description Jerry had given of Judge Brandon. This man was very large, in his mid-fifties, with Native American features, black eyes, dark skin, and a full head of long, gray hair, making him look very distinguished.

The judge rose and said, "Good morning gentlemen. I'm Judge Sam Sheldon, on assignment from Sacramento." Massey and Kane introduced themselves and the judge invited them to sit down, saying, "I'll be sitting in on this murder trial in place of Judge Brandon. The Chief Justice of the Supreme Court finally gave him some relief because of his busy calendar."

Massey looked over at Jerry's face and immediately knew that he was unhappy about the change of judges. With the loss of Judge Brandon, they would be dealing with an unknown deck of cards.

"I'm expecting the district attorney shortly," said the judge while sipping a cup of coffee. "You gentlemen care for any coffee?"

"Thank you, Judge, but I think we're both coffeed out. I've been loading up with caffeine since six-thirty this morning, and Mr. Massey had several cups of coffee on the plane and turned me down for another cup when he arrived," said Kane in response.

A few minutes later, the judge's clerk ushered Steve Aaron, the district attorney, and one of his assistants into the judge's chambers. Massey couldn't help but notice that Steve Aaron walked in with a cocky flamboyance about him. He seemed to be relishing the prospect of trying this case, probably because of all the publicity. He was about five foot seven inches, 150 pounds, and in his early forties. He had a ruddy complexion and beady eyes that could pierce one's soul. *I'll bet he can be merciless,* Massey thought to himself.

Kane leaned sideways and whispered to Massey, "He's a good street fighter in the courtroom. A solid win here would give him the inside track on Judge Brandon's job when the judge retires."

"Gentlemen, we have one week before the trial starts, and I want to know the names of any witnesses who will be testifying."

Kane spoke first. "Your Honor, we will be calling two physicians, Dr. Stanley Tishman and Dr. Scott Smith. They will testify on the defendant's state of mind and her psychological makeup. We also plan to call Mr. Mike O'Malley and Susan Winters who both know the defendant well, as character witnesses. The defendant, Leola Langley, will also testify in her defense. We are still undergoing an investigation and reserve the right to call newly discovered witnesses that have a bearing on the trial."

Massey noted that Kane didn't use the word investigator when referring to O'Malley and also didn't mention the name of Garrity, the superintendent of schools. *Smart. He doesn't want to tip off the prosecution,* Massey thought.

The district attorney rattled off a series of police officers, the county coroner, and several witnesses who were present in the parking lot when Arnold was killed. He reserved the right to call a medical expert, Dr. Wade Clevenger.

The judge remarked, "In fairness to the prosecution, I will require the defense to set forth in writing the

143

names of any additional witnesses as soon as they are discovered."

Massey got a sense that while the judge was cordial, he was mountain tough. Based on his comments so far, he appeared to have plenty of mileage as a judge. Massey told himself, *This judge knows how to take charge of a case and will be no pushover when it comes to rulings.*

Judge Sheldon then looked directly at the attorneys and said, "Gentlemen, have you had any discussions about plea bargaining this case? Since you estimated to the clerk that the trial is going to take three to four weeks, I'll tell you quite frankly that I don't relish being away from my family for that period of time. Let's see if we can make some headway on a plea bargain."

Steve Aaron, the district attorney, opened in a confident tone and said, "With the evidence that the prosecution has, about all we'll be willing to do is to allow the defendant to plead guilty to murder in the first degree without the possibility of parole, and dismiss the special circumstances aspect of the case which would eliminate the possibility of the death sentence. The evidence is overwhelming that the murder was premeditated."

Massey was getting a little irritated at the arrogant attitude of the district attorney. "Your Honor, that proposal is like throwing a glass of water on a raging fire. How could any lawyer for a defendant accept that token offer?"

"Well, counselor, you're whistling Dixie if you think you're going to get her off with any lesser charge," said a cocky Steve Aaron.

That comment sparked Massey's ire. "I've seen a lot of lawyers in my time brag about the merits of their case, and then go home with their tail between their legs. You might be in for a big fall, Mr. Aaron." Then Massey couldn't resist the temptation to add, "It might even ruin your chances to succeed Judge Brandon."

Before the judge could stop the heated Aaron, the lawyer retorted, "Look, big-city lawyer, you're in for the surprise of your life."

The judge was now getting irritated. "Gentlemen,

gentlemen, this is no way to start a trial. Let's quit the personal comments and get on with the business at hand. Remember, we have a woman's life at stake, not a personal battle between a couple of egos."

"Sorry, Your Honor," Massey responded. Aaron didn't say a word as his eyes locked on Massey with venom.

"Suppose I just see each side individually here for a few moments, on the condition that I can speak on a confidential basis so we can talk freely," said the judge. "Before I act in this capacity, I want each side to waive their rights to challenge me when we begin the trial, so that I will still be able to act as the trial judge in this matter."

Both the prosecution and defense lawyers agreed to waive their rights of challenge, and the judge called the court reporter into his chambers to put the stipulation on the record.

Judge Sheldon wanted to talk with the prosecution first, so Kane and Massey left the room. After twenty minutes, the district attorney exited the judge's chambers, and the bailiff beckoned the two defense lawyers. The judge asked them to sit down, pulled out a cigar box from his desk drawer and said, "Would either of you gentlemen like to have a cigar with me? There are only a few times when I get enough peace and quiet to sit down and smoke one of these vile things." They both declined.

The judge pulled a big stogie out of the cigar box, lit it, and then leaned back in his chair. He took a big puff, and finally said with a quizzical look on his face, "Why don't you fellows tell me how you think you're going to get away with a charge less than murder one?"

Jerry took the lead and gave the judge the background of the killing. "In conclusion, Your Honor, the defendant was totally out of her mind when she killed the victim. She had no intent to kill. We have strong medical evidence to support this position."

"I'll be frank with both of you," said the judge. "If you could use the old defense of irresistible impulse, I think you could get her off like Dan White when he killed Harvey Milk, that supervisor from San Francisco.

That jury disliked gays and went out of its way to let White go free when he was clearly guilty of murder. But now that the legislature has eliminated the defense of irresistible impulse, I think your only hope is the insanity defense. You fellows also know how difficult it will be to prove insanity? It takes a raving nut to convince a jury that a killer ought to get off on grounds of insanity. I think you boys have a tough row to hoe. You should seriously consider the district attorney's offer."

"With all due respect, Your Honor," Massey began. "I think we have a good solid argument to use the post-traumatic stress syndrome defense. This woman, when she killed the teacher, was in the exact state of mind as a Vietnam veteran when he kills an innocent person, thinking he is still in the middle of the war. I think the defense will apply."

"I think that's a real stretch, counselor, and unless I have some case support, I would not be inclined to allow such a defense. To my knowledge, case law has confined this defense to the military. So much for your theory, counsel."

On the way out of the judge's chambers, Jerry whispered to Massey, "I think we ought to seriously consider the district attorney's offer and save Leola's life."

Massey had flown up to Susanville early this morning, bringing Leola with him. He left her sitting in the courtroom while they met with the judge. Kane and Massey now took her to a private conference room in the courthouse and Jerry stated, "Leola, the district attorney is willing to save your life and allow you to plead to murder one with no possibility of parole. I think you should accept his offer."

Leola looked at Massey and said, "I don't want to spend the rest of my life in jail. If I can't see my boys grow up and babysit my grandchildren, there really is no sense living any more. I would rather die than rot in jail." Massey couldn't really disagree with her logic.

The two lawyers returned to the judge's chambers and told him of their client's reaction. The judge then called in the district attorney and his assistant, and while

146

all four of them were present, he told the district attorney, "This case isn't as open-and-shut as you might think, Mr. Aaron. I think you should consider murder one with the possibility of parole. The defense is going to come up with some interesting arguments."

Aaron replied, "There is no way I could allow a cold-blooded murderer to have a shot at parole. I have a duty to protect the public."

Massey decided to take Aaron on again. "Wait a minute, this defendant is by no stretch of the imagination a cold-blooded murderer. By the time the defense rests its case, she's going to have a hell of a lot more sympathy from the jury than the victim."

"Who the hell do you think you are, big-city lawyer? People up here don't turn the other cheek when there's a killing. They'll see that justice is done. Mr. Massey, you're going to learn your lesson the hard way, if I have anything to say about it."

The judge interrupted, "Enough of this personal harping. I want you both to think about getting together for a plea bargain over the weekend so that we can dispose of this case."

"There's no way I'm reducing my offer, Your Honor," said Aaron.

"Mr. Aaron, I find your attitude a little offensive. I hope you're as good an attorney as you seem to think you are," remarked the judge with a tone of sarcasm in his voice.

Massey thought, *Chalk one up for the defense; the district attorney is starting to irritate the judge. If he continues with his arrogant attitude, the judge could start pulling for the underdog subconsciously.*

"Well, gentlemen, there isn't any sense in prolonging the agony. I'll see all of you in court, ready for trial, next Monday morning at nine. I'll hear any pretrial motions before the jury arrives at ten."

While the lawyers were rising to leave his chambers, the judge said to Kane and Massey, "Which one of you lawyers is going to try this case?"

"Both Mr. Massey and I are going to try the case and alternate witnesses."

"Not in my court, gentlemen. I want the same attorney to choose the jury, make the opening statement, examine the witnesses, make objections, and make the closing argument. I've had too many bad experiences where there have been multiple attorneys trying the same case, and it usually takes twice as long. Each lawyer tries to outdo the other co-counsel so he can take credit for the win. Egos too often create chaos."

As they walked out of the judge's chambers, Massey could see Jerry Kane's shoulders slump. Massey thought, *He knows he has to be the one trying the case since he is the local boy. The jury will relate to him better than me, a flatlander. Undoubtedly he is troubled by the judge's negative comments about our defenses, and feels the weight of Leola's plight is now squarely on his shoulders.*

Jerry and Massey agreed to meet on Saturday morning to go over jury instructions that Massey's staff had prepared. They would have to give them to the judge on Monday so that he could review them during the course of the trial and decide which ones he would give. Massey also prepared a subpoena which would be served on Garrity when they needed him to appear as a witness. They would notify the judge about the witness sometime in the middle of the trial. By then the cat would be out of the bag about the defense theory. They also planned to go over testimony with Leola. Thankfully, Susan's boss had given her a leave of absence so she could attend the trial and give Leola the support she needed.

Massey turned to Jerry. "Since we had planned on my doing the direct examination of our medical experts, Dr. Smith and Dr. Tishman, you'll have to go over the testimony with them an evening or two before they take the stand." Jerry didn't respond.

From Kane's office, Massey called Big Mike and asked him to do some investigation on the judge's background. "Mike, can you find out what kind of judge he is from some of the lawyers up in Sacramento?"

148

▼

Late Sunday afternoon, Massey invited Kane to have dinner. He was a little worried about Kane's state of mind now that he had to try the case alone. He could feel the pressure mounting in Kane because the outcome was life or death with no in-between. After they had cocktails and had ordered dinner, Massey said to Jerry, "How are you feeling about this case?"

"I'm okay."

"Look, Jerry, I think we have a real chance at getting at least murder two. What jury in the world is going to send this mother to the gas chamber or lock her up for life when the defendant is such a depraved individual? And wait until they hear that Arnold and the superintendent of the school district were involved with a porn shop that specializes in kiddie porn. I think the rednecks up here will go out of their way to help Leola. It is my opinion that the district attorney is about to make a terrible mistake in going only for murder one, not leaving the jury any room to find Leola guilty of murder two or manslaughter."

"Well, I hope you're right. I don't need another death case hanging over my head. It would kill me off."

▼

Monday, October 21, the commencement date of the trial, came quickly. Sam, Leola, Susan, and Massey checked in at the St. Francis Hotel on Sunday evening. They agreed to meet Jerry at 8 a.m. for breakfast at the hotel, then walk over to the courthouse.

Massey and Susan met Sam and Leola for breakfast at the appointed hour of eight. Kane hadn't shown by 8:30 a.m., so Massey called his home and office. There was no answer at either place except for the answering machine. Massey figured he was on his way. Kane still hadn't arrived by 8:45. Massey decided they had better hightail it to the courthouse, figuring that Jerry was running late and had probably gone straight there.

149

When they arrived at the courthouse steps, a handful of pushy newspaper and TV reporters began asking Massey questions about the case and taking pictures of Leola. Massey shouted, "No comment," pushing through the crowd. When Massey walked into the courtroom, he asked the bailiff, "Have you seen Jerry Kane?" The bailiff shook his head.

Massey was growing impatient with Kane for being late. When 9 a.m. rolled around, Kane still hadn't arrived. Massey said to the bailiff, "Could you tell the judge that Kane hasn't arrived, but is expected momentarily? I'll call Kane to make sure he's on the way." Massey tried both his home and office and again got only his answering machines.

The judge invited the district attorney, his two associates, and Massey into his chambers. "Judge, I apologize for the absence of Mr. Kane. I called him and got his answering machine, so he must be on his way here," said a worried Massey.

They all waited until 9:30 a.m., but still no Jerry Kane. Massey had a sinking feeling in his stomach, hoping against hope that Jerry had a good reason for being late. He went outside and made another call with the same results. Massey went over to Susan to request, "Would you go to Kane's office and see if you can locate him? The judge is getting madder than hell."

It was 10:10 a.m. when the bailiff told Massey that there was a call on this line. "Massey," Susan said in an anxious voice, "I just walked into Jerry's office and found him. He's been drinking all night and is totally incoherent. You'd better get here quick."

Massey went back into the judge's chambers and reported, "Mr. Kane has been located. May I have permission to go to his office and find out what his problem is?"

The judge was fuming. "Kane had better have one hell of an alibi or he's going to get some stiff sanctions," growled the judge.

As Massey walked into Kane's office he smelled a foul odor. He saw Susan with a wet towel, cleaning up vomit on the floor next to his desk. Massey looked at

Kane, sitting with his head laying flat on the desk. "Jerry, what the hell has happened?" He looked like he'd been on a three-week drunk with his hollow red eyes and vomit all over his white shirt. He was totally out of it.

Finally Kane raised his head, looked through blood-shot eyes at Massey and muttered, "I can't take it. I'm going to kill myself for being a coward. I'm sorry. I'm sorry. I'm sorry." He started babbling incoherently.

"Susan, make the poor bastard some strong coffee while I throw him into the shower. Let's see if we can sober him up."

Shortly, Massey returned to the judge's chambers and told him, "Mr. Kane has cracked under the pressure of this trial. He has never forgotten the last murder case that he lost. After that case, I understand that he started drinking heavily, but did lick the habit. Apparently, he wasn't strong enough to withstand the recent pressure."

Unexpectedly, the judge cooled down, reached for his desk drawer, pulled out a cigar and lit it. After he blew a big puff of smoke in the air, he looked at Massey and the other lawyers present and commented, "You know, people never realize the responsibility that lawyers and judges have. We are charged with the awesome power to make decisions, financially transferring millions of dollars of companies' and people's assets, incarcerating men, women, and children, and then the responsibility of taking the lives of people."

The judge took another puff on his cigar and continued, "Many lawyers take their losses as personal failures and, over a lengthy period of time, either succumb to the bottle, have mental breakdowns, or simply get out of the business altogether. I sympathize with your co-counsel, although I am going to fine him big time."

Massey stood up. "Your Honor, I respectfully request a continuance in light of Mr. Kane's condition. I'll either have to get him on the wagon or find a replacement. I thoroughly apologize to the court and the district attorney for the inconvenience."

The judge replied, "I know you'd like a continuance, but that's not going to do Kane any good. He's just lost his stomach for trying murder cases. Fortunately,

Mr. Massey, you're up to speed on this case, so we'll just go ahead with the trial without Mr. Kane."

Massey was dumbfounded and replied strongly, "Judge, I haven't tried a criminal case in fifteen years. My last criminal case was a kidnapping case. I have never tried a capital case before. I have to beg Your Honor for a continuance, so I can bring an experienced criminal attorney into this case."

The judge responded, "How long have you been an attorney, Mr. Massey? And how many civil and criminal cases have you tried before a jury?"

"Well, I've been practicing law for twenty-five years and I've probably had between fifty to seventy-five jury trials," he replied.

"Son," the judge smiled, "you probably have more trial experience than the district attorney and ninety percent of the lawyers in the state of California. You're going to try this case. Motion for a continuance denied. I'll let you put this motion on the record. Bailiff, bring in the reporter."

While the bailiff was out of the room looking for the court reporter, the judge turned to Massey and said, "If I refuse to allow a defense attorney to try a capital case because he's had no prior murder cases, in a few years there wouldn't be any lawyers left to handle capital cases. Handling a capital case is nothing more than the trials that you've been handling for years; there's just more at stake."

*Yeah, like a woman's life,* Massey said to himself. *No big deal, Judge. What's a life here and there. What have I gotten myself into. I'm a typical do-gooder who can't say no, and winds up getting in over his head. My first criminal case in fifteen years and a death case to boot. Nice going, Massey!*

The bailiff returned with the court reporter in tow. She set up the stenographic machine, loaded it with paper, and nodded to the judge that she was ready. The judge stated, "Mr. Massey has just made a motion in chambers for a continuance of the trial because his co-counsel, Mr. Jerry Kane, has been taken ill and will need a lengthy time to recover. I have interviewed Mr. Massey, and while he has not tried a capital case, his experience with the trial practice is extensive and his knowledge of this case is intimate. I will grant him a one-day continuance, deny him any further continuance, and will expect him to be ready for trial tomorrow morning at nine sharp. That's all gentlemen. Have a good day."

Steve Aaron looked at Massey with a big smile on his face that said, I'll eat your lunch, Massey.

▼

Massey walked dejectedly out of the chambers and into the courtroom where Leola sat. "Leola, I've got some bad news. Kane's sick and unable to try the case. The judge has ordered me to defend you. I want you to know that I've never tried a murder case before, and I think you should be represented by someone with experience in this field. I can get you a continuance if you fire me, because the judge will have no choice."

Leola stood up and put her arms around Massey. She smiled and said, "Mr. Massey, Susan has tol' me what a wonderful lawyer you are. I have more confidence in you than anybody. You're the only person I want to defend me."

Susan was standing behind Leola. She said, "Good decision, Leola. I have a good feeling about this case." Susan turned to Massey and handed him a report she had just received from Mike O'Malley, the investigator.

Massey looked at the report. It was about Judge Sheldon. The judge was another conservative Reagan appointee. He was known throughout Sacramento County as one tough law-and-order judge and a strict constructionist when it came to interpreting the law. After putting the report down, Massey looked dejectedly at Susan. "Whew, not only am I going to be trying my first capital case, but it will be in front of a very inflexible judge. I was counting on a liberal judge to help us break new ground in interpreting some of the statutes and case law. My spirits are beginning to sag."

Susan put her arm around him to assure him, "You'll do just fine."

Sam and Leola had gone back to the hotel. Massey and Susan went over to Kane's home to see how he was doing. When they arrived, he was passed out. Massey shook him, but he mumbled incoherently.

"We've lost him, Susan. There's no way he'll recuperate by tomorrow, much less face the wrath of Judge Sheldon for screwing up. I think the judge was right. I think Kane has lost his stomach for battle."

"I wish there was a way to help," sighed Susan.

Massey turned to Susan. "Well, you can. Now that I've temporarily lost my legal cohort, could you help me rehearse the jury questions and the opening statement?"

"I'm a novice, but I'll do the best I can."

"You'll be great because you're very sensitive to people. You'll know what appeals to a juror. Put yourself in the shoes of a juror and let me know how I can improve the presentation."

Susan and Massey spent the rest of the day preparing. Massey thought Susan had many great comments about how to approach certain key points from a layman's point of view. He was pleased at his new assistant, and gave her a hug and a pat on the fanny. "Watch your step, counselor," Susan said with a smile on her face.

When they got back to the hotel to get ready for dinner, there was a message at the front desk for Massey to call his office. He got his secretary, Helen, just as she was about to leave for home. "Massey," she said, "I received a call from Sergeant Cardoza, who left a message that Mr. Garrity, the superintendent, was found dead in his home today."

Massey was shocked and sat in silence, thinking about the bad luck he was having. "First, Kane collapses on me. I wind up being ordered to try my first murder case in front of a conservative judge, and now Garrity's dead, depriving us of a very important witness. What the hell's going on?"

Massey immediately placed a call to San Jose, hoping to catch Sergeant Cardoza. He had stayed late and answered the phone. "Skip Massey here. I just heard that Garrity is dead. What happened?"

"Garrity's housekeeper called the department and

said that when she went to work this morning, she found Garrity in his bed. At first she thought he was asleep. She came back an hour later and tried to wake him. She noticed blood on the sheets, and then a bullet hole in his head. There was a handgun next to him. We had the coroner out, and he thinks the death is a murder. There were no powder marks on his head, and it appeared that he was shot at some distance. I understand from his attorney that you took his deposition a short time ago. What do you know about this?"

Massey thought for a second and told Cardoza, "After I took his deposition the second time, I found out about his connection with Arnold and a San Francisco porn business, so I subpoenaed Garrity to testify in Leola Langley's murder trial. Maybe there's somebody out there who didn't want us to dig into their porn business?"

That night at dinner, Massey said to Susan, "Losing a key witness like Garrity is a big blow. I needed to get in firsthand evidence of the slimy kiddie porn business that these pedophiles were engaged in. This type of testimony would get the jury emotionally charged against Arnold. Big Mike can testify what he found out about the two, but that testimony won't have the impact of having a despicable person like Garrity on the stand testifying under cross-examination."

Susan inquired, "Skip, I've always wondered where Arnold and Garrity got the money to buy that porn shop. Teachers' salaries are at the bottom rung of the ladder. I don't see how they could have saved whatever it cost to buy that business. Maybe they had a financial backer. You know, there may be another witness out there to replace Garrity."

"Brilliant, my dear Watson. You might be on the right track. I'll call Big Mike. If he can find a financial backer, I'll subpoena him to come up here and testify. I really want to get the porn shop involvement in front of this jury."

Massey called O'Malley and asked him to drop everything and track down the possible undisclosed partner.

# CHAPTER 19

The bailiff opened the rear door of the courtroom dressed in his tan uniform and hat. "Hear ye, hear ye. Please rise. Department 1 of the Superior Court of Lassen County in and for the State of California is now in session. Judge Sam Sheldon, presiding."

Promptly at 9 a.m. on October 21, the trial of *People v. Leola Langley* began in earnest. The courtroom was packed with potential jurors, the press, and curious citizens. Susan and Sam Langley were in the front row. Leola, an ashen Jerry Kane, who had been fined $1,000 by the judge, and Massey were seated at the defense table to the right of the district attorney and his two assistants. Everyone rose while Judge Sheldon strode into the room and took his place behind the large judge's bench. "Madame Clerk, please call the case before us today."

"The State of California versus Mrs. Leola Langley, case number 68340."

Steven Aaron stood. "Ready for the prosecution, Your Honor."

Skip Massey, dressed in his dark blue pin-striped suit, rose. "Ready for the defendant, Leola Langley, Your Honor." Massey had a huge knot in his stomach. Like most actors before their play, he always suffered severe anxiety before a trial. He thought the malady would pass in time, but it never did.

"Madame clerk, would you place the prospective jurors' names in the ballot box and draw out twelve names?"

The clerk mixed up the slips of paper with names on them and drew out twelve, calling the names of the prospective jurors. As they filed to the jury box, the bailiff showed them their seats.

About two weeks before trial, Kane and Massey had obtained a list of prospective jurors from the county clerk's office and hired a local investigator to check their backgrounds. When the information was gathered, they had a general idea as to whether or not the people select-ed for the jury had served in prior jury trials, what type of trial, and how they had voted. The information also gave a description of their age, jobs and family. This information would be useful in making preliminary decisions regarding whether certain jurors would be favorable or unfavorable to their case.

After reviewing the jury report, Jerry and Massey decided they were going to look for jurors who could identify with Leola's situation. Mothers or fathers of young children would be their best jurors. Also high on their list would be hardworking country people who had come through hard times. These people would be rugged individuals who may have had to take the law into their own hands during their struggle to survive. Not that they weren't law abiding, but many times in the life of hard knocks, there aren't too many rules of the road. Young college kids and older men, they felt, would not be the best jurors, because they would feel that people like Leola can't and shouldn't be self-appointed execu-tioners. Lastly, they wanted a jury with no strong leaders in the group, as many times these people dominate the jury, preventing other jurors from exercising their own free will.

Massey knew the extreme importance of the jury selection. After trying jury trials for the last twenty-five years, he recognized that starting off with a good first impression is an essential tool for any trial lawyer. He knew that good lawyers phrase questions to prospective jurors in such a manner that almost makes a preliminary opening statement.

Steve Aaron, the district attorney, began his ques-tioning of the jurors with a general statement. His goal was to set the stage for a conviction of murder in the first degree. He stood before all twelve prospective jurors.

"Ladies and gentlemen, there's been a killing in our town. One of our townsfolk, a schoolteacher, was shot to death by a woman from out of town. My question to all of you is as follows: Is there anyone on this jury who has any reservation about following the law and returning a verdict of murder in the first degree, which then allows the judge to sentence this defendant to die in the gas chamber?"

*Smart district attorney,* Massey thought. *Intimidate the jurors. No one will raise their hands at that question, because they would be embarrassed by refusing to follow the law.* As expected, nobody in the jury raised a hand.

Aaron continued with his coercive type of questions. "Let me put the same question in another way, but be more direct. Do any of you have any hesitation at all about participating in a legal process in which the state will kill another human being as punishment for the taking of an innocent life?" Again, no hands were raised.

Massey said to himself, *That son of a bitch, he knows many of the jurors would like to raise their hands at that question, but again he had framed the question in such a way that anyone raising his or her hand would feel unpatriotic. Getting a commitment based on loyalty to the community and the laws of the State of California was clearly his objective.*

"Now, I want to ask some individual questions." He began to ask about the background of each juror, their spouses, and their family in order to get a sense of their intellect as well as their sense of fairness. He finished with the toughest question for any juror to answer, but Massey knew he had to know the answer now—not after the jury deliberated—so he could weed out the weaker jurors. "If you bring in a verdict in the first degree, and the judge sentences this woman to death, a woman who, by the way, is a mother of two young children, will any of you feel any guilt or remorse if she is executed?"

Massey figured the question would test the resolve of many of the jurors, particularly the women. Seven jurors raised their hands; some of the women and a couple of men said that they would feel some degree of remorse in having participated in the killing.

Aaron decided to further pursue this line of questioning. "If I told you that you were carrying out the law of the State of California, would you still feel remorseful?" Four jurors continued to raise their hands.

Massey was dying to get in a question or two. The district attorney was solidifying the jury to vote for murder one, which can lead to the death sentence. Massey knew that any juror who said she or he would feel remorseful would be excused for cause, and the judge would grant the district attorney's request. It took Aaron about four hours to examine the jurors, including four newly selected prospects who replaced those who raised their hands and were removed from the panel.

Finally, it was Massey's turn. "Ladies and gentlemen, it is now my turn to ask questions of each of you. I will not be as time-consuming as Mr. Aaron, but I do have some important questions to ask. First, let me introduce you to my client, Mrs. Leola Langley." He asked Leola to stand up and face the jury. He realized he had to get the jury acquainted with her. It was going to be a significant task to get their sympathy, but the more exposure that Leola got, the easier it would be. Leola was wearing a simple blue cotton dress, with little makeup on her face, and looked like an average housewife.

When she stood up, Massey could see that the prospective jurors didn't yet have much sympathy as many just glanced at her for a second or two. Others, however, stared at her for quite a while. He could imagine the jurors asking themselves, *What caused this mother to go out and shoot a teacher in cold blood?*

Massey continued, "Now that you have been introduced to my client, let me tell you that she is married, the mother of two children, and lives in Los Gatos, where her husband works for a company known as Spartan Electronics. Let me ask all of you the following general questions, and if your answer would be yes, would you kindly raise your hand: Have you ever been so angry and upset that you've said things to another person that you never really meant?" Most of the jurors raised their hands.

His next question: "Have you seen or heard of people who become so enraged and angry that they do things that they never really intended?" Several of the jurors raised their hands.

"Let me ask you if any of your close relatives or friends have ever experienced any mental illness?" Jurors number two and seven raised their hands, and Massey took down their seat numbers, planning to go into depth with them later in order to set up the defenses.

"Now the judge, at the end of this case, is going to instruct you about various legal defenses that mitigate the charge of first degree murder. Will each of you promise the defendant, Leola Langley, that you won't make your mind up until you hear the judge's instructions, and then retire to the jury room to discuss the law and the facts with the other jurors?"

Based on Massey's trial experience, getting jurors to wait until the end of the case before they make up their minds is very difficult, but he knew it was imperative to convince the jury not to prejudge the case based on the prosecution's evidence, which was presented first—a big advantage for the State.

Massey then proceeded to ask the prospective jurors about their individual circumstances in order to get a picture of their backgrounds. Massey needed to find out the potential for bias. He asked each person: "Did you previously serve on a criminal jury? If so, did you vote to convict or acquit? Are you married to or related to any person in law enforcement? Has any member of your family or any acquaintance ever been wounded by gunfire? Has your family ever been victimized in any crime? Has any member of your family or any acquaintance had any mental illness?"

After an hour, Massey went back to juror number two. "Mrs. Layman, you raised your hand when I asked if any person in your family or any friends had ever had any mental illness. Could you tell me more about the illness?"

"Well, my aunt had Alzheimer's disease when she was older. It got so bad that she would go driving in her car and get lost. Near the end of her life, she didn't remember any of her family. It was really sad." Massey thought this answer didn't help much, so he thanked her and moved on to juror number seven.

"Mr. McNitt, you also raised your hand to the question about mental illness. Would you tell me about the situation in your family?"

"Well, my father lost our family farm in the 1950s when there was a drought in Oklahoma. After he lost it, he went into a deep depression and wound up committing suicide."

"I'm sorry to hear of that tragedy, Mr. McNitt. What kind of man was your father?"

"He was a good, hardworking Christian man, a great father to his six children, and he treated my mother well," said the saddened juror.

"Do you think he really meant to kill himself?" Massey asked, having a good idea what the answer would be.

"No, not really. When he went off the deep end, it was like somebody else was inside his mind. He was a totally different person." Massey thanked the juror for his candor. As Massey walked back to his chair, he said to himself, *Man, I couldn't have written the script any better. That juror set the stage for our trial.* He didn't ask any further questions of the jury.

The prosecution and defense can each excuse twelve jurors for any reason whatsoever without having to reveal the reasons. The prosecution excused mothers and fathers of young children, and then Massey excused people without young children and older people in general as he knew they normally don't get too emotional. He did, however, keep grandparents of young children as they would be apt to react strongly to the sexual abuse of a young child. He also wanted as many churchgoers as he could get, because they too would be incensed when they heard the evidence of the pornography twist in this case.

The final jury consisted of six women and six men. Most were ordinary country folk, hardworking, Christian, conservative, and by and large Massey thought they would be repulsed by what they were going to hear.

Kane, who had been sitting quietly next to Massey all morning, leaned over and whispered to Massey, "I think the jury that was just selected is great. I can't believe the district attorney left so many parents of young children on the jury, particularly four mothers."

Massey chuckled and whispered back, "Aaron has no idea how bad the evidence is going to be regarding the young boy's sexual abuse by the victim and the extent of the involvement of the teacher and his boss."

# CHAPTER 20

Now that the jury selection was finished, it was time for the opening statements from both attorneys.

District attorney Steve Aaron rose from his seat, walked over to the jury box and began, "Ladies and gentlemen, opening statements are a time when the attorneys tell the jurors what evidence they expect to produce so that the jury can get an overall view of the case. During the course of a trial, witnesses are examined and cross-examined, many objections are made, and a trial does not flow as smoothly as one would expect. For this reason, opening statements are exceedingly important. The clearer an attorney can paint the big picture, the easier it will be for you to follow the case."

Massey thought, *This guy is good. He's no country cowpoke. He can try a case. I've got my work cut out for me.*

Aaron continued, "Ladies and gentlemen, the main issue in this case is that citizens can't take the law into their own hands and kill someone whenever they have a grievance against a person. We've all seen what happens to a society that allows this to happen. Look at Yugoslavia, with armed bands of people killing, raping, and slaughtering their neighbors."

The district attorney let that thought sink into the jurors' minds while he went back to his seat and poured himself a glass of water. He returned to the front of the jury box. "The state will produce the police officer who arrived at the scene of the crime and arrested the defendant while she still had a gun in her hand and was standing over the victim; witnesses who saw her shoot the victim; a subsequent confession by the defendant which was not coerced, in which the defendant admitted killing the victim, and then stated that she would do it all over again if she had a chance; the county coroner, who will testify how the death occurred; and lastly, a psychiatrist who will testify that the murderer was of sound mind when the killing occurred and knew the nature of her act. The evidence will be overwhelming that this evil act was a premeditated murder."

Massey surmised that the district attorney, after his hour-long statement, was convinced he had an absolute winner. Massey thought he might be right, but was hoping he was wrong. He felt that this case was going to turn on several key rulings from the judge during the course of the trial.

The judge then asked, "Mr. Massey, do you wish to make an opening statement?"

Massey rose and stated, "Your Honor, I will wait until the prosecution rests its case before I decide whether or not to make an opening statement." Massey was willing to forego the advantage of a good opening statement, because he didn't want to allow the prosecution time to prepare for the surprises that he was going to present into evidence.

"Ladies and gentlemen," said the judge, "it's late in the day. We'll recess now, and I'll see you at nine in the morning when the evidence phase of the trial will begin."

On his way out of the courthouse, Massey stopped at the pay phone in the hallway and called Big Mike. "Mike, any luck in tracking down Garrity's financial backer?"

Mike responded, "I'm running into a lot of dead ends. Garrity's Executor hasn't sold his home yet. I got into Garrity's home in the middle of the night, checked his address books, got into his telephone records, but failed to turn up any connection with a potential financial partner for the porn business. I revisited the porn shop in San Francisco and picked up some additional kiddie porn films and some informational brochures and posters. I'm going to review the material to see if I can come up with any leads."

"Mike, if there is a financial backer, I need you to locate him this week," said a dejected Skip Massey.

"I haven't let you down yet. I'll track this guy down."

▼

The next morning at nine, the district attorney called the county coroner as his first witness. "My name is Dr. James Gilley, the county coroner. I performed an autopsy on the victim, Mr. Edward Stewart, on Thursday, July 11, 1991, at approximately three in the afternoon. The victim died of a gunshot wound from pellets fired from a 20-gauge shotgun which penetrated the lungs and the heart. I took pictures of the deceased which I have in my briefcase."

Aaron then asked, "May I have the pictures that were taken of the deceased so that I can pass them among the jury?" The coroner pulled out a dozen ten-by-twelve-inch reproductions and handed them to the district attorney. After the pictures were inspected by Massey and then properly marked as exhibits, the district attorney went over to juror number one and slowly handed her one picture at a time.

When juror number one looked at the first picture, she audibly gasped. It showed the deceased covered with blood, a gaping hole in his chest. Juror number one held up the picture to study it, and juror number seven looked over her shoulder. When juror number seven saw the picture, she winced in horror and let out a groan. To Massey, the more horrific sight was the ghastly expression of pain on the defendant's face. When both jurors looked directly at Leola, a look of disdain in their eyes, Massey knew the next ten minutes were going to be painful for the defense.

As the pictures were passed one by one among the jurors, the silence hung so thick in the air you could have sliced it with a knife. The jurors were visibly shaken by what they saw and gazed solemnly at Leola, some wondering why she would resort to such a brutal act, others just looking with contempt on their faces and hate in their eyes.

165

The district attorney then produced three eyewitnesses who testified they heard the blast, looked up, and saw the defendant standing near the victim holding a shotgun.

Following these witnesses was Sergeant Dick Clark, the supervising police officer from the County Sheriff's Department, who was on the scene right after the murder occurred. The sergeant was sworn in and testified about what he had observed. "It was twelve-thirteen in the afternoon, Thursday, June 11, 1991. I was patrolling Main Street in my police vehicle when I received an emergency call from headquarters indicating that there was a reported shooting in the parking lot at the local elementary school. I immediately turned my car around and sped toward the school. As I turned into the parking lot, I noticed a crowd of people sixty or seventy feet away from a woman who was standing alone over a body on the ground beside her. She had a shotgun in her hand."

"What did you do next, Sergeant Clark?"

"I immediately called for a backup patrol car, which I learned was already on its way. Within a few seconds, the patrol car arrived with two other officers, Officer Smith and Officer Carmichael. I got out of my patrol car and directed Officer Smith to clear the crowd out of the area. I told Officer Carmichael to cover me. I approached the woman with the gun in order to disarm her. I identified myself and then told her to place the shotgun on the pavement and raise her hands in the air. Instantly, the woman dropped the shotgun to the ground and raised her hands. I approached the woman, and told her not to move or I'd shoot."

"Officer, who was the woman holding the shotgun?"

Sergeant Clark pointed his finger at Leola. "That woman sitting there at the front table next to her lawyer, Mr. Massey." All eyes of the jury shifted from Sergeant Clark to Leola.

"What did you do next?"

"I picked up the shotgun and ordered her to lie face down on the ground with her hands behind her back, which she did immediately. I pulled out a set of handcuffs and placed them around her wrists. At this time Officers Smith and Carmichael came running up. I ordered Officer Smith to radio for an ambulance, and directed Officer Carmichael to take the woman to the back of my patrol car while I checked out the victim on the ground."

"What was the condition of the victim?"

"When I went over to the victim on the ground, I grabbed his arm to see if there was any pulse. After feeling none, I began to give the victim mouth-to-mouth resuscitation until the ambulance arrived about four minutes later."

"What happened when the ambulance arrived?"

"The medics scrambled out of the ambulance with a defibrillator and applied it to the victim's chest. As soon as the first jolt of electricity hit the body, it jerked and continued to jerk as they repeatedly tried to revive the victim. While applying the defibrillator, they simultaneously put the victim on a gurney, wheeled him into the back of the ambulance and sped away toward the hospital. My understanding was that they were unable to revive him at the hospital and pronounced him dead."

"And after the ambulance left, what occurred next?"

"Officer Carmichael and I took the suspect in my patrol car down to headquarters. Upon arrival, I had the suspect booked and then escorted her to the interrogation room."

"What occurred in the interrogation room?"

"I started off by reading her the Miranda Rights."

Massey thought this good-looking officer with his mustache was a very credible witness. When he spoke to the jury, he looked straight at them, a sign of a good witness. His testimony was going smoothly and there wasn't much that Massey could tear apart.

The district attorney continued, looking as though he was enjoying the smooth delivery of his witness, "Officer, did you obtain a voluntary statement from the suspect that afternoon?"

"Yes, sir."

"Did you have her statement typed up and have her sign it after she read it?"

"Yes, sir. I have it with me."

Aaron took the signed document from the police officer, turned to the judge and said, "Your Honor, I would like to introduce this two-page confession as our next exhibit."

The judge admitted the document as the prosecution's next exhibit.

"Officer, did you make a tape recording of the conversation you had with the suspect that afternoon, and did you bring it with you today?"

"Yes, sir." The officer reached into his briefcase and then held the cassette up for the district attorney.

After the district attorney had the tape admitted into evidence, he placed a table in front of the jury box and set a cassette player on top.

"Officer, would you mind inserting the tape in this recording machine that I've placed on the table in front of the jury and play it for us?"

The sergeant got up from the witness chair, inserted the tape into the recording machine, and pushed the play button.

This tape is being transcribed at the Lassen County Jail in Susanville, California, on Thursday, June 11, 1991, at 1:15 p.m. I am Officer Dick Clark of the Lassen County Sheriff's Department. In attendance is Mrs. Leola Langley, the suspect in the murder of Mr. Edward Stewart. Also present are Officers Smith and Carmichael. I am going to ask Mrs. Langley, Do you consent to my taping this conversation?

Yes, I do.

Mrs. Langley, I am going to ask you if the statements you are about to make are of your own free and voluntary will, and are you willing to make them without your attorney present?

Yes.

Has there been any coercion used by any of us in order to have you answer the questions being put to you this afternoon?

No.

Now Mrs. Langley, about thirty minutes ago, we were in the parking lot at the local elementary school here in Susanville. Is that correct?

[There was silence, then Officer Clark spoke again.]

Mrs. Langley, you can't nod your head. Instead, please speak audibly and directly into the microphone in the middle of the desk.

Yes, we was in the school parking lot.

And when we arrived, did you have a 20-gauge shotgun in your hands?"

Yes, I did.

Next to you was the body of a man lying on the ground next to a car. Tell me what happened?

Well, I drove up here and hid behind a bush so that horrible man wouldn't see me when he went to his car. When he got near the car, I rose and pulled the trigger on mah shotgun and let him have what he deserved.

Massey noted that she was speaking in a matter-of-fact voice.

Why did you kill him?

Because he deserved to die, and I would do it again if I had a chance.

And why did he deserve to die, Mrs. Langley?

Because he was a vile individual and a terrible man.

Massey knew the officer would pursue the question, because he wanted her motive for the killing.

Why did you consider him a vile and terrible person?

[There was silence for sixty seconds.]

Mrs. Langley, did you hear my question?

[Again, there was silence.]

169

Mrs. Langley, I would like to know why you killed the teacher?

I'm not talking any more.

All right then, Mrs. Langley, I am going to have one of our secretaries type a copy of this recording, and I will ask you to read it over and then sign it so that you can acknowledge the truth of your answers.

[The testimony ended and then after a break, the tape recording went on with Officer Clark speaking.]

Mrs. Langley, our secretary has just transcribed the tape. I am going to hand it to you and ask you to read the transcript for its accuracy. If you find the transcript to be correct, would you then sign the document on the line that says that this confession is true and correct. Let the record reflect that I am handing the document to Mrs. Langley. She is reading the transcript and now is signing the document. Mrs. Langley, is that your signature that appears on the transcript, and is the transcript a correct statement of your confession?

[Leola's response was barely audible.]

Yes.

Aaron stood with a look of arrogance and said, "Thank you, Officer, for your splendid testimony."

Throughout the prosecution's production of their key witnesses, Massey kept his questions to a minimum. He thought that there was no lawyer in the land that could shake down any of these witnesses.

The prosecution finished presenting its case after only three days of trial. Massey was stunned for a moment when Aaron rested his case, because the prosecution had not called their medical expert to testify on the defendant's state of mind. Then he realized Aaron's tactic. *Smart move, Mr. Aaron. He's figured that he has plenty of evidence for a premeditated murder without having his expert testify now. He wants to have his expert be the last witness so he can prepare his expert for any unexpected surprises. But more importantly, he wants to have his medical expert be the last witness in the case, because juries always remember the fresh testimony better.*

"Ladies and gentlemen, we will now recess until tomorrow morning when the defense will present its case," ordered the judge. Massey noticed that as jurors left the room, they looked at Leola as if she were the lowest form of life. Massey had a sick feeling that if they voted at this moment, she would get the gas chamber.

When Massey got back to the hotel, he hopped into the telephone booth and placed a call to his investigator. "Mike, how are you coming on the search for Garrity's partner?"

"I may have something, but I need more time," was Big Mike's answer.

"Time, I'm running out of. You've got to find this guy in the next day or two."

"Hang onto your pants, I've got a lead and may be able to pull a rabbit out of the hat if I get lucky," Mike commented. "I'm in a hurry. I gotta go and follow up on the lead." With that he hung up, leaving Massey with more unanswered questions.

# CHAPTER 21

The court session began again the following morning promptly at nine.

"Mr. Massey, do you wish to give an opening statement for the defense?" asked the judge.

"Your Honor, I have decided to pass on an opening statement for the defense."

Massey wanted to surprise the hell out of the district attorney with evidence of Leola's motive for killing Arnold. He was fairly confident that the district attorney never discovered the fact that the deceased had molested her child.

"The defense will call its first witness, Dr. Stan Tishman."

The Stanford psychiatrist, nattily dressed in a tan pin-striped suit, rose from his seat in the first row and walked past the jury on his way to the witness stand. The clerk stopped him before he reached his seat. "Doctor, I would like to swear you in as a witness. Please raise your right hand."

The doctor took the witness chair, placed the briefcase he was carrying on the floor beside him, and looked up through his glasses.

In order to qualify the doctor as an expert witness, Massey asked Dr. Tishman about his qualifications. The doctor recited the litany of his medical degrees and experience; the judge then ruled that the doctor was qualified to act as an expert.

"Dr. Tishman, how long have you treated the defendant and her family?"

"For approximately seven weeks prior to her arrest,"

was the doctor's answer.

"And what was the reason for the defendant seeking your services?"

"You referred her to me after her son was sexually molested by his teacher."

"And who was the teacher that sexually molested her son?"

"At the time of the molestation, the teacher's name was Stanley Arnold, but he changed his name, moved to Susanville, and went by the name of Edward Stewart," he answered.

Massey looked over at the district attorney. Aaron looked as though somebody had just stabbed him in the ass with a pitchfork. Members of the jury looked surprised, and there was a commotion in the gallery.

After the noise quieted, Massey continued, "Doctor, were you able to verify that the person who was shot in the school parking lot by the defendant was the teacher from Los Gatos named Stanley Arnold, who allegedly molested the defendant's son?" Massey held his breath, waiting for the doctor's answer.

"Yes," said the doctor emphatically.

Again the courtroom gallery started buzzing. Massey looked over at the jury, who looked shocked.

"Order in the courtroom," shouted the judge as he banged his gavel.

The district attorney jumped up from his chair, his face crimson red at the turn of events. "Your Honor, I request permission to examine this witness on *voir dire*."

"Permission granted, Mr. Aaron," replied the judge.

Leola looked at Skip Massey quizzically and then whispered, "*Voir dire*. What's that all about?"

"That's Latin for 'speak the truth.' It means he's going to cross-examine the doctor to see if he has the background to answer the questions I just put to him."

A very disturbed Steve Aaron approached the witness. "Doctor, how do you know that Mr. Stanley Arnold and Mr. Edward Stewart were one and the same person?"

"I obtained the dental records and fingerprints of both men. They both matched."

"Do you have those records with you today?"

"Yes, I do." Tishman reached down and pulled two sets of dental records and fingerprints from his briefcase, offering them to Aaron.

The district attorney grabbed the records, hurriedly went back to his chair and reviewed them with his associates. After a couple of minutes he returned the documents to Dr. Tishman, apparently satisfied that they matched. "No further questions of this witness," uttered the dejected district attorney.

Massey then rose from his seat and continued his line of questioning. "Was Mr. Stanley Arnold the fifth-grade teacher of Mrs. Langley's son, Billy?"

Before the doctor could answer, the district attorney jumped to his feet again. "Objection, Your Honor, on the grounds of relevancy." Massey looked at Steve Aaron. He looked like he was in a state of shock, and was obviously trying to prevent any more surprise testimony.

Judge Sheldon peered down from his pulpit and asked the lawyers to approach the bench. When they got in front of him, the judge whispered to Massey so the jury couldn't hear the question, "What's the relevancy, counsel?"

Massey whispered back, "State of mind, Your Honor, which supports our defense of absence of the requisite intent to kill. The doctor will testify that the child was sexually molested by the victim over a lengthy period of time. The child developed severe emotional trauma, causing the mother to go into a state of depression to such an extent that at the time of the shooting, she was so mentally incapacitated that she was incapable of forming a premeditated intent to kill."

The district attorney looked as if he had been hit with a sledgehammer. "Your Honor, the prosecution has no prior knowledge of these facts. The State respectfully requests a continuance so we can depose the doctor in order to rebut his testimony."

Judge Sheldon looked at Steve Aaron and smiled. "So you want a continuance right in the middle of trial, while twelve jurors wait for you to prepare your case? You should have prepared your case before trial, counselor. Your request for a continuance is denied, and your objection to this line of questioning is also denied. Proceed with your witness, Mr. Massey."

Massey had guessed right; the district attorney was oblivious of the sexual abuse of Billy because Leola had never mention the subject to the police or to the prosecution's medical expert. He had felt quite sure that Leola would not reveal the family's dirty secret to anyone.

The district attorney then pleaded with the judge, "Your Honor, may we take the deposition of this witness this evening?"

"Mr. Aaron, did you ever wonder what the motive of this mother was?"

"Your Honor, we never could figure out why the woman came up here and murdered the teacher. We thought she may have been an ex-girlfriend, or was having an affair with him. Since we had such an ironclad case, we thought her motive would have little bearing on the outcome," replied the somber district attorney.

"You're in for a surprise, counsel. One that I think you richly deserve for not preparing this case any better than you did," retorted the judge. "Your motion to take the doctor's deposition is denied. You'll have a chance to cross-examine him and find out what is really going on in this case."

As the district attorney returned to his chair, Massey stood between the jury and his witness. "Doctor, how many times have you interviewed the defendant and her family?"

The district attorney swiftly rose to his feet and once again tried to impede the line of questioning. "It is my understanding that the doctor is seeing the boy for treatment and not the mother, and hence he would not be in a position to render an opinion on the mother's state of mind."

The judge peered down at Mr. Aaron, obviously displeased with his tactics. "Mr. Aaron, if you had been listening to the testimony instead of trying to interrupt this trial with your constant objections, you would have heard the doctor testify that he has been seeing the mother for seven weeks. Objection denied."

"Dr. Tishman, please continue with the history of your treatment of the Langley family," said Massey. He was enjoying the sight of Aaron squirming and groveling before the judge.

"As I testified a moment ago, the family had been referred to me by you, Mr. Massey. I believe you were representing them at that time. You stated that the reason for the referral was an incident in which the boy's teacher, Mr. Stanley Arnold, had sexually molested the boy, and thereafter the teacher had reputedly committed suicide. You told me that the boy was suffering from depression and that you thought the family needed medical attention."

Aaron could have validly requested the judge to strike all the hearsay included in the doctor's answer, but he didn't. Massey figured Aaron didn't want to incur the judge's wrath anymore.

"How long had the teacher's sexual abuse of the Langley boy been going on?"

"For a period of at least six months," replied Dr. Tishman.

"What was the nature of the sexual abuse?"

"Well, the boy has been fairly close-mouthed about his relationship with his teacher, but he did admit that the teacher had fondled his private parts and said that on one occasion he was sodomized by the teacher, although he didn't use the word *sodomize*," was the doctor's response.

There was dead silence in the courtroom after the doctor's answer, except for the weeping of Leola. Massey purposely waited about thirty seconds to allow Leola to gain control of herself. He even returned to their table to pour her a glass of water. He wanted the jury to notice the extent of the pain this mother was suffering over the incident that had occurred to her son. For the first time since the trial started, the jurors began to look at Leola as a victim. Perhaps there was a rational explanation for this killing.

Massey then continued, "How often did you see the family?"

"On the average of twice a week during the

seven-week period."

"And how did the treatments progress?"

"Well, I would have to say that my treatment didn't seem to be of much assistance. The family could not get over what happened. Each member of the family began deteriorating mentally and physically after the discovery of the son's sexual molestation and then the reported suicide of the teacher. Billy Langley became severely depressed and refused to talk about his emotions and feelings. Much of this change in his condition can be attributed to the fact that his classmates blamed him for the death of the teacher. As a result, he was receiving physical and emotional abuse from his peers at school. On top of that, word had gotten out that he was sexually involved with the teacher, and the kids began calling him names like queer and fag."

"Did the mother take any steps to curtail the abuse the boy was taking?"

"The mother had him transferred to a different school, but soon the word leaked out to his new class-mates and the taunting began anew. The boy lost interest in school, and his depression manifested itself by his withdrawing not only from his school, but also his family. Furthermore, he refused to eat, to such an extent that I had to hospitalize him for anorexia to try to save him from starving himself to death."

"And did other members of the family have difficulty?"

"Well, the father, Sam Langley, began to deny that anything occurred. He refused to talk to his wife about any subject connected with the incident or any of the subsequent events that were occurring with the boy. The father's escape was to pour his full energy into his work. He would leave for work before the family arose in the morning and return after the evening meal. In addition, he started drinking heavily. His behavior was affecting the marriage and put even more pressure on his wife, as she was the only one ostensibly worrying about the child."

"Did you notice any change in the mother, Leola Langley?"

The doctor turned and looked at Leola, then looked back at Massey. "Leola Langley began deteriorating rapidly. She was not responding to treatment, so I prescribed Valium to lift her out of her depression, but the medicine didn't seem to help her. At my last session with her, I considered hospitalizing her to stabilize her condition. She spent most of our hour-long session weeping uncontrollably. She didn't respond to my questions in a rational manner, but instead, broke down and sobbed every time I asked a question. She had been much better a week earlier, and her sudden mental deterioration puzzled me. Rather than hospitalizing her, I decided to let her husband take her home and told him to let me know if she started acting irrationally."

"Did you ever tell the mother and father what effect the lengthy sexual molestation of their son might have on his future development?"

"I had to inform them that the boy would need a long and intense period of treatment. Once a child of this age begins to enjoy the sexual sensation of his contact with the adult, he is overcome with a desire to recreate that satisfying sensation when he becomes an adult, and often becomes a child molester himself."

Dr. Tishman's testimony hung in the air. Massey turned and looked at the jury, noticing a change in their faces as they glanced at Leola. No longer did they give her looks of disdain.

"That's all the questions I have for Dr. Tishman, Your Honor." Massey purposely didn't ask Tishman all of the questions he had for him, because on cross-examination the district attorney would open a couple of doors for him; then Massey expected to make some good mileage on redirect.

The district attorney rose and walked to the witness box. "Doctor, when did you first see the family, and when was the last time you saw the defendant?"

"I started seeing the family Wednesday, May 15, 1991, and my last visit with Mrs. Leola Langley was Wednesday, July 10, 1991, which I believe was the day before the shooting of Mr. Arnold." Massey thought that testimony hurt the prosecution because his medical expert had seen the defendant so close to the date of the killing. His testimony on her state of mind would be tremendously significant, particularly since the prosecution's medical expert hadn't seen her until several days after the killing.

"During your treatment of Mrs. Langley, did she seem to understand your questions?" pursued the district attorney.

"Yes, except for the last occasion, when I really couldn't tell if she understood me or not."

"Based on your dealings with the defendant, did you understand that she knew the difference between right and wrong?"

"My answer would be generally yes, except I really couldn't get much out of her during the last treatment session. She appeared to be delusional and, frankly, was hardly able to function as a person."

"Doctor, do you have your notes of that last session with you, and may I see them?"

The doctor again reached down to his briefcase and pulled out the client file of Leola Langley which contained his daily notes. He handed them to Aaron, who read through them silently.

"Doctor, I'm looking at your notes taken on her last visit. When you asked Mrs. Langley how she was doing, she answered 'Not very well.' Is that correct?"

"Yes, but when I asked her why, she began to weep uncontrollably and never gave me an explanation. For the rest of the session, that was the kind of response I received, sobbing and weeping in a most uncontrollable fashion."

"But she did understand your first question and answered it, correct?"

"She just said she wasn't doing very well. I originally thought the reason for her depressed state was the hospitalization of her son the night before she visited me. I really don't know if she understood any of my questions, because in my opinion, she was in the midst of a mental breakdown. In retrospect, I should have hospitalized her then and there."

The district attorney wouldn't let up. "Now, doctor, she really did understand your question because she told you she wasn't doing very well, and hence, she understood on that day the difference between right and wrong. Correct?"

The doctor paused and then said, "I really can't answer that question, because after I asked her why she wasn't doing well, she couldn't function. Thereafter, I don't know whether she understood the questions I was asking or even had the capacity to understand."

"So you can't testify that on the day you saw her, that she didn't know the difference between right and wrong?"

"I really can't."

"Your witness, Mr. Massey." Aaron, now a little more cocky than before, returned to his seat.

Massey rose and stood before the witness. "Doctor, you stated that you were considering hospitalizing Mrs. Langley during her last visit. Why?"

"Because I was concerned whether or not she could function. She seemed disassociated from reality, and I was fearful for her safety. As I testified previously, I let her go home in the care of her husband. I took him aside and told him of my concerns and made him promise to call me and tell me how she was doing. I didn't get a call back the next day, so I assumed she had improved."

Massey paused to look at a note Kane had just passed to him. "Ask him about her character," it read.

"Doctor, you treated Leola Langley for seven weeks. During that treatment period, were you able to gain an insight into her character?"

"Certainly," he replied.

"Is the killing of Mr. Arnold by Mrs. Langley consistent with the type of character traits that you witnessed during your treatment of her?"

"Based on my period of treatment, it is my opinion that she is a kind and loving mother. In a rational state of mind, I really don't think she would intentionally kill anyone. It's out of character."

"Do you believe she would ever act out of vengeance?"

"No, she is not a vengeful person, and she never talked about revenge."

"Your witness, Mr. Aaron," Massey concluded and returned to his seat. The district attorney was clearly not a happy camper. Massey was frankly surprised that Aaron didn't ask the judge to strike the doctor's speculative answers, as those would have been valid objections. Massey surmised that Aaron had been intimidated by the judge over his efforts to block the doctor's testimony and was worried about irritating the judge further.

Steve Aaron now rose and approached the witness, saying, "Doctor, do you know if Mrs. Langley had found out that Mr. Arnold was not dead, but in fact alive, when you saw her that day?"

"No," stated the doctor.

"It could have been several weeks before her last visit with you, could it not, and by the time she saw you in your office, she had already planned to travel to Susanville the next day to kill him?"

"I don't think so," replied the doctor, "but I don't know for sure."

The district attorney's beady eyes now pierced the doctor. "But doctor, you don't know that for a fact, do you?"

"No, I don't."

"No more questions," said the district attorney, strutting to his seat.

The judge then announced, "Ladies and gentlemen, while it's early in the afternoon, I'm going to recess the court for the remainder of the day as Judge Brandon has asked me to handle several short hearings this afternoon. We will reconvene at nine tomorrow. Please remember the admonition that I gave you about not discussing this case with anyone, including your fellow jurors."

# CHAPTER 22

Susan, Kane and Massey walked back to the St. Francis Hotel after the court recessed, while Leola and Sam stopped to make a telephone call to their children. Massey asked, "How do you think we're doing?"

Susan was the first to respond, "Okay, but not great. I thought Dr. Tishman was a good witness, but I think the jury is having a hard time buying the story that Leola had a complete mental collapse which justifies her killing of Arnold. It sounds more like a revenge killing to me."

Kane added, "I'm worried as well. When we come to the post-traumatic stress syndrome defense, we're going to have a hard time getting the judge to buy our argument that Leola may have been traumatized like a Vietnam veteran and suffered a flashback."

Upon reaching the St. Francis Hotel, they went into the bar for a round of beers to further discuss the day's events. When Susan and Massey finally got back to their room, Susan noticed the red message light on the telephone. She picked up the receiver, listened, and then said to Massey, "Big Mike wants you to call as soon as possible."

Massey dialed Mike's number hurriedly. "Skip Massey. What's going on?"

"Great news, I found the son of a bitch. I'm going to Fed Ex the report up tomorrow morning, but I thought I'd better call you right away so that we can serve the guy with a subpoena tonight if you need him to testify."

"I've got plenty of time to talk. The judge let us out early today. Hold on a second." Massey slid off his shoes, pulled off his coat and tie, and lay on the bed.

He was tired after the intense day in court. After a short pause, Massey returned and continued, "Hi Mike, I'm back on the line. What have you come up with?"

"Well, it wasn't easy, but I got a good break. I told you I had hit a stone wall in finding out who backed the purchase of the porn shop, and that I went back to the shop to see if I could get any more leads. I gathered more of those kiddie porn movies and some posters. When I got back home, I started looking at the posters. Young kids posing nude. I could tell that whoever did the printing spent a hell of a lot of money. The images were as clear as I had ever seen on a poster."

"Very interesting. Tell me more?"

"I visited a friend in the printing business and showed the posters to him. When he first looked at them, he told me that the machine that printed those color posters had to be one of those new expensive printing presses. The more dots per square inch that are used in the printing process, the higher the quality. He showed me a color copy that his press turned out and compared it to the poster I found at the porn shop. The difference in the clarity was amazing. My friend said the new presses cost about two and a half million dollars, so there wouldn't be many of them in the Bay Area. He told me that one expensive printing press was a German printing machine called the Heidelberg, and that was probably the press used. He couldn't remember the manufacturer, but suggested I contact several major printing firms in the Bay Area."

"You sound like a hound dog who's closing in on the fox."

Mike continued, "It gets better. I haven't even started. An old-time company named Heidelberg turned out to be the manufacturer and is located in none other than Heidelberg, Germany. I called the plant in Germany and got the sales department. I told them I was a potential buyer and wanted to visit a printing house in the Bay Area for a demonstration."

"You are the biggest B.S.'er I know," Massey said with a chuckle.

"Listen to this. The guy on the other end of the line checked his computer and said there were only three in the area, one in San Francisco, another in San Jose, and the last one in Cupertino. He gave me the names of the companies and their phone numbers. I contacted the three, pretending I was looking into firms that would do some printing work for my company. Each one of these companies was doing extremely well financially because they specialize in annual reports and brochures for the high-tech and bio-med companies in the Bay Area. All three companies were corporations, so I called the Corporations Commissioner's office in San Francisco, talked to one of the deputies, and got the names and addresses of the officers and directors."

"Now, I think you've got the scent of the fox."

"I then got the idea to run a property check on the officers and directors to see if they owned any property in the Saratoga-Los Gatos area. Only two names popped up. I figured that whoever our man was had to have some connection with the schools because of Garrity and Arnold, so I went down to the Los Gatos School District Administrative office and talked to the people in the office to see if they recognized any of the names. It didn't take long. The guy's name is Fillmore."

"You're kidding, you don't mean Gary Fillmore?" Massey said in a stunned voice.

"Oh yes, I do. But wait until you hear the rest of this story. So, I go to investigate his properties. One is a big fancy home in Los Gatos, probably worth two to three million bucks. Then he has an office building in Cupertino where his business is located. I visit his other property, and damned if it isn't a cabin located up on Big Basin Highway about two miles from Saratoga, up in the Santa Cruz Mountains. The cabin is located in a remote hideaway. You take a narrow crooked road off the highway for about a mile to get to the cabin. It's surrounded by redwood trees. There isn't another home within half a mile. Nobody's there, so I make the obvious move and gain access. You'll never guess what I found. Christ, there was a movie studio with all of the expensive gear for making movies. After looking at some of the videotapes and posters, I discover that this place is the production center for Youth Fantasies Productions, Inc."

"Man, you are one smart son of a bitch. Great work! The fox nailed his prey. I'll call my friend Levitt and have his pilot meet you at the airport in an hour and fly you up here this afternoon. I need those posters and videotapes right away."

"You're on. I'm ready any time," said the pleased investigator. Massey could imagine a wide smile on Big Mike's face.

"Before you leave, however, I'm going to call my secretary, Helen, and have her prepare a subpoena for Fillmore to appear tomorrow afternoon. Would you stop by the office, pick up the subpoena, and then serve the son of a bitch? Lastly, knowing what a good sleuth you are, I assume you took pictures of Mr. Fillmore's filth palace in the mountains?"

"You betcha, I took plenty of them, and also of his palace in Los Gatos and even his business headquarters. It will be my absolute pleasure to serve this creep with the subpoena."

After Massey hung up the telephone, he said to Susan, "Listen to this bombshell. Mike found the financial backer. You won't believe it. Gary Fillmore."

Susan shook her head and exclaimed, "Can it be true? It's beyond my imagination. If so, now we know why he got so mad at us for trying to get Arnold suspended and investigated, and why Garrity and Fillmore went out of their way to protect him. The puzzle is starting to fit. Didn't Mike include a videotape with that first report that he gave us when he located Arnold in Susanville? We never did look at it."

"Well, that is a very intriguing question. I always wanted to look at it, but never had time. I don't know if it will shed any light on this case, but let me call Mike and have him stop by our place and pick it up."

The plane touched down shortly after eight. Massey picked up his favorite investigator and drove him to the hotel. Mike, the thinker, had also brought along a VCR, which he plugged into the TV. Mike gave Massey the tape he had included in Arnold's original folder.

Massey put the tape in the VCR and pressed the play button. Sure enough, a video entitled *Play Time* appeared on the screen. First they saw large redwood trees with the sun shining through them, and then the camera focused in on a small cabin. Massey put the VCR on pause and asked Mike to pull out the pictures of Fillmore's cabin above Saratoga. He produced half a dozen. This cabin appeared to be the same cabin that was in the movie.

"This is unbelievable."

Massey turned the video back on, and several minutes later three children appeared on the screen inside the cabin. Almost instantly, Susan said, "My God, that's Billy on the left." Massey pushed the pause button. Sure enough, it was Billy, dressed up in a clown costume. He pushed the play button and the film began again. After about two minutes of idle chatter among the three children, an adult clown with a mask appeared in the scene. When the camera got a close view of the adult clown, Massey pushed the pause button again. "Do you recognize him, Susan?"

"No, not with all that makeup on and the mask." Massey pushed the start button again. After five minutes, the older clown got the kids to undress and began touching their private parts. All the kids were young boys about Billy's age, eleven or twelve.

Before long, the older clown had unzipped his fly and pulled out his erect penis. He invited the children to kiss it, which they did, including Billy. "Massey, I don't think I can take much more of this sick and disgusting movie. Poor Billy. If Leola saw this tape, no wonder she went off the deep end. I can also understand why she didn't want anybody to know what her son had done. No wonder she kept this so secret." Susan excused herself and went to get a glass of water in the bathroom.

Massey continued the movie and soon all of the participants were completely naked and dancing. Then to everyone's disgust and amazement, the older clown started sodomizing Billy Langley.

After Susan calmed down, she came back into the room and started watching the film again. After a few moments, Susan said, "Stop this awful film, Skip, and go back a couple of frames."

Massey slowly went back, and Susan told Massey to hit the pause button. She then exclaimed excitedly, "That's him! The adult clown is Arnold. I recognize the tattoo. He had a Marine tattoo on his left forearm, just below the elbow, that he was proud of and used to show his pupils, including my daughter. I saw his tattoo when I was in his office for a parent-teacher conference, when he was wearing a short-sleeved shirt. Little did I know what a low-life he was."

Susan shook her head in sorrow. "You know, Skip, if Leola saw this tape, it could have sent her into orbit."

# CHAPTER 23

Massey immediately placed a call to Dr. Scott Smith. "Scott, Skip Massey here. Sorry to call in the evening, but we just discovered some new evidence. We have a tape of Billy Langley's teacher, Arnold, sodomizing the kid. If Leola ever looked at the tape, which she could have discovered with Mike's original investigative report, I wonder whether this might be what sent her into the psychological tailspin? Could you meet us at our hotel right away? I want to show you this tape and then have you interview Leola and see if you can find out if she saw that tape. If so, I need your opinion on whether or not this event could have started the flashback episode."

"Sure," said the doctor, "but I'll probably need an hour or so to get the answer out of her. It won't be easy. Her fragile psyche probably can't handle the scene of her son getting abused by Arnold. I'll bet she's buried that godforsaken memory."

Fifteen minutes later, Dr. Smith met Massey in the hotel's foyer. "Thanks, Scott for being so prompt. I've arranged with the hotel for you to interview Leola in one of the conference rooms on the first floor. I'll go get Leola and bring her down. Do the best you can, because this evidence would be an important breakthrough for us. I think the jury would really relate to this mother's reaction. After I play that tape, I want them convinced that Arnold deserved what he got."

Five minutes later, the phone in Massey's room rang. "Massey, this is Scott. Could you bring down the videotape and the VCR?"

Massey promptly took the video player and tape to the doctor.

About forty-five minutes later, Dr. Smith called Massey from the lobby and asked him to meet him downstairs again. He was standing in the main lobby when Massey saw him, and the door to the conference room was shut.

"I think I've just struck gold. Leola had a very difficult time reviewing the pornographic tape involving her son, but does recall finding the Arnold investigation file in your dresser drawer when she was putting away the clothes she had just washed. She says she read the investigator's report and found the videotape. She didn't remember viewing the tape. I had a hunch she was not telling all she knew, so I put the tape on. When the video got to the scene where her boy was being abused, she went ballistic. After I calmed her down, she said she remembered seeing her son on the video being raped by Arnold that day. I asked her if she knew the date when she discovered the report. She couldn't remember the date, but did remember that it was the day before she saw Dr. Tishman for the last time."

"Scott, what a break for our case. That evidence will kill the prosecution."

"There's more. I got her to recall that she was sexually molested by her father for years as a child. It's not unusual for victims to bury these sordid memories and not remember them for years until some event triggers the mind to release them. Now there is no question in my mind that on the day she discovered the Arnold file at your condo, the sudden realization that Arnold was alive, and then seeing her son on video being raped by his teacher, was the catalyst that put her into orbit. The shocking scene caused the flood of painful memories to suddenly surface. She had a true flashback like the Vietnam veteran, went into a hallucinatory state of mind, drove up to Susanville and killed Arnold."

"I'll tell you, Doc, this is the best news I've had in months. If I can get this testimony into evidence, you watch this jury turn around. They'll now have a damn good reason to understand why she killed him, and

I'm sure that many of them will think the bastard got what he deserved."

"I agree," said Dr. Smith, and he rose to leave.

"I'm going to put Leola on the stand tomorrow. Her testimony may take most of the day, and then I'll put you on the stand the following day."

"That's fine," said Smith.

"Incidentally, let's not get into the post-traumatic stress syndrome defense until the end of the questioning," said Massey. "If we start off with the PTSD testimony, the judge might be tempted to strike all of your testimony, thinking that the only purpose for calling you was to present this defense. I want to get the catalyst testimony into evidence on the theory that she didn't have the requisite intent to kill. Make sure you stress that she did not understand the nature and quality of her actions after she went into orbit. As you probably know, the judge won't let you give an opinion of her state of mind at the instant of the killing, but your testimony on the catalyst issue which occurred the day before is admissible. Thanks again, Doc. Great job."

Massey went upstairs, opened the door of room 202, and said to Susan and O'Malley, "You won't believe what Doc Smith was able to pry out of Leola's mind." He immediately launched into what the doctor told him.

# CHAPTER 24

Prior to coming to court that morning, Massey called Leola at six and asked her to meet him and Susan in the coffee shop downstairs so they could go over the testimony she would be giving that morning. Leola arrived at seven-thirty, sat down at their table and ordered a cup of coffee.

Massey saw that Leola looked very tired. "I want to put you on the stand this morning. Now, you don't have to testify, but unless we can explain away that confession, I don't think we have much of a chance of getting an acquittal, much less a manslaughter charge."

"I'm willin', if you want me to."

"That's great. It's very important that the jury find out who you really are. That you are not a cold-blooded killer. They also need to know what happened between your son and Arnold. I know this is painful, but they need to know about your discovery of the Arnold file in my condo and your viewing of the tape where Billy was abused, and what impact that had on you."

Leola looked down at the floor a long time and finally said in a low tone, "I don't know if I can hold up without going to pieces."

Susan took her hand. "Leola, I know you can do it."

Massey looked Leola in the eye and with a quiet voice said, "I want permission to ask questions about your past life."

"What do you mean . . . ?"

"I mean about your father abusing you as a child."

Leola looked down at the floor and tears welled in her eyes. She replied, "I can't, it's too painful and embarrassin'. I really can't. Mah mind buried those awful memories for so many years. Now that mah mind remembers all the pain and agony of mah childhood, I would just like to forget about it all."

Massey reached over, took her hand, and gently said, "I will respect your wishes, but let me be blunt. If you want to see your boys grow up to be young men, marry, and have children, then you're going to have to be brave and go through the agony of recounting those horrible events."

She was silent a moment, and slowly nodded her head as tears kept falling. Massey leaned over and put his arm around her. "I'm sorry to put you through this ordeal, but I know you will want to enjoy those young men, particularly when they have children, and you get to be a grandma and be a part of your grandchildren's lives. Believe me, it will be worth all the suffering and humiliation that you will go through today."

"Thank you. I'll do the best I can. Make sure you bring plenty of hankies," she said, and the edges of her mouth turned up ever so slightly, the nearest thing to a smile he'd seen in months. Massey knew she was visualizing her role as grandma.

For the next hour, Massey went through other areas of questioning that he was going to cover in her testimony and then looked at his watch. "Well, it's time to get ready for court," he announced.

They all got up, and Susan gave Leola a big hug. "You'll do great. We'll meet in the lobby in a few minutes and walk over to the courthouse."

Massey and Susan met with Kane before the morning session began. Massey excitedly told the local attorney about their discovery of the evening before. Kane now appeared excited for the first time since the trial began and was even smiling. "God, that's the break we've needed. This evidence will really rock that jury."

"I hope you're right," said a happy Susan.

Five minutes before the court session was to resume, the bailiff told the district attorney and Massey, "The judge wants to see both of you in his chambers right away."

Once inside the chambers, Judge Sheldon turned to Massey. "Mr. Massey, I got a call a few minutes ago from an irate lawyer in San Jose. He stated that his client, a Mr. Gary Fillmore, was served late yesterday afternoon with a subpoena to appear today in this court at 2 p.m. Don't you think that Mr. Fillmore might have some business to tend to? How do you expect him to get up here to testify on such short notice?"

"Well, I apologize, Your Honor, but I didn't discover the witness until yesterday afternoon when I got a call from my investigator. We have been looking for this witness for several weeks, but were unable to locate him."

The judge retorted, "What is so special about him that he can't testify on Monday?"

"I need him to lay a foundation for the introduction of videotapes that were made prior to the time of the murder, which will shed light on why the defendant went off the deep end. The evidence will go to the defendant's state of mind at the time of the murder to show she did not have the requisite intent. My next medical expert will be testifying tomorrow, and he wants to use these tapes as one piece of evidence to confirm his observation of the defendant."

"May I inquire as to the nature of the tapes, counselor, and what your new witness has to do with them?"

"Your Honor, these tapes are child pornography tapes which include the defendant's twelve-year-old son and Mr. Arnold. It shows the child kissing and sucking the penis of his former teacher, Mr. Arnold, and also being raped by the teacher. The witness that is under subpoena is the owner of the studio where the film was produced, the custodian of these tapes, and the one who did the filming of these sordid acts."

The district attorney was red as a beet and hot under the collar. "Judge, you cannot allow these tapes to be introduced. They will absolutely inflame this jury, and their admittance would be highly prejudicial to the prosecution's case. In addition, the prejudice would greatly outweigh the probative value of the evidence."

"Mr. Massey, would you go out and get the tapes. I want to see them before I make a ruling," said the judge.

Massey brought the video equipment into the judge's chambers and turned on the tape. During the film, Massey noticed the judge shaking his head in disbelief. When the tape ended, the judge looked up solemnly. "Well, gentlemen, there is no question that these tapes will inflame this jury against the victim. Mr. Arnold, however, is dead, while the defendant is fighting for her life. I will allow the tapes."

Massey tried to conceal his excitement. "Thank you, Your Honor."

"Now, I will grant Mr. Fillmore and his lawyer until Monday to get up here. If you finish with your witness early today, we'll recess. I've got plenty of work to do, and I can get home for the weekend earlier than I expected."

After filing out of the judge's chambers with a significant victory, Massey returned to the courtroom to get ready for what he hoped would be the successful testimony of his client. Massey leaned over and whispered to Kane, "Score one for our team. The judge is going to allow the videotape."

Kane grinned and gave him the thumbs up.

As the judge returned to the courtroom, the bailiff gave his usual pronouncement, everybody rose and then sat down. Judge Sheldon peered at Massey. "Who's your next witness, counselor?"

Massey rose to his feet. "Your Honor, my next witness is the defendant, Mrs. Leola Langley."

All eyes in the courtroom looked at Leola as she rose from her seat and walked to the witness chair. As she neared the chair, she turned and raised her right hand.

The clerk stood, "Ma'am, do you swear to give the whole truth, and nothing but the truth?"

"I do." Leola took her seat and looked at the jury.

"Your Honor, I have explained to the defendant that she does not have to testify in her defense, but she has agreed and waives her right against self-incrimination."

*We have reached the point of no return,* Massey thought to himself, fussing with papers on the table to steady his nerves. *We just rolled all the dice by putting Leola on the stand. The gamble is that if she is logical and coherent, will the jury believe that she was delusional when she killed Arnold and buy our argument that she didn't know the nature of her act? On top of that, the district attorney will try to discredit her testimony with her confession when he questions her on cross-examination. I hope she can hold up under his tough line of questioning.*

Massey moved over to the witness stand. "Mrs. Langley, let's start with your background. Tell the jury about your family?"

"Well, I was born in Abbieville, Georgia, and married mah husband Sam when I was eighteen. We all moved to California a year after we was married and had Sammy, and then we had Billy two years later. We live in Los Gatos. Mah husband works for a company called Spartan Electronics as a supervisor on the production line. I take care of mah kids and babysit and do housework to make ends meet. We're church-goin' Southern Baptists, try to make church every Sunday, though we don't always manage."

"In March of this year, what school did your son, Billy, attend, and what was his grade level?"

"Los Encinos Elementary School in Los Gatos, and my boy was in the fifth grade."

"Who was his teacher?"

Leola looked down. "A man by the name of Stanley Arnold."

"In March of this year, did you find out something disturbing about your boy, Billy, and the teacher, Mr. Arnold?"

Leola hesitated, then looked over at Susan, who gave her a smile, and then looked back at Massey. "One of Billy's classmates, his daddy called. He said the teacher put his hands down his boy's pants, and he also said that there was somethin' goin' on with the teacher and our Billy."

"What did you do after hearing this news?"

"My Sam went down to see the principal and got nowhere. Then the next day he went to the superintendent and the superintendent walked out on him."

"Mrs. Langley, what was the next course of action?"

"After gettin' nowhere, we decided to contact you,

195

Mr. Massey, to help us. We all went to the next school board meetin'. They wasn't any better and refused to do anything. You served them with some kind of papers. After that the police got involved."

"What happened next?"

"My understandin' was that the police were goin' to arrest the teacher, but before they could, they said he committed suicide."

"What happened to your son after the teacher's so-called suicide?"

"Billy's classmates blamed mah boy for the death of the teacher and began teasin' him and beatin' him up. He didn' want to go to school and then stayed in his room after school and weekends. He didn' even want to come to supper. Soon he started losin' weight from not eatin'. We was seein' Dr. Tishman, but Billy was gettin' worse."

Her voice was beginning to quiver and Massey saw she was having a hard time holding herself together, so he paused, poured a glass of water, and took it to her.

After a momentary pause, he went on. "When did you and your family start to see Dr. Tishman?"

"Sometime in May, this year."

"Did the doctor ever relate to you and your husband any opinions on whether or not there would be any lasting effects on the development of Billy?"

Leola hesitated a long time before giving her answer. Massey could see that she didn't want to get into this line of questioning, because the thought of Billy becoming a pedophile in the future was so repugnant to her that her denial system couldn't admit to even the remote possibility. Tears welled up in her eyes. Massey went over and handed her a box of tissues.

"Please proceed, Mrs. Langley," said the judge.

"Well, he said that my son would have some long-lasting effects."

"What long-lasting effects?" Massey asked.

In a whisper, she said, "That there was a good possibility that poor Billy would turn out to be . . ." And she paused, unable to go on.

"What?" Massey asked.

Leola took a deep breath, and then lamented, "A child molester." With that answer she started to sob, putting a tissue to her eyes.

Massey looked up at the judge. "Your Honor, can we have a few minutes while the witness calms down?"

"Ladies and gentlemen, let's take our morning recess early. We will reconvene in ten minutes," said the judge, a shred of impatience in his voice.

Leola regained her composure during the recess. Massey whispered, "You're doing great, keep it up."

The judge returned to the courtroom after ten minutes and Massey began questioning his witness again. "Mrs. Langley, how did the incident with the teacher, coupled with the doctor's opinion that your son might turn out to be a child molester, affect you?"

"I quit sleepin', worryin' about my little boy. Then I got an ulcer and started coughin' up blood. It hurt so much to see my Billy comin' home from school with bruises on his body. Then he refused to talk even to me, and he quit eatin'. I worried about his health. I tried switchin' schools, but the word got out, and the kids began teasin' him all over again. After a while Billy began losin' more weight. It was awful," she said, tears welling in her eyes again.

"How did your husband react to all of this?"

"Mah husband, Sam, refused to even discuss the matter. He started goin' to work at six in the mornin', and then came home most of the time after supper, sometimes after havin' one too many beers. Before too long, he was like a stranger livin' at home."

"Mrs. Langley, you mentioned that your son wasn't eating. What did Dr. Tishman finally have to do with Billy?"

"The doctor put him in the hospital because he was losin' so much weight. He said Billy was goin' to starve hisself to death if he didn't put him there."

"How long had you and your family been seeing Dr. Tishman?" Massey inquired.

"About six or seven weeks, two times a week."

"When was the last time you visited him?"

"The day before the shootin'."

"Prior to your visit to Dr. Tishman, did you discover that the teacher was in fact alive?"

"At first I got suspicious because I noticed that there were no death notices in the paper. I called you. I never heard nothin' after that, but about a month later when I was puttin' your wash away, I opened a drawer in your bedroom and found a file in there with that teacher's name on it. I shouldn't have looked, but I was curious."

"What did you find in the file?"

"There was an investigator's report in there. It said Mr. Arnold, the teacher, was alive and living in Susanville. I never heard of the place before. Not only that, but the report said he went by the name of Stewart and was teachin' little children all over again. I started shakin' all over. I was shocked and terrified that the evil man would come after my Billy again. It was horrible."

"Besides the investigator's report, what else did you find in the file?"

Leola hesitated, and then in a soft voice said, "A videotape."

"Mrs. Langley, you have to speak up. The jury can't hear the answer."

"A videotape," she answered in a slightly louder voice.

"Was there a title on the videotape?"

"I don't remember."

"Did you view the tape after you found it?"

Her mouth started to quiver. She wiped her eyes with a tissue, took a deep breath, then answered, "Yes."

"What did you see on the tape?"

Leola held the tissue in both hands and put them to her eyes, and quietly sobbed, then answered between her sobs, "Mah little boy being raped by his teacher." Her hands were shaking violently, and she took a deep breath trying to hold herself together.

"What happened to you after you saw that scene with your boy and his teacher? Take your time."

"I completely went to pieces. Mah mind started fillin' up with childhood memories that I'd forgotten all about."

"What memories?"

"About mah daddy," she answered in a soft voice.

"What about your father?" She remained silent.

"Mrs. Langley, you've got to answer this question." Massey looked over and saw the jury leaning over in their seats, waiting to hear her response.

Tears squeezed out of Leola's eyes. In a low voice, hardly audible, she said, "My daddy was rapin' me again."

"Mrs. Langley, you've got to speak louder so the jury can hear you. I know this question is embarrassing to you, but they need to hear this evidence."

In a slightly louder voice, she said, "My daddy was raping me again."

"In real life, had your father raped you when you were a child?" Massey asked. That question brought forth an outburst of emotion. Leola began to sob like a child and was rocking back and forth in her chair.

The judge interrupted this time, showing even more impatience as he said, "Let's take a recess, Mr. Massey, while your client regains her composure."

Massey went over to Susan during the break. "Poor Leola, she's having a hard time getting though the story."

Susan asked, "Why is the judge so impatient with her?"

"Most judges know that a crying woman tends to evoke a lot of jury sympathy, and the emotion they see tends to cloud their objectivity."

"You can hardly blame her for breaking down," answered Susan, who went to console Leola.

After about ten minutes, Leola got control of herself, and Massey started again. "Mrs. Langley, did your father rape you as a child?"

"Yes," she said looking down at the floor.

"What age were you when he started raping you?"

"Seven years old." Massey looked over at the jury and could see many of the jurors shake their heads with a look of bewilderment Several women were opening their purses and taking out hankies.

"How long did he continue to rape you?"

"Until I was fifteen, when I went to live with my aunt," she mumbled.

"How often did he sexually abuse you?"

Leola was now on the verge of tears again, but managed to answer softly, "One or two times a week."

"Louder please?"

"One or two times a week." With that answer, she completely broke down and began to tremble all over, sobbing at the same time. The judge again called a recess. His voice wasn't so impatient this time, because Massey could sense that the judge was shocked by the testimony he had just heard.

When the questioning began again, Massey asked, "Mrs. Langley, I know how sensitive this line of questioning is, but I have to go on. You began to tremble before the recess. Why?"

"I was thinking of all of the years of pain. It was terrible. I couldn't tell anybody. It hurt so badly. Mah daddy would rape me for so long it seemed like forever. I would bleed and beg him to stop. He treated me worse than his animals. But what was even worse was that my momma could hear me screaming for help and never came to help." She began to quietly sob again.

Massey looked over at the jury. Most of them had tears in their eyes, unable to comprehend the years of barbaric pain and humiliation that this woman had endured as a young girl.

He paused for a few moments so that Leola's testimony could really hit home, and then continued, "Let me change the subject and go to a confession that you gave to the sheriff after Mr. Arnold was killed. Do you remember talking to Sergeant Clark, the arresting officer, the day Mr. Arnold was killed?"

"No," she responded.

"Do you remember shooting Mr. Arnold?"

"No," she answered again.

"Do you know why you can't remember anything about the events during this period?"

"It's like I lost my memory. Mah last memory was findin' out that Mr. Arnold was alive and seein' the tape. I don't remember any shooting. I don't remember any arrest or any confession. The next thing I remember was being in jail in Susanville. God, I hope mah mind isn't going."

"That's all the questions I have, Your Honor," Massey said. He turned and took his seat at the counsel table. There was dead silence in the courtroom except for the quiet sobbing of Leola.

Steven Aaron rose and asked the judge if he could approach the witness. "Permission granted," said the judge.

Mr. Aaron rose from his chair, holding a copy of Leola's confession.

After Leola quieted down, Aaron walked to the witness stand. "Mrs. Langley, I'm going to hand you a confession which was given by you and ask that you read it to yourself."

Leola read the confession and then looked up.

"Mrs. Langley, is that your signature at the bottom of the document?"

"Yes, it does look like it."

"Your confession states that you acknowledged hiding behind a bush while holding a 20-gauge shotgun in the school parking lot, and as Mr. Arnold approached his car, you rose from your hiding spot, pointed the gun at Mr. Arnold, and pulled the trigger. Isn't that correct, Mrs. Langley?"

She looked at the confession again and took some more time reading it. Finally she looked up and said, "Well, that is what this paper says, but I don't have any recollection of shootin' anybody."

Steve Aaron placed a tape player on a small table in front of the jury. "Mrs. Langley, let me play a recording for you." The district attorney then punched the play button. The voice on the tape began,

Why did you kill him?
Because he deserved to die, and I would do it again if I had the chance.

The district attorney then pressed the off button and asked, "Mrs. Langley, is that your voice?"

"Yes, it sounds like mah voice," she answered.

"Mrs. Langley, you're trying to tell this jury that after you found the file about Mr. Arnold and discovered he was alive, that you have no recollection of any shooting or any confession whatsoever, isn't that right?" The district attorney was looking straight at the jury when he asked this question, hoping they would understand the ridiculousness of her answer.

"As I live and breathe, that's the truth," she answered and looked at the row of jurors herself. None of the jurors reacted, and Massey couldn't tell how her answer was received. The memory-loss alibi was a big hurdle. Massey hoped his next witness, Dr. Scott Smith, could put the pieces of the puzzle together.

"That is all, Mrs. Langley," said Aaron, returning to his seat.

"Mr. Massey, do you have any redirect?" inquired the judge.

"No, Your Honor."

"The witness is excused. Ladies and gentlemen, the hour is approaching for our evening recess. I have another calendar to take care of this afternoon, so we will reconvene Monday morning. Remember my admonition not to talk about the case among yourselves."

Massey, Susan and Kane walked back to the St. Francis Hotel. On their way, Massey reflected, "God, I knew her confession was big trouble for our case. The taped statement made it clear that she knew the consequences of her actions when she pulled the trigger. She knew she would harm the victim. Aaron will argue to the jury that her not remembering the event now is of no consequence, because it's the state of mind at the time of the killing. Being in an altered state of mind is irrelevant."

Kane said, "Yeh, I'm afraid he has a valid argument, ever since the state legislature eliminated diminished capacity as a defense to murder in the first degree."

Massey stated, "I think our defense is left with only two small openings. First, we can try to convince the jury that she was incapable of forming any intent at all when the shooting occurred because of her mental illness, or second, get the judge and jury to buy the PTSD defense on the flashback theory."

"Sounds like an uphill battle to me, gents," chimed in Susan.

# CHAPTER 25

Back at the hotel, Massey called Dr. Smith. "Scott, we are finished with Leola's examination. There will be a few brief witnesses Monday morning, and I'll be calling you sometime late that morning or early afternoon. Why don't you join Kane, Susan and me for dinner tonight at seven, and we'll go over what Leola had to say? Free meal, pal."

Dr. Smith walked into the St. Francis Restaurant and Bar a little after seven. As he neared their table, Massey looked up and saw him. He'd had his curls clipped, shaved his beard, and wore a coat and tie and a regular pair of shoes instead of sandals. "Hey Doc, I'm impressed. You look fashionable. Those ladies on the jury will fall in love with you," said a smiling Skip Massey.

Susan exclaimed, "Mmmm, I think I'll just dump Massey, and see if I can get your attention."

"Flattery will get you nowhere, ladies and gents. I hated to clip my hair and my beard. That's what I hide behind. Now, I feel naked with no hole to climb in," exclaimed Dr. Smith, embarrassed by all the attention.

The four of them went over Leola's testimony during dinner and planned the strategy for Smith's testimony.

▼

When Massey arrived at the courthouse Monday, he walked up the stone stairs to the courtroom. As he turned the corner, he spotted Gary Fillmore and his attorney standing in the hallway, waiting for the bailiff to open the courtroom door. He noticed that Fillmore no longer looked like the cocky school board member who had made the motion to retain Arnold in the classroom. Instead, he was pacing back and forth. *He looks nervous as hell,* Massey said to himself. Fillmore couldn't possibly know the extent of the information that Massey had on him, but he was probably fearful that Massey had discovered something.

After the court session was convened, Massey rose and announced to the court, "Your Honor, I would like to call Mr. Gary Fillmore to the stand."

A distinguished-looking man rose from the front row and addressed the court. "Your Honor, my name is Richard Darby. I am Mr. Fillmore's attorney. I want to introduce myself and my client to the court and to the jury."

"Thank you, Mr. Darby. Be seated up here at the counsel table, and we will start this morning's testimony," the judge responded.

Massey rose from his seat. "Your Honor, I would like to cross-examine Mr. Fillmore as an adverse witness whom I have subpoenaed to attend this trial."

"Permission granted, Mr. Massey."

"Mr. Fillmore, you were a member of the Los Gatos School Board in March of 1991, were you not?"

"Yes."

"Did you know a Mr. Stanley Arnold, and a Mr. Roland Garrity?"

"Yes." His attorney had obviously told him to keep his answers to a simple yes or no as much as possible.

"Who were they?"

"Mr. Arnold was a teacher at Los Encinos Elementary School, and Mr. Garrity was the Superintendent of the Los Gatos School District."

"Were you ever in business with either of these two gentlemen, or did you help finance their business?"

"No," he replied, showing no emotion.

*You lying bastard,* Massey said to himself. "What is your business, Mr. Fillmore?"

"I am in the printing business in Cupertino."

"Does your business own a printing press called the Heidelberg?"

There was a puzzled look on Fillmore's face as he answered, "Yes."

"What is the cost of such a press?"

"Approximately two and one half million dollars."

"Why so expensive?"

"Well, it is the best printing press in the world, because it produces high quality images," he answered again with a quizzical look on his face.

"Let me show you a poster, and I will ask you if this poster was printed on a Heidelberg press?" Massey reached down and pulled out one of the posters that Big Mike had obtained from the porn shop depicting young children in the nude.

"Your Honor, I would like to mark this exhibit as the defense's Exhibit 1." The clerk marked the exhibit and returned the poster to Massey.

Several of the jurors were trying to get a glimpse of the poster while he was carrying it to Fillmore and then spreading it in out front of him. Fillmore was visibly shaken when he saw it.

"Mr. Fillmore, let me show you this poster and ask you if it was printed by a Heidelberg printing press?"

"I can't tell," he answered nervously. Massey could see the jurors in the top row stretching their necks to get a peek.

"Did your firm print this poster?"

"Absolutely not," replied a now flustered Fillmore.

"Would you read the inscription at the bottom of the poster?"

Fillmore took the picture and said in a low voice, "It says, 'This poster is produced by Youth Fantasies Productions, Inc.'"

"Isn't that a company owned by you, Mr. Fillmore?"

"No." Sweat was forming on his forehead.

"Do you own any real property in the County of Santa Clara?"

"Yes."

"Could you tell the jury the location of each property?"

"Yes, my office building is located in Cupertino off

of Highway 280 and Highway 9, and my home is located in the town of Los Gatos."

"Is that all of the property that you own in Santa Clara County?"

"Yes," he said nervously. Fillmore started to get twitchy and could hardly sit still in his seat.

"Let me mark our next exhibit as number 2," Massey said as he gave the document to the clerk. "Now I'll show you a deed from the county recorder's office and ask you to read it to yourself silently."

Fillmore took the deed and looked visibly shocked when he read it. "Now, Mr. Fillmore, does this document refresh your recollection about a cabin you own?"

"Yes," said Fillmore, with more beads of sweat building on his forehead. His face reddened.

"This document is a certified copy of a deed in your name alone, which shows you own a parcel of land located above Saratoga on Big Basin Road. Is that correct, Mr. Fillmore?"

"Yes, I forgot about it since I haven't visited the property for months."

"Please describe the property."

"Well, it's a small cabin in the hills above Saratoga."

"Is it secluded?"

"Yes."

Massey had the clerk mark a series of ten pictures as Exhibit 3, a through j.

"Let me show you some pictures. Massey handed a few to him. "Do you recognize your cabin?"

"Yes, that is the cabin." He was now sweating profusely. He quickly loosened his tie and unbuttoned his shirt.

"Let me now show you a picture of the inside of the main room in the house, which shows movie-making equipment. Do you recognize that picture as depicting the inside of the main room in the cabin?"

"Yes."

"This is your production studio, isn't it, Mr. Fillmore?" Massey asked, eagerly awaiting his answer.

"Well, I have a hobby of taking pictures. I just left some of the equipment around."

"Isn't that overhead mike in the right-hand side of the picture used in making movie pictures?"

"Yes," he answered, as his Adam's apple bobbed up and down.

Massey walked to the clerk and gave her a videotape which was marked Exhibit 4.

"Mr. Fillmore, I am going to show you Exhibit 4, a videotape. It is a pornographic tape entitled *Play Time*, and it was produced by Youth Fantasies Productions, Inc., according to the credits on the videocassette. Have you ever seen this tape before?"

Before Fillmore could answer, he started stammering. He was looking at the floor like he wanted to dive underneath it. Finally, he looked up, took a deep breath and said, "No."

"In fact, Mr. Fillmore, you had a copy of that tape stored on a bookshelf at your cabin, didn't you?"

"Absolutely not," he answered in anguish.

"Let me show you a picture, marked Exhibit 5, and ask you if that's the bookshelf that is currently located in the living room of the cabin?"

"It could be."

"What do you mean, 'could be'? Look at the picture carefully. That is your cabin, and that is the bookshelf that sits in the living room. Correct?"

"Yeh," Fillmore answered. His voice sounded defeated and his head was down.

"Let me show you the picture marked Exhibit 6. It's a blowup of the bookshelf. Read me the title of the tape, the third from the left on the top shelf."

Fillmore looked at the blowup and was horrified at what he saw. He looked at his attorney with eyes that were pleading with Mr. Darby to come to the rescue.

Darby saw his client's distress signal, rose and shouted, "Objection, the question is irrelevant and immaterial."

The judge peered down at Darby and said, "Objection overruled. Proceed Mr. Massey."

"Mr. Fillmore, did you hear my question? What's the title of the tape, third from the left on the top shelf?"

Fillmore put his hands over his face and mumbled, *"Play Time."*

The judge angrily turned to the witness. "You, sir, answer that question louder so this jury can hear the answer."

"*Play Time,*" Fillmore said in a louder voice while shaking all over.

"Mr. Fillmore, I am going to put up a screen and show the video clip and then ask you some questions."

Aaron rose suddenly. "For the record Your Honor, this tape is objectionable as its highly prejudicial content outweighs its probative value."

"Mr. Aaron, as we discussed already in chambers, the tape is admissible. Proceed with your line of questioning, Mr. Massey."

Massey thought to himself, *After that line of questioning, poor old Fillmore is reeling and is probably on the verge of having a heart attack. This scumbag deserves everything he is getting.*

"Your Honor, before I proceed with the showing of the video, I must warn the jury that the tape is very graphic."

"Please proceed, counselor," commanded the judge.

Massey set up the video player and the screen. He had the bailiff dim the lights only slightly as he didn't want to miss the expressions of both Fillmore and the jurors. He began to roll the film. First the title appeared, *Play Time.* Soon the name of Youth Fantasies Productions, Inc. appeared on the screen. The initial part of the film showed the sun gleaming through the tall redwoods and then focused on a cabin. He stopped the film with the pause button.

Massey asked the witness, "Do you recognize that cabin as being your cabin?"

"Yes," said Fillmore, plainly gagging.

Massey then punched the play button, and soon the three young boys in clown costumes came on the scene and walked into the cabin. Before too long, a man appeared in a clown costume. After a few minutes the children were kissing his penis, and then the man fornicated a young boy from the rear. Massey looked over at the jurors, and there were horrified looks on all their faces.

Leola was sobbing with her head in her hands. Massey hated to do this to her, but her life was at stake. He knew at this moment that she hated him for exposing her son and revealing the much hidden secret. Even so, Massey punched the pause button on a scene that clearly showed Billy and Arnold in a compromising position.

"Mr. Fillmore, did you take those movies?"

"Objection, Your Honor. My client is going to invoke his Fifth Amendment right against self-incrimination," shouted a heated Mr. Darby.

"Granted," said the judge.

That was okay with Massey. He had been able to get into evidence the full horror of the movie so that the jury could now better understand the cause for Leola's actions.

Massey moved in front of the witness again and glared at him. "The man raping the defendant's son is Mr. Stanley Arnold, isn't it, Mr. Fillmore?"

After a long pause, the witness replied, "I don't know."

"Sure you do. You took those movies, didn't you, Mr. Fillmore?"

Darby stood up and shouted, "Same objection, Your Honor."

"Granted," said the judge. "Don't get into that line of questioning again, Mr. Massey."

"One last question, Mr. Fillmore. Mr. Arnold and Mr. Garrity owned a porn shop in San Francisco, and your company, Youth Fantasies Productions, Inc., distributed that movie to their porn shop, didn't it?"

"Objection, my client will take the Fifth," shouted Darby again.

"You don't have to answer that question, Mr. Fillmore," said the judge, who was looking at Fillmore with disgust.

"No more questions," Massey said and sat down.

Massey knew that the district attorney wouldn't want to touch this issue with a ten-foot pole. And he was right; Steve Aaron had no questions for the witness. When the court excused Fillmore, he ran out of the courtroom like a mouse fleeing a cat.

# CHAPTER 26

"My next witness is Mr. Mike O'Malley, Your Honor."

Big Mike rose from the first row and waddled to the witness stand. After taking the oath, he soon discovered his hips didn't fit between the arms of the witness chair. The judge peered down at Big Mike's predicament. "Mr. Bailiff, would you bring a chair without arms for the witness." Big Mike was red as a beet with embarrassment, but most of the jurors were smiling at him.

After Mike was finally seated, Massey began his questioning. "Mr. O'Malley, your occupation is a private investigator, and you were engaged by me to investigate several matters pertaining to this case. Is that correct?"

"Yes." Mike managed a smile and looked at the jury, many of whom smiled back because of his awkward beginning.

"Where did you obtain the poster that I had marked as Exhibit 1?" Massey rose, got the poster, and showed it to Mike. Once again, he could see several jurors trying to get a peek, obviously very curious about the poster.

"From a pornography shop known as the Adam and Eve Porno Shop in San Francisco."

"And who owns the porn shop?"

"A Mr. Stanley Arnold and a Mr. Roland Garrity."

"How do know that fact?"

"I obtained the business license for the porn shop with Garrity's home address listed as the owner. Then I heard a telephone conversation between the two men acknowledging their relationship."

The district attorney was on his feet. "Objection, Your Honor, I move to strike the part about the telephone conversation. This detective undoubtedly overheard the call using an illegal wiretap."

The judge leaned forward and peered at Big Mike. "Is that true, Mr. O'Malley?"

"I'm afraid it is, Your Honor."

The judge gave Mike a nasty look. "The part of the testimony referring to the telephone conversation is hereby stricken and the jury will disregard that portion of the testimony."

Massey had the business license marked as Exhibit 7 and showed it to Mike. "Is this the business license that you obtained on the Adam and Eve Porno Shop?"

"Yes, it is. And the address of two twenty-one Peabody, San Jose, California, is the home of Mr. Garrity."

"How are you sure it is the home of Mr. Garrity?"

"The home address was listed in the telephone book under Mr. Garrity's name. In addition, I was employed by you to conduct a surveillance on Mr. Garrity, and I saw him during the month of June 1991, entering and exiting the residence on several occasions."

Massey picked up the deposition of Roland Garrity from the table and had the deposition marked Exhibit 8. "Your Honor, I would like to read into the record from page 85, lines 2 though 4, the deposition of Mr. Roland Garrity, which was taken in my office in Palo Alto, California on June 18, 1991."

Mr. Massey: Question, Mr. Garrity, did you and
Mr. Arnold own the Adam and Eve Porno Shop?
Mr. Garrity: Answer, Yes.

Massey looked at the jury and several were shaking their heads. Putting the deposition down, Massey returned to his witness. "Did you purchase the videotape marked Exhibit 4, entitled *Play Time* and produced by Youth Fantasies Productions, Inc., at the Adam and Eve Porno Shop?"

"Yes."

"Did you visit Mr. Fillmore's cabin in the Santa Cruz Mountains?"

"Yes."

"Did you take pictures of the cabin through the windows, showing the filming paraphernalia?"

"Yes."

"And are these the pictures that you took that are marked Exhibit 3, a through j, and Exhibits 5 and 6, which I've already shown to Mr. Fillmore?"

Mike went through the pictures one by one, then responded, "Yes."

"Did you notice any videotapes when you were taking the pictures?"

"Yes, there was a whole bookshelf filled with videotapes on a wall opposite the window where I was taking shots. I got my zoom lens, located the video *Play Time*, and photographed it."

Massey looked again at the jury. Several jurors nodded at Massey. It was evident that they had put two and two together and concluded that the three men were in business together.

"Your Honor, I'd like to introduce into evidence all Exhibits 1 through 8."

Steve Aaron conferred for several moments with his two associates, then finally stood up. "No objection, Your Honor."

Massey breathed a sigh of relief. The district attorney probably could have made objections to several pictures because Massey was sure Mike had taken them illegally by trespassing on private property. The deposition, poster, and the tape in particular were clearly admissible and the most damaging, so Massey surmised that the district attorney didn't want to irritate the jury by appearing to want to hide something from them.

"Exhibits 1 through 8 will be admitted into evidence," ruled the judge.

Massey then took the poster and the pictures and passed them one by one to the jury. As the poster went from hand to hand, a look of shock appeared on each juror's face. They studied each picture carefully.

When the jury was through viewing the exhibits, Massey said, "Your Honor, I have no more questions of this witness."

Now the district attorney rose. "Mr. O'Malley, you tapped the telephone of Mr. Garrity and illegally overheard his telephone conversations, did you not?"

"Yes, sir, that's part of my business."

The judge looked at the witness with scorn.

"And you trespassed on Mr. Fillmore's property to take those pictures, didn't you?"

"I didn't think I did. There was no gate, and the road looked like a county road to me."

The district attorney thought he had a real opening to eliminate all of the previous embarrassing testimony. "Your Honor, I move to strike all of the testimony regarding the videotape since the witness trespassed on private property without a search warrant."

The judge peered down at O'Malley. "Were there any No Trespassing signs posted on the property?"

"No, sir," answered O'Malley, looking down at the floor.

"Was there any gate before entering the dirt road?"

"No, sir."

"I'm going to allow the testimony to stand since the witness said he thought it was a county road, no signs were posted indicating the property was private, and no gate blocked his entrance to the road. In addition, he didn't break into the property."

"No further questions," said the district attorney.

Massey had just two more questions himself. "Mr. O'Malley, how long have you been in the private investigation business?"

"Fifteen years, sir."

"Have you ever been charged with any crime in connection with your business practice?"

"No, sir."

"That's all the questions I have for this witness, Your Honor," said Massey. He returned to his chair, very pleased at the way the evidence was flowing.

"The witness is excused," said the judge.

Big Mike got up from his chair and waddled in front of the jury. He waved his hand and smiled at them. They were smiling back. They obviously liked the witness.

"Your Honor, my next witness is Susan Winters."

Susan rose from the front row and walked to the witness stand. After she was sworn in, she sat down.

"Mrs. Winters, were you able to view the tape, *Play Time?*"

"Yes, much to my chagrin."

"Did you recognize any of the individuals in the tape?"

"Yes, one of the young boys was Billy Langley, Leola's son. The other person I recognized was the adult male, Mr. Stanley Arnold, who was dressed as the clown and who sexually abused the young boy, Billy, in the film."

Massey saw several jurors bow their heads and put their hands to their faces to hide their emotions.

"How were you able to identify each of these two?"

"I've known the Langley family very well over the past four years. Billy has been in my home and I have been in his home many times when he was present. I easily recognized the boy. With regard to Mr. Arnold, my daughter was in his class six years ago, and during a parent-teacher conference I saw the Marine tattoo on his left forearm. When the clown undressed himself, his build and height were the same as Mr. Arnold, and the Marine tattoo was in the same location on his left arm where I saw it six years earlier."

"That's all I have of this witness, Your Honor."

The district attorney passed on cross-examination.

Massey's next witness was Chuck, the owner of the Starving College Student Movers, who identified Garrity in a picture as the man who moved the furniture from Stanley Arnold's apartment.

"Ladies and gentlemen, time for our lunch break. Be back at one-thirty. Remember the admonition."

# CHAPTER 27

When court reconvened after lunch, Massey called Dr. Smith to the stand. After the doctor had finished testifying on his background and his credentials, he was qualified by the judge as an expert witness.

Massey asked, "Doctor, how many times have you seen the defendant, and who else have you consulted?"

"I've seen Mrs. Langley three times, including last evening, and have consulted with Dr. Stan Tishman at the Stanford Hospital on two occasions."

"What did you discuss with Dr. Tishman?"

"He told me that he had been treating Mrs. Langley for a period of seven weeks, and during that time she was very distressed by what had happened to her son. During the period of treatment, she was generally rational and understood what she was doing. He did reveal that on the last visit, which was the day before the killing, she seemed disassociated, wasn't able to function, and he wasn't sure she understood what she was doing. He said he almost hospitalized her, but let her go home with her husband."

"In your conversations with Mrs. Langley, were you able to ascertain if there was a traumatic incident that occurred prior to her seeing Dr. Tishman?"

"Yes, on the day before her last visit with Dr. Tishman, she discovered an investigative file in your home, Mr. Massey. The report revealed that Mr. Arnold had not committed suicide, but in fact was living in Susanville. In addition, she saw a videotape in which her son was being raped by his teacher."

"Objection, Your Honor. I move to strike the hearsay answer of the doctor."

"Mr. Massey, what's your answer?" inquired the judge.

"Your Honor, it is my understanding that hearsay is admissible, because the law allows the expert to use hearsay in formulating his opinion."

"Very good answer, Mr. Massey. Objection to strike is overruled."

"Did you discuss with Dr. Tishman his visit with Mrs. Langley while she was in jail in Susanville after the killing occurred?"

"Dr. Tishman related to me that he saw Mrs. Langley seven days after the killing, and that she could not remember the killing or making a statement to the police or signing a confession."

Massey looked over at the jury. Several members were taking copious notes of the doctor's testimony. Others had blank stares as if they weren't buying Leola's testimony that she didn't remember the killing or the confession.

"Doctor, when did Mrs. Langley discover the investigative report and videotape?"

"Two days before the killing."

"When did you have the opportunity to first discuss the existence of a videotape with the defendant?"

"I met with the defendant two nights ago and asked if she ever saw a pornographic videotape entitled *Play Time*. At first, she couldn't recollect such a tape. I then obtained a tape player and showed her the scene where Mr. Arnold was raping her son. She was so shocked that she went into convulsions. This episode jarred her suppressed memory, and she was able to recall seeing the tape before at your home when she discovered your file on Mr. Arnold."

"Do you have any opinion as to why a person, such as Leola Langley, can't recall past events, but later is able to remember them?"

"It's a syndrome that the experts call shrinking retrograde amnesia. When a person suffers a high degree of stress, excitability or fear, the brain can become overloaded, and memory and learning deteriorate. When these conditions become intense, a region in the brain called the hippocampus, where long-term memory is stored, may shut down, causing memory loss. When a person suffers repetitive trauma and fear, this portion of the brain may be injured, causing a blank darkness shrouded in terrible feelings."

"Do people who have been sexually abused during their childhood often suffer this type of amnesia?"

"Many victims of repeated child abuse can recall little of their childhood. It's a very common phenomenon. However, another part of the brain, called the amygdala, perceives, comprehends, and retains the psychological pain of the sexual and emotional experience. A severely sexually abused child may forever feel traumatized, but not know why because the brain has suppressed the memory of the brutal abuse."

"Once the young child suppresses that childhood abuse, can he or she ever recall that childhood trauma?"

"Later in life, the forgotten memory may return to the surface of the brain and be remembered. These forgotten memories may resurface when the person is jarred by a catalytic event which may resemble an event that occurred to them years ago."

"When these buried memories suddenly resurface, what type of reaction does such a person have?"

"The reactions vary from individual to individual. They can show up in the form of revulsion and disgust, and range to the extreme of irrational and violent behavior."

"What is the explanation for such a wide variation in reactions?"

"During the lengthy period when a person can't remember the suppressed memories of the painful past, the part of the brain that retains the trauma keeps eating away at the underlying psyche. The extent to which the person absorbs and retains that pain during this lengthy period determines the severity of the reaction when the forgotten memories suddenly do resurface."

"In your opinion, did Mrs. Langley suffer from shrinking retrograde amnesia?"

"Yes, in my opinion, during the period of eight years when she was being violently raped by her father, the pain was too much for her long-term memory to handle and she suppressed the memories of the horror that she endured."

"In your opinion, did a catalytic event suddenly cause her long-term memory to surface these childhood memories?"

"Oh yes. When she saw her son being raped in the video scene, it was the catalytic event that caused her mind to recall the nearly identical painful incidents that she suffered at the hands of her father."

"And what type of reaction did Mrs. Langley have?"

"Upon the sudden recollection of her past childhood, Mrs. Langley had a severe reaction. Her mind took on a sudden and significant personality change known as an 'altered state of mind,' commonly referred to as a state of hallucination. This is a state of mind wherein that person has no conception of what he or she is doing, but is totally divorced from reality. People in this state are not masters of their actions."

"Is there any similarity to a flashback situation that other types of people may have?"

"Mrs. Langley's personality change was very parallel to what Vietnam veterans went through years after they came home from the war. This syndrome resulted in an altered state of mind, and when some catalytic event suddenly caused the painful war memories to resurface, many veterans thought they were on a battlefield, being attacked by the enemy."

"Objection, Your Honor," shouted the district attorney. "The witness is testifying about the post-traumatic stress syndrome defense, which is used in some cases where a Vietnam veteran is involved. This defense is not applicable in this situation, because she is not a veteran. I request the court to strike the last answer."

The judge beckoned both attorneys to approach the bench for a conference. "Your Honor," Massey began, "the witness is merely making an analogy, comparing the Vietnam veteran's situation with the experience that the defendant went through, in order to make it clear to the jury as to what caused her reaction and change in personality."

"May I respond?" the district attorney asked.

"Certainly, Mr. Aaron," said the judge.

"Her confession is a clear indication that she intended to pull the trigger and cause harm to the victim. At the moment she pulled the trigger, she knew that she would inflict harm. It is the prosecution's position that at the time of the killing, even though she may have had diminished mental capacity, this type of situation is no longer a defense to murder in the first degree in the State of California."

Massey spoke up. "And it is the opinion of the defense that the testimony should be allowed as we are attempting to show not diminished capacity, but a mental breakdown so severe that she couldn't formulate any intent whatsoever to cause harm."

The judge held his head in his hands for a few seconds, then responded, "Gentlemen, this issue seems to be the crux of this case. I am going to allow the testimony, but I will make it clear to the jury, through jury instructions, what the law is regarding the requisite intent or state of mind at the time of the killing."

The district attorney spoke. "I would like to *voir dire* the medical expert in chambers regarding his knowledge of and his work with Vietnam veterans, because the court decisions are very strict in requiring the medical expert to have extensive knowledge and experience in this field."

Massey knew that Aaron had the right of *voir dire* to interrupt the cross-examination of Smith so that he could question his qualifications to testify on the post-traumatic stress syndrome defense. Aaron certainly wanted to keep this testimony from the jury.

Both attorneys, the judge, and the court reporter retired to the judge's chambers, and the district attorney soon found out about Dr. Smith's extensive work and treatment of Vietnam veterans. The judge had no trouble in ruling that Dr. Smith could testify in this area, and they all returned to the courtroom.

After asking about the doctor's extensive medical background and his experiences in Vietnam, Massey then stated, "Doctor, you were beginning to compare the defendant's mental state with what happens to some Vietnam veterans, years after they have returned home from the war. Please continue with your answer."

"During the Vietnam war, soldiers saw all kinds of atrocities—massacres of innocent women and children, the killing of their own buddies—and all experienced the dread that they might be the next to die. The impact of these horrific events was often too much for their psyches. Many of these men suppressed the memories of their painful experiences, but still retained in their subconscious mind the pain they had suffered during the war, not knowing in later years why they were in such pain. Frankly, that is why so many of these veterans turn to hard drugs. They're trying to relieve the underlying pain that their brain has retained."

"What may occur thereafter?"

"Years later, some catalytic event occurs, and some veterans will have a flashback to their war experiences. Often they hallucinate and become violent. In their altered state of mind, they truly believe they are reliving a battle. They try to defend themselves and on occasion strike out and kill an innocent bystander."

Massey continued, "Does the defendant's situation parallel the violent reactions that sometimes occur with Vietnam veterans when they have flashbacks?"

"Yes, I think that she suffered a significant and an ugly reaction as evidenced by the killing that occurred."

"Do patients who have buried significant tragedies in their lives have any control over their behavior when the buried painful memory suddenly resurfaces?"

"Most often, persons with deep-seated suppressed pain become walking time bombs. They have little control over themselves when an event triggers a significant personality change. They, like the Vietnam veterans, have flashbacks, and many times they exhibit very irrational behavioral patterns."

"When a person suffers such a violent reaction and kills another person, do they know what they're doing when they point a gun at a victim and pull the trigger?"

"As I said a few minutes ago, when a person's mind is in a state of hallucination, they are divorced from reality and have no control over their actions. However, their mind in the hallucinatory state does intend to kill the victim."

"Thank you, doctor, that is all the questions I have for you."

The district attorney rose and said, "Dr. Smith, the plain fact is that Mrs. Langley, when she pulled the trigger of the shotgun, probably intended to kill the teacher. Isn't that correct?"

"Yes, but as I have answered, she had no control over herself. She was out of touch with reality."

"Dr. Smith, I have a simple question for you. Did you read the confession of the defendant and hear the voice tape taken when she made the confession?"

"Yes, I did," replied the doctor.

"Now this tape was taken of the defendant only forty-five minutes after the murder. Isn't it clear to you after reading her signed statement and hearing the voice tape, that the defendant was in complete control of herself, understood the questions and gave rational answers?"

"Yes, that is true, but it is my opinion that when a person is hallucinating, they can appear to be in total touch with reality, just as you and I are right now. But in truth, they are not masters of their minds and actions."

"I have no further questions of this witness, Your Honor."

Massey rose. "Dr. Smith, what is the meaning of the word 'hallucinating'?"

"It's a false perception of reality. One who is hallucinating is out of touch with reality. They are in an altered state of mind."

"Doctor, when a person is hallucinating, do they have an ability to distinguish between right and wrong?"

"No, they are out of touch with reality," finished the doctor.

Massey rested the case for the defense. He thought the case had ended on a high note, at least from a strategic standpoint. When he sat down, the jury could see Leola sobbing quietly. At this moment in time, he was sure the jury thought that the teacher deserved everything he got, and that if they were in the defendant's shoes, they would have done the same thing.

However, Massey had learned over the years that jury temperament can change quickly. Whether the jury would be in this frame of mind when they went to deliberate this case was anybody's guess.

Massey also knew there was trouble ahead in two areas. The district attorney had wisely decided to postpone the examination of his own medical expert and use him as a rebuttal witness at the very end of the trial. His expert could go to school on the defense's medical experts, and then, when called to the stand, would refute what they had to say. Jurors also tend to remember the testimony of the last witness more than previous witnesses. Secondly, the judge's instructions were going to play a big part in the outcome of the trial. That phase of the trial would occur after both parties rested their case. Massey figured the next witness would be very challenging to their defense.

# CHAPTER 28

A confident-looking Steve Aaron stood up. "Your Honor, my rebuttal witness is Dr. Wade Clevenger." Dr. Clevenger walked to the witness stand and was sworn in. In his mid-fifties, the doctor was dressed in an expensive gray flannel suit and a silk tie. He was a good-looking man with a solid head of dark hair.

The district attorney asked him about his credentials. They were impeccable: a graduate of Stanford Medical School, an internship at UCLA Medical Center, with his residency at the University of San Francisco Medical Center. He was board certified in the field of psychiatry and had testified in more than twenty murder cases, primarily for the prosecution, but occasionally for the defense.

"Dr. Clevenger, have you interviewed the defendant, Mrs. Leola Langley?"

"I saw the defendant seven days after the murder for about two hours, and then again a week later for a period of four hours."

"What were your observations of the defendant?"

"On both occasions, she was coherent, able to understand my questions, and her answers were clear and well reasoned. She did not, however, recall the murder or the confession that she gave to the sheriff."

Mr. Aaron continued, "Doctor, have you reviewed the confession that she gave the afternoon of the murder?"

"I reviewed not only her signed confession, but also the voice tape that was recorded during her interview."

"Did she sound coherent and able to understand the questions that were asked of her by the officer the day of the murder?"

The doctor responded, "Yes, based on her answers to the questions posed, she clearly understood what she was doing during the course of that interview."

"At the time she made the confession, from your review of the transcript of the confession, did she seem to understand that she had killed the victim?" pursued the district attorney.

Massey rose, "Objection, Your Honor, the expert cannot testify as to the state of mind of the defendant at the time of the killing."

"Overruled," said the judge. "The question posed was not the state of mind at the time of the killing, but when she made the confession."

Massey felt the judge was probably correct, but his ruling really hurt the case. The district attorney continued, "Doctor, let's have the reporter read back the last question."

Massey thought to himself, *Good tactic, Aaron. Having the reporter read the question back to the jury gets the jury really focused on the ultimate answer.*

The court reporter read back, "At the time she made the confession, did she seem to understand that she had killed the victim?"

"Her answers indicated that she clearly understood the interrogator's questions, and her answers were logical, revealing her soundness of mind. In addition, she stated she had intended to kill him and said she would do so again if she had a chance."

"Based on the confession transcript, what is your opinion of whether or not she understood the difference between right and wrong?"

"Based on her statements, it is my opinion that she was able to comprehend the difference between right and wrong at the time of the killing," answered the doctor.

Massey jumped out of his seat and shouted, "Objection, Your Honor, the district attorney and his witness are out of line. May I approach the bench?"

The judge nodded his head, and Massey and Aaron approached the bench. The court reporter moved herself and her stenographic machine over to them so she could record the conversations.

"State the reason for your objection, Mr. Massey."

"The doctor's answer is totally inappropriate because he has just given the jury the answer to the question that they alone must decide, which is to determine the state of mind of the killer at the exact instant of the killing. Both he and the district attorney know full well that this answer is not proper, and they tried to sneak it in before I could object. The doctor's testimony severely prejudices the defendant's case."

The judge looked at Steve Aaron with fire in his eyes. "Mr. Aaron, you and your expert witness are over the line. You know very well that the doctor's opinion is not admissible on this issue. I will order the last sentence of the doctor's testimony stricken. I know it is difficult for the jury to forget the testimony when I tell them to disregard it. One more abuse of the rules of evidence, and I will declare a mistrial and sanction both you and your expert."

As counsel returned to their seats, the judge ordered, "Ladies and gentlemen of the jury, I am ordering the last sentence of the doctor's testimony stricken. It is your decision alone to decide the defendant's intent at the exact time of the killing. An expert's testimony on this very issue is not admissible."

The district attorney resumed his questioning of the doctor with a little less enthusiasm. "Doctor, how long after the murder did Mrs. Langley make her confession?"

"According to the coroner's report, the victim died about ten after twelve in the afternoon, and according to the tape, the recording started at one-fifteen."

"Based on your interview with the defendant, coupled with her taped conversations and her confession, what was the motive for the killing of the victim?"

"Objection, Your Honor, there is no way the doctor can testify as to motive based on that tape. The testimony is pure conjecture," Massey argued.

"Sustained," said the judge.

The district attorney was not going to give up. "Doctor, based on your interview with the defendant, the tape and the confession, do you have an opinion as to her motive?"

"Same objection, Your Honor," Massey remarked.

"Mr. Aaron," said the judge, "ask the doctor if there is anything in the tape or the confession that sheds any light on a motive for the killing."

The district attorney repeated the judge's question. The doctor said, "No, but I have learned that during this trial, there has come to light some evidence that the victim had sexually molested Mrs. Langley's son. I believe revenge was her motive," said the doctor. "It is the strongest of human responses. A mother getting even with somebody who has hurt her child. The eye-for-an-eye rule has permeated society for centuries."

"I have no further questions for this witness, Your Honor." Mr. Aaron sat down.

Massey knew he had to be careful with Dr. Clevenger so as not to anger the jury by being too rough with him. He knew he must couch questions in a nice manner and hope the doctor would go out on a limb, stretch his testimony beyond reason. Massey rose from his chair and stood before the witness. "Doctor, do you have the notes that you took when you interviewed the defendant? And may I see them?"

The doctor went through his file, which was before him, and handed the notes to Massey. Massey went to his seat and studied them for a few moments.

He then rose. "Doctor, I reviewed your notes and your opinion of the defendant's mental condition. The opinion expressed in your report and in your testimony today is based only on your interviews with the defendant and the notes of Dr. Tishman. Is that correct?"

"Obviously," was his curt answer.

"Now, while you haven't been allowed in the courtroom during the testimony of the defendant and her medical experts, have you received information from any source as to the content of their testimony?"

"Yes, Mr. Aaron told me about the testimony of the defendant and her medical experts."

226

Massey then asked, already knowing what his answer would be, "Doctor, after you received this information, did you make any changes in your opinion that the defendant was of sound mind before the killing?"

"Certainly not."

"Well, when you formed your opinion of the defendant's mental condition, you didn't have all the facts, did you?" Massey knew again what this egotist's answer would be.

"I had all the facts I needed to form my opinion. My interviews and the confession were more than sufficient," he stated with conviction.

"During your interview with the defendant, did you find out that she had been sexually abused by her father from the age of seven to the age of fifteen?"

The doctor answered curtly, "No."

"During your interview with her, did you know that her father raped her one to two times a week during her adolescence?"

"No," snapped the witness. It was obvious he didn't like rendering opinions without knowing all the facts, and he was now chagrined because this subject never came up during his examination of Leola.

"Were you ever able to find out if she had psychiatric care to heal the pain and suffering she endured for eight years as a young child?"

"Well, I know she was treated by Dr. Tishman of Stanford for a seven-week period," stated the witness.

"Are you aware that the defendant never revealed to Dr. Tishman the abuse that she received from her father?"

"Well, I didn't see anything in his notes that indicated she revealed this information."

"When you interviewed the defendant, did she tell you her son had become a scapegoat at school for the death of Mr. Arnold, and that her son's classmates ridiculed him and even physically assaulted him?"

"No, but the notes of Dr. Tishman revealed that the mother was alarmed about the abuse her son was receiving at school."

"Do you know what impact this situation had on the boy?"

"I knew that he became very depressed, withdrawn, and then began refusing to eat his meals, to the point where Dr. Tishman thought the boy was suffering from anorexia and eventually hospitalized him."

"And what impact did the boy's deteriorating condition have on the mother?"

"Dr. Tishman's report indicated she became mentally depressed and physically ill."

"When you interviewed the defendant, did you find out that her son had been raped and sodomized by the victim?"

"No," the doctor stated impatiently.

"Doctor, could any of these events that I've just described have an impact on Mrs. Langley's mental condition when the killing took place?"

"I'm not sure."

"Could these events have prevented Mrs. Langley from forming an intent to kill the teacher?"

"Absolutely not. Based on her confession, she knew exactly what she was doing when she killed the man," said the arrogant doctor.

"Do you know what the mental state of the defendant was when she was last seen by Dr. Tishman, the day before the killing?"

"Dr. Tishman stated in his notes that she didn't act normally during their last interview."

"In fact," said Massey, "his notes reveal that he thought she was, in effect, not there, oblivious to her surroundings and, in Dr. Tishman's opinion, not able to comprehend what he was saying or what she was doing. Is that correct?"

"That's the essence of what he said," Dr. Clevenger reluctantly replied.

"The sixty-four thousand dollar question, doctor, is that you don't have any clue as to the defendant's state of mind at the time of the killing, do you?"

The district attorney jumped to his feet. "Objection, Your Honor, counsel is now asking the same question about her state of mind at the time of the killing."

"Objection sustained. If you ask that question again, Mr. Massey, I will allow the doctor to testify on his opinion of the defendant's state of mind at the time of the killing. I know you don't want me to allow that question."

Massey continued, "Doctor, do you know how long the defendant continued in her hallucinatory state of mind after she left Dr. Tishman's office?"

"I can't answer that because I didn't see her until several days after the killing. In reviewing Dr. Tishman's notes, I find that he never came to the conclusion that she was in a state of hallucination. However, based on the confession given later that day, her answers didn't sound like she was in a trance or hallucinating. Rather, her answers were rational. She responded to the interrogating officer in a cogent manner, and in my opinion understood that she would cause bodily harm to the victim when she pulled the trigger."

Massey was angry. "Your Honor, the doctor just violated your admonition to him not to render an opinion on the defendant's state of mind at the time of the killing. I find his behavior contemptuous, and would ask the court to reprimand the witness."

The judge responded, "Objection sustained. The jury will disregard the doctor's testimony on the defendant's state of mind at the time of the killing." The judge then leaned over the bench and looked directly at Dr. Clevenger. "Doctor, I have already warned you once not to testify about the state of mind of the defendant at the time of the killing, and you just now blatantly disregarded my order. I will therefore schedule a contempt hearing immediately after this trial where you will learn what happens in my court when you deliberately disregard my order."

The doctor seemed taken aback by the severity of the judge's remarks as he put his hands to his temples and shook his head.

Massey waited for a few moments for the impact of the interchange to sink in. "Doctor, people suffering from hallucinations eventually return to their normal state, don't they?"

"I seriously doubt that she hallucinated. She was out for revenge."

"Your Honor," Massey said angrily, "The answer is nonresponsive. I request it be stricken."

Once again the judge leaned over the bench and gave the doctor a very stern look. "The jury will disregard the doctor's last comment. Doctor, you are bordering on some heavy sanctions. You just answer the question asked. You do not, in my court, offer gratuitous comments that are prejudicial to the other side. No more deviations from the question."

"Doctor, have you ever heard of the post-traumatic stress syndrome defense?"

"Yes."

"Given the same amount of stress that the Vietnam veterans suffered, don't you think that a female, with the same degree of stress, might also suffer flashbacks similar to those experienced by men fighting in that war?"

"Certainly, but I think the situation would have to parallel the experience of those veterans, which was very severe, very extreme."

"Have you ever treated a battered wife?"

"Objection, Your Honor," stated Steve Aaron.

"Approach the bench, counselors," the judge replied.

"Mr. Aaron, what's the basis for your objection?"

"Your Honor, the PTSD defense has never been extended to a battered wife or to any party other than Vietnam veterans, and hence this question is irrelevant."

"What's your reply, Mr. Massey?"

"Your Honor, there are two battered wife syndrome cases up on appeal, where wives killed their husbands. At least one of the two cases will be decided imminently. I think it would be prejudicial to the defendant not to allow this testimony on the record, particularly if the appellate courts determine that this defense is valid."

"She's not a battered wife, so counsel is really stretching the argument. This type of testimony is very prejudicial as it invokes sympathy for the defendant and gives credibility to her actions," replied the district attorney vociferously.

"One last comment, Your Honor," Massey stated quickly, before the judge could make his ruling. "It isn't the question of whether she is an abused wife or abused child, it's a question of the degree of abuse that the psyche suffered which triggers the violent action of the psychologically impaired person."

The judge was silent for several seconds, looked up at the ceiling, and then looked at Massey. "I am going to allow your question, Mr. Massey, primarily for appellate purposes, so that you can preserve on the record testimony concerning this defense."

The attorneys returned to their seats. Massey was pleased with the ruling. He noted on his yellow pad, *Call office and find out status of battered wife cases.*

"Ladies and gentlemen of the jury, I am going to overrule the prosecution's objection and allow the testimony."

"Thank you, Your Honor," Massey replied. "Now doctor, let me have the reporter read back the question to refresh your memory and that of the jury."

The reporter read back the question, asking the doctor if he had ever treated a battered wife in his practice. "Yes, several times."

"Were any of these women severely battered over a period of years?"

"Yes."

"And they came to you because they needed treatment for their current psychological condition?"

"Yes."

"Doctor, can you imagine a situation wherein the physical and mental abuse inflicted by a husband on a wife over a lengthy period of years would equal the same abuse suffered by those veterans on the battlefield in Vietnam?"

"No, not even close," said the confident doctor.

Massey looked over at the woman jurors. One caught Massey's eye and shook her head as if to say, *What a ridiculous answer. What a putdown to women.*

"Please explain the reasoning behind your answer."

"Well, in my opinion, I don't think any amount of marital abuse can equal the sight of seeing innocent women and children slaughtered. In addition, these veterans saw their buddies killed before their eyes.

They witnessed slow and agonizing deaths. Lastly, every night when they tried to sleep and couldn't, they listened for some Viet Cong soldier sneaking up to slit their throats. They lived in constant fear."

"So, you don't believe that a woman who has been raped and beaten to a bloody pulp for years, who lives from day to day in constant fear of the next beating which may end her life, whose self-esteem has been shattered for so many years that she feels like she's a nonentity, has suffered mental trauma equal to that of the veteran you just described?"

"No," answered the doctor with conviction.

"Thank you for your testimony, doctor. That is all the questions I have for this witness."

Steve Aaron rose, knowing that some of the jurors had been disturbed by the doctor's answers. "Dr. Clevenger, you served your country in the army during the Vietnam war, is that correct?"

"Yes, as a young psychiatrist."

"Did you actually witness the horrors of war?"

"Oh, yes, I had firsthand knowledge of the impact of that war on the minds of the men who served."

"Thank you, doctor. No more questions," said the district attorney. He sat down, confident that he had rehabilitated Dr. Clevenger.

Massey was on his feet immediately. "A couple more questions, Your Honor." The judge nodded.

"Doctor, have you ever witnessed firsthand a wife beating, in which the husband pulverized the wife so that her face was turned into a bloody pulp?"

"Obviously not. I only see the battered wife as a patient after the damage has been done," retorted the irritated witness.

"So your previous testimony about the mental trauma suffered by a battered wife is all based on second-hand information, which has been given to you by a battered client."

"That's partially correct, but I also used my experiences during the war. I do see the end result of the trauma when I treat the battered wife."

"I believe your testimony was that the trauma that

a battered wife suffers isn't even close to that of the Vietnam vets you described previously. Correct, doctor?"

"That was my testimony," answered the doctor curtly.

"And, you've never witnessed firsthand a child being raped by her father to such an extent that her vagina was raw and bleeding?"

"No, I haven't."

"Do you have an opinion on whether or not a child who receives this type of extreme abuse over an eight-year period would have an equal or greater amount of damage to her psyche compared to the Vietnam vet you described?"

"Objection. Mr. Massey's question is asking for the doctor to speculate," said the district attorney.

"Sustained."

"I have no further questions of the witness." Massey turned and sat down. He frankly didn't care what the doctor's answer was going to be. He thought he got the message across to the jury that Leola had just as much right to use the defense as did a soldier of war.

The judge dismissed the doctor as a witness. As he walked in front of the jury box, Massey noticed that none of the jurors were looking at the doctor.

Steve Aaron rose. "I have no more witnesses, Your Honor."

"Mr. Massey, do you have any rebuttal witnesses?"

"No, Your Honor."

"Ladies and gentlemen of the jury, the trial phase of this case has now ended. I'm going to call a recess until tomorrow morning at ten. I will be busy early in the morning, going over jury instructions with the attorneys. The attorneys will present closing arguments as soon as we finish preparing the instructions. Thereafter, I will give instructions to you, and after that you will commence deliberating."

*Now comes the moment of truth,* Massey said to himself.

# CHAPTER 29

When Massey returned to the hotel with Susan, he immediately picked up the phone in the room and dialed his office. "Helen, please connect me with Dan Hult in library."

Dan answered and Massey spoke with a tone of urgency, "Dan, Massey here. We just finished the trial and will be arguing jury instructions tomorrow morning. I need you to call the clerks of those two appellate courts handling the battered wife syndrome cases and find out their status. Give me a call back this evening or early tomorrow. By the way, I liked the jury instructions you sent up this week. I sent them on to the judge with very few revisions."

"Thanks, I'll get on it right away."

Twenty minutes later Dan Hult was again on the line. "Good news, Mr. Massey. I called the clerks of the two appellate courts. The clerk of the First Appellate District in San Francisco told me she had heard that the battered wife case had been decided. The decision was somewhere between the judges, their secretaries, the deputy clerk, and the reporter of decisions. Unfortunately, the exact whereabouts of the decision is unknown. She thought it was in the judge's hands for review before the final decision is published."

"Dan, get the name and phone number of the head clerk of the judge that wrote the opinion, and I'll stick Big Mike on this."

At about five minutes to five, Dan called back with the clerk's name and her telephone number. Massey hung up and dialed Mike O'Malley. "Mike, I'm in a bind.

We finished the Langley trial this afternoon, and I have to argue the case tomorrow morning. There is an important decision concerning the battered wife defense that was just decided in the First Appellate District in San Francisco, but nobody knows exactly who's got it. Let me give you the name and the phone number of the head clerk. See if you can track down the decision and get me a copy?"

Mike hung up with, "Let me at 'em."

That night, Massey worked his buns off preparing his closing argument, reviewing the case law and drawing a chart that he always displays to the jury, setting forth the issues to be decided by them and important evidence bearing on those issues.

▼

The next morning, the phone in Massey's room rang early. He rolled over from a dead sleep, rubbed his eyes, and picked up the phone. "Hope I didn't get you up too early, Massey." It was Big Mike.

"Not if you have good news."

Mike continued, "I must admit, I've been lucky in this case. I was able to reach the chief clerk last night. She was very reluctant to help out and almost hung up on me. But after I told her the story of Leola, then she couldn't help enough. She contacted the presiding judge at his home and found out that he had just given the decision to his secretary, having finally proofed it and gotten it approved by the other judges. The clerk promised me that the secretary would forward the transcript of the decision via the computer first thing in the morning, and that I could pick up a copy at 8 a.m. today. I'm calling from my car in front of the courthouse. I should have it soon, and I'll fax it up shortly."

"Mike, if you were a woman, I'd give you a great big kiss. Maybe this will turn out to be huge break."

Promptly at nine, Massey walked into the judge's chambers where he and the district attorney were having a cup of coffee. "Coffee, Mr. Massey?"

235

"Yes, thanks. No cream or sugar." Massey took the cup of coffee from the judge's clerk and sat in the vacant chair in front of the judge.

"Gentlemen, I've read the proposed jury instructions that each of you submitted. There are a few issues that I would like to discuss before I make my final decision."

Massey raised his hand like a school kid. "Your Honor, I received a supplemental case this morning that I would like to submit in support of the defense's request for the post-traumatic stress syndrome instruction. It was published this morning at eight in the First District of the Appellate Court." Massey handed a copy to the judge and district attorney.

The judge grinned and looked at Massey. "Impressive, counselor, the ink on the pages of this decision is still wet." The judge took several minutes reading the decision, then looked up. "Very interesting."

The judge reached into his drawer and pulled out a cigar. "Vile things. I normally wait until later in the day, but since this will take a while, I'll have time to enjoy every puff on this fine Cuban." Massey took a sip of his coffee, eagerly awaiting the judge's remarks about the new case.

Judge Sheldon pushed his chair back from his desk, leaned back, took a big puff with his huge hands clasped behind his neck, and said, "Gentlemen, let me tell you both about my approach as a judge to the case law of this state. I happen to be a strict constructionist when it comes to the United States and California state constitutions. I believe strongly in the separation of powers between the three branches of government. I do not favor legislators curtailing the powers of the judiciary, nor do I favor judges attempting to act as legislators in passing new laws from the bench on the excuse that they are merely redefining or interpreting a statute."

The judge continued, "Mr. Massey, the case you just handed me makes strong inroads into Penal Code 28, which abolished diminished capacity as a defense to murder. Our appellate courts were all over the block on the interpretation of Penal Code 28 until Judge Edward

236

Panelli of the State Supreme Court wrote his decision earlier this year in *People v. Saille*. The Supreme Court concluded, and let me quote from page 1113, 'Once the trier of fact finds a deliberate intention unlawfully to kill, no other mental state need be shown to establish malice aforethought.' This decision means that if a mentally ill person kills somebody, but knows at the time of the killing the consequences of that action, he or she is guilty of murder in the first degree."

Skip Massey felt sick to his stomach, because he knew where the judge was headed.

"Now, Mr. Massey, with regard to our case, there is clear evidence from her confession and her voice tape that the defendant knew the consequences of her actions when she pulled the trigger. While your medical experts support the theory that she was in a trance or in an altered state of mind or was suffering a flashback, the evidence is clear that she intended the defendant harm. There is no contradicting evidence."

"Judge, she's no cold-blooded murderer. How can the law be so blind?"

The judge continued, "Mr. Massey, I know how you feel. Two very recent appellate decisions have broadened Judge Panelli's opinion and have allowed the use of the post-traumatic stress syndrome defense in the case of Vietnam veterans having a flashback. Unfortunately, I can't allow your client to use such a defense as there is no precedent."

"But, Your Honor, how about the battered wife case I just gave you? The court has broadened the defense and applied it to nonveterans."

"Mr. Massey, the case that you gave me this morning is very interesting. It certainly broadens the use of the PTSD defense even further to include not only the veterans but battered women."

Massey looked up, thinking that maybe the judge would get gutsy and extend this battered woman theory to Leola.

"My reaction to your new case is that if we applied this defense to your client, we would be broadening the defense even further to the non-wife situation such as yours. However, I am not about to act as a legislator and stretch this defense even further than it has already been stretched by the First Appellate District Court. Undoubtedly, this appellate case will be appealed to the State Supreme Court. This appellate decision is far from final. The judges in this case are from the liberal San Francisco area where they think they are legislators and make laws instead of adjudicating. I am not going to make law. I will apply only the existing law."

Massey suddenly felt like upchucking on the judge's desk.

"In light of the evidence presented, namely the confession and tape which show the defendant had a clear understanding of the nature of her act when she pulled the trigger, I am not inclined to buy the theory of the 'altered state of mind' as a defense to murder, no more than I would allow the irresistible impulse defense theory which is almost an identical theory. The legislature in my view did away with these psychological defenses. These issues are relevant only in the penalty phase of the case and cannot be used to show that the defendant did not have the requisite intent to kill."

Massey felt as if the judge had just stuck a sharp knife in him and twisted it.

The judge then read to the attorneys the instructions he intended to give to the jury. Not one of Massey's instructions was included.

Massey knew he was bleeding all over the floor. He was worried sick about Leola's defense. He rose from his seat in total frustration. "Your Honor, you can't be serious. You leave no room for the jury to find the defendant guilty of voluntary or involuntary manslaughter, much less an acquittal. Surely there is sufficient evidence for the jury to find that she did not have the requisite intent."

"Mr. Massey, manslaughter is reserved for negligent killings, or heat of passion killings where there is no cooling-off period. The facts of this case do not fit into the manslaughter category. I am sorry, Mr. Massey. I have great compassion for your client. She has suffered probably more than any defendant that I have had in my courtroom. Her long-standing suffering will be given great weight in the penalty phase of this case, but not in the guilt phase of this case."

"Judge, may I excuse myself? I'm not feeling well."

When the judge nodded, Massey packed his legal memo and jury instructions into his briefcase and walked out of the judge's chambers.

Massey approached Susan and Kane with a look of dismay on his face and whispered, "I've just been scalped by the judge. There is no room for the jury to move. Second degree murder is the best I can hope for. Even if great weight is given to her suffering during the penalty phase of the case, Leola will still spend considerable time in prison. A jail sentence would crack this fragile woman into a million pieces that could never be gathered and put back together."

Kane look at Massey and put his hand on his shoulder. "I know how you feel, but don't give up. We've got a lot going for us."

Massey sat dejectedly in his chair at the counsel table, realizing that he would have to make some drastic changes in his closing argument. Since the judge had just gutted his case, Massey didn't have much law to discuss. He knew that when your case is weak on the law, then you have to spend most of the time talking to the jury about the facts of the case, trying to evoke sympathy. Today, that would be the only possible approach.

Court was soon reconvened and Judge Sheldon announced, "Ladies and gentlemen, we are now ready for the closing arguments of counsel. The prosecution will proceed first, then the defendant, and then the prosecution will return to rebut."

Steve Aaron rose, walked up to the lectern in front of the jury where he placed his notes, and looked into the eyes of the jury panel.

He began in a quiet voice, "I'm very aware of the tremendous amount of sympathy you all have for this defendant because of all the suffering she has endured during her lifetime, probably more than any person that I can remember. Unfortunately, she killed a person. The judge will read you an instruction shortly, instructing you that sympathy has no place in a courtroom of law. As TV's Joe Friday used to say, "Just the facts, ma'am."

Aaron put his hands on the lectern and leaned over it so as to get closer to the jury. "I know that some of you may feel that the victim, Mr. Stanley Arnold, got what he deserved, and that the defendant had a right to inflict harm on him. In many countries throughout the world, for centuries, the prevailing rule has been 'an eye for an eye, and a tooth for a tooth,' but that is not the law in this country. The United States of America is a constitutional government ruled by laws, just like those God set forth in the Ten Commandments, one of which is 'Thou shall not kill.' In countries where constitutional law does not rule the land, the people take the law into their own hands, and the result is chaos."

Massey noticed that members of the jury were all paying strict attention to Aaron. He was scoring points.

"I told you in my opening argument what has been going on for centuries in Yugoslavia. I want to reiterate that point because it's the crux of this case. In that part of the world, when one family member is killed, then the remaining members of the deceased family and their relatives go out and murder someone from the killer's family. There is a snowball effect and before long, entire families are killing other families. The net result is that the society breaks down into a state of anarchy and constant civil strife. Our forefathers, who framed the Constitution of this land, were well aware of the chaos that can result from this eye-for-an-eye rule. That is why they were so insistent that this country be governed by laws preventing random killings by people with grievances against other people."

Aaron paused and poured himself a glass of water to let the last point sink into the jurors' minds. He continued, "When I first asked you questions on *voir dire*, I asked each of you if you would follow the laws given by the judge at the end of the trial and not make up your own rules. Each of you promised me that you would follow the law and the judge's instructions. I am going to ask each of you to recommit yourself to this promise, because all of you are human. I am sure you have great compassion toward the defendant. However, you can't bend the rules because of sympathy and compassion.

The law is the law, and it applies equally to all persons, whether they are cold-blooded killers or persons in the same capacity as the defendant. Today, you are the law. You are the ones who will decide if the law given by the judge applies in this case."

Steve Aaron walked up to the chalkboard in front of the jury. "Ladies and gentlemen, the state must prove the following beyond a reasonable doubt." He began writing on the board. "First, a human being was killed. Second, the killing was unlawful; and third, the killing was done with malice aforethought. 'Malice aforethought' is defined as an act that was deliberately performed with knowledge of the danger to, and with conscious disregard for, human life."

Now Aaron approached the barrier that separates the jury box from the courtroom and rested his hands on top of the railing. "Let me ask you, ladies and gentlemen of the jury: Has the State proven beyond a reasonable doubt that the victim was killed by the defendant, when she knew that pulling the trigger of that shotgun would harm her victim? Based on the defendant's confession, the tape, and her acknowledgment that the voice on the tape was her voice, your only answer must be a resounding yes!" Aaron pounded his fist on the railing to emphasize his point, and then paused to let the message sink into the minds of the jurors.

Aaron paced back and forth in front of the jury and continued, "The judge will soon instruct you that mental illness does not apply as a defense to murder in the first degree when the defendant knows the consequences of her act of killing. Her confession makes it clear that she knew the difference between right and wrong."

Massey couldn't help but notice that the jurors were intently listening to Aaron, almost as if they had already made up their minds in favor of convicting Leola.

"Let me end my argument by saying that your only task is to bring in a verdict for first or second degree murder. The judge will not give instructions on involuntary or voluntary manslaughter. Those degrees of murder are not an option for you, the jury, because they are defenses to negligent homicides—which, of course, this is not."

Massey noticed some of the jurors raise their heads and blink in disbelief.

"I want to thank each of you for your attention and for your service to the state by being part of the jury system. Do your duty and bring in a verdict for murder in the first degree," Aaron concluded. He took his notes from the lectern and went to his seat looking supremely confident.

Massey didn't rise from his seat immediately as he was deep in thought. *Now it's my turn. My first murder case, and the damn judge just ruined my case by eliminating my defenses and narrowly defining the mental illness defense. I'm going to chuck my planned oral argument and prey on their emotions. What the hell, let it all hang out. We've got nothing to lose.* He knew that the jury felt sorry as hell for Leola, and probably thought Arnold got his just desserts. But he also realized he had to give them a way to reach the right result, which meant convincing the jury that they shouldn't follow the law.

Massey rose slowly and walked toward the jury box, thinking about what he was going to say. He stood before the jury without any notes and looked directly into the eyes of those few jurors who he thought might be in his camp. "Ladies and gentlemen of the jury. You, today, now have the awesome power to participate in the possibility of the killing of a human being. Her name is Leola Langley, a mother, a wife, a good citizen all of her life, who is now faced with a possible death sentence as a result of killing a man who did dastardly acts to her son, a man she believed was ruining her family. Death. Is that a just result? You are the sole judges of her guilt or innocence in this matter, and no court can take away this power."

Massey looked up and saw a frown on the judge's face. He was actually glaring at him, ready to jump down his throat if he went any further with this type of argument.

Massey walked to the jury barrier. "Let's look at the law and the facts of this case, ladies and gentlemen. I am convinced that common sense will lead all of you to a verdict of not guilty. I'm not going to reiterate all the suffering that was inflicted on young Leola Langley, except to ask, can any of you imagine any greater pain and suffering than what this woman went through as a child? If you agree with me that this woman was subjected to extreme and excruciating suffering, then you will also agree with me that the mental damage to the young girl had to be devastating. Those painful memories of her father pumping his penis into her bleeding vagina over an eight-year period. That ghastly memory was like hot molten lava simmering for years under Mount St. Helens. Then one day the volcano erupted and exploded when she saw, on tape, her own son being raped by his teacher. The explosion brought forth the ghastly memories and triggered a severe personality reaction. She became another person, totally unconscious of the realities of life."

Skip Massey looked up and down the rows of jurors. Their rapt attention was evident. All eyes were on him, and they were listening to every word he said. A couple of women took out their hankies from their purses. *Good, I may be getting to their raw nerves,* he surmised.

"Ladies and gentlemen, look at the defendant. Look into her eyes. Leola Langley is no cold-blooded killer. She is no different from a Vietnam veteran who's lived the horrors of war and years later has a flashback and thinks he's on the battlefield. At the time of the killing, she was incapable of formulating an intent to kill. She simply wasn't the Leola Langley that you see before you today. She simply was, for all intents and purposes, unable to formulate any intent to kill."

Massey poured himself a glass of water in order to let those last remarks sink in.

"As a result, the State has failed to prove beyond a reasonable doubt that Leola Langley had the requisite intent to kill the decedent. Leola Langley did not understand the nature of her act when she pulled the trigger of the 20-gauge shotgun. I ask you to return a not guilty verdict for the defendant." All eyes of the jurors followed Massey as he returned to his seat.

Massey was concerned about the rebuttal argument which Steven Aaron was now about to give. He had always felt it was grossly unfair to give the prosecution rebuttal time when the defense is limited to only one argument.

The district attorney rose and began his final summation to the jury. "Ladies and gentlemen, Mr. Massey has misquoted and misinterpreted the instructions that the judge will give you shortly. The 'other person,' 'altered state of mind,' 'hallucinating' theories are not defenses to murder. Leola Langley admitted in her confession and on the transcribed tape that she intended to kill the defendant. End of case. The State has proven beyond a reasonable doubt that she had the requisite intent and that she knew the nature of her act.

"If Mrs. Langley had a mental problem, that is an issue for the penalty phase of the case, not this phase. The judge will undoubtedly take this fact into account when she is sentenced. Ladies and gentlemen, do your duty and follow the law as the judge gives it to you. You must return a verdict of guilty in the first degree."

Massey watched the jury as the D.A. finished his argument, telling them what they had to do. He could sense that some of the jurors didn't like being told how they had to decide this matter. Steve Aaron had invaded their territory. Not a smart thing to do.

For the next forty-five minutes, the judge read jury instructions. Jury instructions are extremely important, but after the judge reads for about ten minutes, most jurors' minds begin to wander. This jury was no exception. The last instruction tells the jury to go into the jury room and select a foreperson. With that instruction completed, the bailiff took the jury into the jury room to deliberate.

As the jury filed into the jury room, Massey turned to Leola and put his arm around her shoulders. "Say a little prayer. I hope they do the right thing."

"I'll be a-prayin' as hard as I know how."

When the bailiff came out of the jury room, Judge Sheldon got up from the bench to go to his chambers, but turned and looked in the direction of both lawyers. "Well done, gentlemen. You both tried an excellent case."

# CHAPTER 30

Now commenced the period of the trial that most lawyers dread: sitting outside the jury room, unable to do anything more to affect the outcome, unable to quell the guessing that goes on the longer the jury is out. During this period, all lawyers think about the arguments they forgot to use, the ones that might have swayed the jury. Skip Massey was no different.

He walked out of the courtroom with Susan and Kane, saying, "Now's the toughest part of the entire case. Not knowing what is going on inside that jury room, thinking about all the questions I should have asked, and what I should have said in my closing argument. I'll be thinking about these things in the middle of the night for months to come."

Kane said enthusiastically, "Massey, you put on a great trial, a hell of a lot better than I could have done. I appreciate your taking me off the hook."

Susan then grabbed his hand. "Skip, I owe you a big thanks for standing up for my friend. Win or lose, you did great, the best you can do. The jury was listening intently when you were talking. You gave the district attorney a run for his money."

"They won't be back for quite a while. Let's all go have a glass of wine so I can settle my nerves."

"Good idea. Wine will help to soothe the savage beast. God, you were good," remarked Kane.

Massey told the bailiff where they'd be, and he, Kane and Susan went to the hotel.

At 5 p.m., rather than call it a day, the judge wanted the jury to keep working hard while the evidence and arguments were still fresh. Consequently, he sent the bailiff into the jury room to ask if they wouldn't mind deliberating until 7 p.m. The bailiff reported that a few made phone calls home, then agreed to stay longer.

▼

The next day the jury reconvened at 9 a.m., and the judge again sent them to the jury room. Judge Sheldon told the lawyers, "Gentlemen, I want you to be within a distance of no more than five minutes, in the event the jury reaches a decision or needs any question answered."

Massey went back to Kane's office with Susan while Sam and Leola went to the hotel. At 11 a.m., the bailiff called and said the jury had a question.

When all attorneys were present, the judge called the bailiff to bring the jury out. Once seated, the judge asked, "Who is the foreperson of the jury, and will he or she let me know what your question is?"

Juror number seven raised her hand and stood. Massey quickly looked at his jury chart. It was Merrill Cannon. Massey thought she was in her early fifties, nice looking, dark-haired woman. His notes indicated that she was a married mother of two children who had gone back to work as a computer programmer for a small company in the area after her kids grew up. *Good choice, jurors,* he thought to himself. *She really paid attention to me during the trial.*

"We have a question, Your Honor, that we have written down." Mrs. Cannon handed the written question to the bailiff, who took the note to the judge.

The judge read the note, then looked up at the attorneys. "Gentlemen, can I see both of you in chambers?"

Aaron and Massey followed the judge into his chambers. When all were seated, the judge said, "Gentlemen, the jury wants to know, 'Can the defendant be convicted of murder if she was another person at the time of the killing?' You both know my feelings on this matter. I am not going to change the law. I will tell them that an altered state of mind or being another person because of a mental condition is not a defense to murder."

246

Massey protested, "Judge, the defendant didn't have the ability to mentally formulate an intent to kill because of her mental condition. The jury should be given the option to decide this issue."

The judge replied, "Mr. Massey, I instructed them that if they found the defendant was mentally ill and didn't know the consequences of her act, they could find that she didn't have the necessary intent and in that case acquit her."

"With all due respect, Your Honor, I think that you have interpreted that issue too narrowly."

"That's your opinion, Mr. Massey, not mine. Let's go back out."

Once he returned to his seat behind the bench, Judge Sheldon told the jury, "Ladies and gentlemen, in answer to your question, an altered state of mind caused by a mental illness is not a defense to murder unless the person causing the harm didn't know the consequences of her act at the moment of the killing."

The judge instructed the bailiff to retire the jury to the jury room.

▼

Late that afternoon, Massey heard another knock on the door from inside the jury room. The bailiff opened the door and was handed a slip of paper.

"Looks like they have another question, gentlemen," the bailiff said as he hurried into the judge's chambers.

Massey looked at Susan. "That's great. The longer they take, the better it is for our side."

The bailiff came back out, saying, "Gentlemen, the judge wants to see you again without calling the jury."

Massey and Aaron again sat before the judge in his chambers. "Well, gentlemen, the jury wants to know why the post-traumatic stress syndrome defense instruction wasn't read to them. They also want to know if that defense is applicable to women who are not veterans. I knew that I was treading on thin ice when I let that type of testimony in, but I did it in order to allow the

247

defendant a reasonable opportunity to have a record for an appeal. This is a death case, and I want to afford any defendant the opportunity to put potential defenses into evidence, in case the higher courts wish to reverse and create a new law."

Massey thought to himself, *If Leola had been tried before a liberal judge, I'd have gotten her off scot-free. Those guys love to make new law.*

The judge had the bailiff call the jury back into the courtroom. "Ladies and gentlemen, the post-traumatic stress syndrome defense would apply to women only if they were Vietnam veterans who were severely mentally affected by their experiences in the war. It's late in the day, so I'm going to recess. Please return Monday morning at nine. Remember my admonition about talking to anybody about this case."

With a weekend ahead of them, Massey, Susan, Sam and Leola flew back to Los Gatos. It gave the Langleys and Susan a chance to be with their children before they had to return to court bright and early Monday morning.

▼

The weekend passed quickly. When the court convened Monday morning, the judge again sent the jury to deliberate. After the jury room door closed, Judge Sheldon looked at both attorneys. "They're getting to crunch time now and dealing with the real issues. We should have a verdict soon."

Massey's stomach turned sour. He didn't like the judge's comment.

Some forty-five minutes later, Massey and the bailiff, who were talking, heard a male voice yelling in the jury room. Next, a woman's voice began shrieking. Then they heard a man and woman yelling at each other. Soon several women's voices joined the fray.

"That doesn't happen very often in there, but once in a while, those jurors get into a real donnybrook. Even had a couple of males come to blows last year," said the bailiff. "I'd better go tell the judge."

The bailiff returned shortly and approached Massey with a smile. "He said to let 'em go at it. They're resolving some issues."

While they listened, the jury room became quiet. Right before lunch, there was knock from inside.

Once again, the judge called counsel into his chambers and addressed the lawyers with irritation in his voice. "The jury wants to know why they can't render a verdict of involuntary manslaughter or voluntary manslaughter. I'm going to tell them that those two defenses are reserved for killings where the defendant was negligent, or in a heat of passion. That the heat of passion defense requires a prompt response as a result of the anger arousal."

As the judge was speaking, Massey was getting butterflies in his stomach, thinking about what the jury really meant by such a question.

Back in the courtroom, the judge looked down at the jury. "Ladies and gentlemen, this case does not involve a negligent act or heat of passion. Hence, a manslaughter conviction is not a proper verdict in this case. For a valid heat of passion defense, the anger arousal which caused the irrational action of the defendant had to be instantaneous, thereby causing the defendant to immediately kill the victim. The best example is that of a husband who finds his wife in bed with another man, becomes enraged, loses his temper, and kills the interloper."

After the jurors returned to the jury room, Susan came up to Massey at the counsel table. "What's that all about?"

"They don't want Leola to get the death sentence or spend the rest of her life in jail. That's why they want to compromise and come in with a verdict of manslaughter where she would only spend a short time in jail." Then he added dejectedly, "The judge just foreclosed that option."

▼

It was now late Monday afternoon. The judge called in the two attorneys and the bailiff. "I don't know what's taking so long. Mr. Bailiff, let's ask the jury if they're making any headway."

The bailiff knocked on the door and asked the jury to take their places in the jury box.

The judge entered the courtroom and asked the forewoman, "Mrs. Cannon, are you making any progress arriving at a decision?"

"Well, Your Honor, we are divided, although I took a recent poll of the jurors and there is some movement toward a decision."

"Keep trying to reach a decision. The bailiff reported to me earlier that a few of the jurors were overheard raising their voices. Please be reminded that such actions will only result in solidifying the other person's position. Madame Forewoman, I need to know if the jury reaches an impasse. Right now, it's getting late in the day. We're going to recess a little early so you all can come back refreshed tomorrow," said the judge.

▼

Massey was present when the jury returned the next day. As he watched the jurors file into the jury room, they looked grim and very serious. Just before lunch, the bailiff brought another note from the jury. When the judge read the question from the jury, he frowned, clearly uncertain about what to say. He called both attorneys in. "This jury has a mind of its own," he grumbled. "You'll never believe it. They want to know if they are subject to any crime or penalty if they don't follow my instructions on the law. I practiced law for fifteen years and now I've been judging for ten years, and I have never heard of a jury asking this kind of question. I don't know what the hell I'm going to tell them. Any suggestions?"

The district attorney spoke in a loud voice. "Judge, tell them that they took an oath to follow the law and are bound to their promise."

Massey stood up and leaned toward the judge. "Your Honor, there are a couple of cases. They cover the issue of jury nullification. If I could have ten minutes, I can dig out a case on the issue."

250

"Mr. Massey, go to the library down the hall and find the case."

It didn't take long for Massey to find *United States v. Berrigan* 417 F.2d 1002 (1969). As Massey looked up jury nullification in the index of Corpus Juris Secundum, he found it right away, grabbed the 417th volume of the second edition of the federal appellate court cases, checked it out, and took it to Judge Sheldon.

The judge read the case, looked up, and said, "This case stands for the proposition that the jury has the power to disregard the law when they feel that the law is unjust. But the opinion also says I have to tell them that they must abide by the law. What perplexes me is that this jury wants to know also if they can be penalized for not following the law. I let the cat out of the bag if I tell them that they can't be penalized. This is one hell of a catch-22 situation."

As Massey walked out of chambers, he could see a worried expression on Aaron's face.

The court reconvened and the judge instructed the jury, "You must follow the law that I gave to you. The jury, however, cannot be penalized if you do not follow the law."

Massey came over to tell Susan the latest turn of events. "The jury's up to something strange. They wanted to know if they could disregard the law. The judge just told them the equivalent of 'yes and no.' Keep your fingers crossed."

Just before 5 p.m., the bailiff heard a knock on the jury door. "Mr. Bailiff, we have reached a verdict," said Mrs. Cannon.

The bailiff informed the judge, and he and his staff, and the cadre of lawyers all took their seats and waited for the jury to come into the courtroom. Suddenly there was another knock on the door in the jury room. The bailiff marched over and went inside. After a few minutes, he came out and told the judge, "The forewoman said that they need a few more minutes, Your Honor."

After a half hour, the judge told the bailiff to find out how much more time would be needed. He returned and reported that the forewoman told him another five or ten minutes.

"Somebody must have changed their mind," surmised the judge.

By now, Massey's nerve endings were raw. He had no idea what the jury was up to. He certainly didn't need a mistrial. He knew by the questions the jury had been asking that many of the jurors were sympathetic to Leola. They were having a hard time. Massey knew they didn't want to punish Leola too severely. However, the judge's instructions left them no middle ground. It was another thirty minutes before the bailiff heard a final knock on the jury door. "We're now ready, Mr. Bailiff."

After the jury was seated, the bailiff took the verdict from the forewoman and gave it to the judge. The judge opened the verdict, looked at it, and with a look of consternation, addressed the jury. "Ladies and gentlemen, I have read your verdict. You have exceeded your powers. You have the right to find the defendant guilty of voluntary manslaughter despite my contrary instructions, but you don't have the right to make probation, with no jail time, a condition of your verdict. Whether or not the defendant serves jail time and/or probation is within my jurisdiction. Now go back to the jury room and bring in a proper verdict."

The forewoman, Merrill Conner, stood and announced in a loud voice, "Your Honor, if our verdict is not acceptable, then we have another verdict which will be acceptable. We anticipated the possibility that our verdict might not be proper, and that is why we spent the extra time in the jury room. Here is the alternate verdict, which you will find in order." She handed the alternate verdict to the bailiff, who took it to the judge. The judge glanced at the verdict, then looked at them with a scowl on his face and handed the verdict to the clerk.

The clerk opened it, read it, smiled, and then stood and announced, "We the jury find the defendant not guilty."

Skip Massey jumped up and went over to Leola, Sam and Susan. All four began hugging each other and smiling through tears of joy.

"Order, Mr. Massey," bellowed the judge.

The judge then addressed the jury. "Ladies and gentlemen, while I don't agree with your verdict, you have the right to reach this result. I wish to thank you for your services. You are now dismissed and free to discuss this case as I lift the previous admonition."

Most of the women on the jury went over to Leola and told her they hoped she would be able to enjoy the rest of her life. As expected, Leola was overcome by their verdict and their comments. She mumbled through her tears, "Thank you, thank you, God bless y'all."

Massey looked over to see Steve Aaron and his associates in a state of shock. They slowly gathered up their briefcases and marched out of the courtroom without saying a word to Massey.

Jerry Kane came up and put his arms around Massey. "Christ, you did the impossible. I can't believe it. I knew you could pull it out."

"Jerry, you deserve a lot of credit for this result, as do Susan, Leola, and Big Mike. I couldn't have done it without every one of you."

As Massey escorted Susan, Sam and Leola out of the courtroom, they were met with flashbulbs blurring their vision and reporters asking questions. Massey stopped, turned to the clamoring press and said, "My only comment is that this case was about discrimination. The jury obviously thought that this woman should have the same rights as men to use the post-traumatic stress syndrome defense. I hope the state legislature takes notice of what the jury did in this case and amends the law accordingly."

As the four freed themselves from the press and strolled back to the hotel, Massey thought about how this trial had impacted his life. He had found the woman of his dreams, and no longer was he going to allow his business to dominate his life. It was time to start smelling the roses and appreciate the world around him. The victory indeed had been sweet, but he would have a difficult time forgetting the stench of the lasting personal destruction wrought on a family by a pedophile's sordid actions against a youngster. He wondered what the future held in store for this family and for the others involved in this tragic affair.

# EPILOGUE

Skip Massey and Susan Winters were married at the Ventana Inn in Big Sur, California, two months after the trial. Massey settled the civil case against the school district and Gary Fillmore on behalf of the Langley family for six million dollars. He and Susan then moved to Carmel Valley, California, where Massey opened a small law office. They took up golf and enjoy their low-key lifestyle together.

Sam and Leola Langley separated and were divorced six months after the trial. Several years later, their oldest son's wife gave birth to their first grandchild. Leola currently loves her role as a grandmother.

Judge Sam Sheldon was appointed by Governor Pete Wilson to the California State Supreme Court shortly after the trial. He now leads the conservative wing of the court.

Steve Aaron, despite the trial's political setback, succeeded Judge Brandon as a Superior Court Judge.

Gary Fillmore was convicted of the murder of Roland Garrity and sentenced to life imprisonment without the possibility of parole.

# ABOUT THE AUTHOR

Frank "Skip" Crist was born in Palo Alto, California. He was raised in this small college town adjacent to Stanford University when there were only 9,000 inhabitants. Skip was educated in the Palo Alto school system and, upon graduation, went across the street and began his college education at Stanford University, first as an undergraduate and later at Stanford Law School. During his undergraduate years, he was a four-year letterman on the Stanford football team.

Skip began practicing law in 1959 at the firm of Crist, Peters, Donegan and Brenner, which was located in downtown Palo Alto. He specialized in trial practice and became recognized as an excellent trial lawyer.

Skip retired from the practice of law in 1992, but his passion for writing about the unique episodes that occurred during his trial practice led him to write his first novel, *Fatal Flashback*.

He and his wife, Carolyn, live in Carmel Valley, California, enjoying the climate, golf, and their family. They are proud parents of eight children and nine grandchildren with more to come.

While the novel is mostly fiction, the story originates from a case Skip handled in early 1977.